THE END OF TIME

BOOK THREE OF THE
TIME TOURISTS TRILOGY

SHARLEEN NELSON

GladEye Press

Springfield, OR
www.gladeyepress.com

© 2024 Sharleen Nelson
The End of Time

All rights reserved.

No part of this publication may be reproduced in any form, by photocopying or by any electronic or mechanical means, including information storage or retrieval systems, without permission in writing from both the copyright owner and the publisher of this book.

Published by: GladEye Press
Interior Design: J.V. Bolkan
Cover Design: Sharleen Nelson
Marketing and Publicity: Kaylee Crum
ISBN-13: 978-1-951289-17-1
Library of Congress Control Number: 2024945954

This is a work of fiction. All names, characters, places, and events are either a product of the author's imagination or are used fictitiously. Any resemblance to real persons, businesses, organizations, or events are totally unintentional and entirely coincidental.

10 9 8 7 6 5 4 3 2

"What is grief, if not love persevering?"
~ Vision, "WandaVision" (2021)

"Science is magic that works." ~ Kurt Vonnegut

PROLOGUE

September 5, 1937

Despite the copious cocktail of drugs flowing through her veins, Tiffany Rose was slightly cognizant of her surroundings—the detached shrieks, the delirious laughter; the high-pitched *screech screech screech* of the gurney wheels as it crawled along the extended hallway; her head lobbing back and forth in tandem with each halting, wonky movement. And when they rolled her into the room beneath a blinding sky of fluorescent light, even in her current state she recognized it. She had been here before, maybe not this exact room, but one like it. Her mind stumbled to hold on to that thought. She couldn't be certain about anything anymore really. It all looked and smelled the same anyway—drab walls in puke green, dingy floors, and curtains reeking of urine and Ammonium and Hypochlorite and Peracetic Acid. In these rooms they administered the electroshock treatments; ostensibly to keep her sweet and docile, to quell any ounce of rage she might still harbor after years of confinement, most of them spent in the isolation of a padded room wearing the white linen jacket of no escape.

    Squeezing her eyes tightly shut to quell the harsh light, an automatic defense mechanism that helped her mind escape to somewhere else, she listened to the low buzzing disembodied voices resonating somewhere overhead, although today a different and new one rose above the murmur of the rest. "Can you hear me, Tiffany? a masculine voice asked, his soothing tone as soft and gentle as music or ocean waves or falling rain. This was different, she thought. This time they hadn't violently connected the cold conduits to her head or jabbed the hard metal piece into her mouth to bite down on when the hot electric current sent convulsive shock waves coursing through her body.

    Tiffany didn't know this, but the man behind the voice was Dr. Freeman, a new doctor at Crestview Sanitarium. Freeman specialized in a new miracle procedure called lobotomy. Why bother with endless shock treatment sessions to keep intractable patients in line, when a simple technique rendered patients docile, forever? Of course, there were side effects—the patient might need to be fed and maintained; someone had to mop up their drool spills and change their shitty diapers, but it was much more efficient and less dangerous for their overseers. Over the course of his career, Freeman, who had no formal surgical training, would go on to perform as many as 4,000 lobotomies in twenty-three states, 2,500 of which were performed using an ice pick, but who was counting?

    This voice, intermingling with the others, began to fade as she floated in and out, and then, burning off like morning fog, a series of disconnected memories—of a childhood that inexplicably happened in the future. Was that right? The way Saturday mornings felt. Full of possibility. A bowl of cereal and cartoons. Shopping at the mall with mother, Christmas time and Halloween and summers spent running barefoot through the park.

Flashes of Simon. What had become of her sweet boy? He was only seven when they came to the house and snatched him away from her. Was he happy? Did he remember her? Her thoughts were a swirl of discombobulation. From the day they brought her to the asylum in 1892 and lopped off her curly mane, leaving it in a muddled pile on the cold tile floor for the janitor to sweep up, through dozens upon dozens of shock therapy treatments, up until this morning when they had pumped her full of drugs, strapped her to the gurney and rolled her across the hall to this sterile green room for a procedure called a lobotomy, Tiffany Rose remained resolute. "I'm from the future," she insisted when the plastic cap was roughly shoved onto her head.

"Of course, you are dear," the nurse said as she patted her small, clenched fist. "Relax now, it'll be over soon." A sharp prick in her arm and a comforting cloud of shadowy nothing began to creep in around the edges. She never felt so calm. As she quietly drifted away to a place where dreams go to die "… from the future," she whispered softly. She did not hear the commotion outside the door, the muffled voices shouting, footsteps running, a metal pan of surgical devices crashing to the floor nor feel someone lifting her off the table.

1

The screen faded to black as the final credits rolled by, ending fifteen seasons of *Supernatural*. Imogen, Niles, and Fletcher looked at each other and expelled a collective sigh.

"That was a good ending," Imogen said reaching for the remote. "What's next?"

Niles grinned. "Well, there's always *Love Island Australia*."

Fletcher frowned. "I'm sick of *Love Island*, and really, everything!" he announced. Rising from the sofa where he and Imogen had been sharing a blanket, he wandered over to the window to peer out at the blurry, wet world outside. Big, soppy raindrops pelting the glass. It had been like this for days and days.

Imogen was a little surprised. Fletcher hardly ever got annoyed. "So ... what? You're sick of *Love Island*? Really?" she teased.

"Seriously Imogen," he said, turning around to face her. "What the hell are we doing here anyway? Why have we been sticking around the house making bread and watching Netflix, when we ... well you ... have friggin' time travel at your disposal?"

Imogen shrugged. Niles picked at a piece of fluff poking out of the sofa cushion. "You guys ..." he whined, "we have the whole world to explore. We could go anywhere, do anything," he continued, his voice rising as his agitation grew. "Heck, we could be drinking margaritas, blowin' out a flip-flop on the beach in Cancún in 1963 or watching trapeze artists perform in a big tent at a Barnum & Bailey circus in, oh, I don't know, nineteen hundred something! He flung his hands in the air over his head with dramatic, exasperated flair.

Admittedly, this whole quarantine business was starting to get old. Her brain was turning to mush. Imogen hadn't picked up a book since she couldn't remember when and secretly, she longed for some fresh air, a hike in the forest, but the unusually rainy spring had kept them indoors. Fletcher was right, of course. What *were* they doing here? What were they waiting for?

The unexpected outbreak in February of the deadly COVID-19 virus had taken everyone, including their wholly unprepared government, by surprise as it spread rapidly across the country, killing thousands, forcing schools and businesses to close, sending everyone scampering into quarantine and forcing people to wear masks, which had ignited a firestorm of protests and anger and division in an already volatile political landscape. They had watched it unfold on the news as they cloistered in the safety of home, blithely removed and out of touch but not sorry for it. And for Imogen, it had been a convenient excuse to avoid the elephant in the room. The elephant being, of course, Simon.

Two months ago, right before the whole world fell apart, they had said their goodbyes to each other as he boarded a plane for Chicago, to Daguerreian Society headquarters … for tests … they said. But it was hard to dismiss the uneasy, unspoken tension between them before he left. As difficult as it was to separate, Imogen sensed they were both anxious to spend some time apart from each other.

Shortly after, she found out she was pregnant, and Simon still did not know because there had been no contact with him since. She had tried calling many times, but the calls went immediately to voicemail; and sent dozens of texts that went unanswered, except for one weirdly detail-free message, written in a voice unlike the Simon she thought she knew:

Hey Imogen. Arrived safely in Chicago.

Testing is going well. Take care. Simon.

So, filling up the time with games and TV and activities with Fletcher and Niles had been her solution for avoiding thinking about him or about their crumbling relationship. Not to mention the weird things that were happening to her body; the morning sickness and severe fatigue that left her too tired to get out of bed some mornings.

Without asking, Fletcher had gone to the kitchen and now returned with a warm mug of coffee with cream and hazelnut syrup, the way she liked it. After handing it to her, he gave her another throw pillow to prop her feet up.

"Are you feeling okay? he asked.

Imogen smiled. "Better now." He was always so thoughtful. He seemed to know what she needed even when she didn't know herself. And it made her slightly uncomfortable. Like they were becoming too comfortable—like a couple, even though they weren't. But he was so good and kind and comforting; it stirred up old feelings that she knew she should squash.

Aside from everything though, the time had not been entirely wasted. It had given her time to reconnect with Niles—the father she had not seen since she was nine years old—but who, amazingly, looked the same age as when he'd left—which at the same time was tremendously weird and off-putting, the consequence of a time traveling individual getting stuck in a time loop as Niles had been for eighteen years. She had lost so much precious time with him, and he was still a bit scrambled from the ordeal, but slowly, as they played scrabble and baked bread, and rediscovered his sweet vinyl record collection together they began to get to know one another on a new and changed level—as one adult person to another.

Imogen and Niles also discussed the time each had spent on the remote island of Bakunawa in the Andamon Sea and their mutual friend D'ar, who had recognized her as daughter of Niles, and the diaries and other personal items that Niles had left there. Niles had found solace on the island once and, like her father, she discovered Bakunawa at a time when she had needed it most.

Her two previous time trips had been nothing short of disastrous. The first, to Kansas 1946, had left her distraught and disillusioned and questioning whether time travel was even worth it. Was she hurting more than helping? She had attempted to tamper with the universe, to change the recorded fate of two teenage sisters who ended up dying in a train accident anyway despite her efforts. Another trip to New York 1921 had culminated with her being assaulted in a hotel speakeasy. Broken, upset, her relationship with Simon in shambles, she had found the bundle of photographs of the remote island in her dad's desk drawer. Perhaps they should go there together.

Imogen remembered the wonderful drink the natives had concocted and felt a sudden craving. Being pregnant, she wouldn't be able to partake, of course, but she knew Fletcher would love it. She worried though how the natives might receive a stranger. Would they be hostile? They could always go to Kauai where she and Simon had visited—what seemed like ages ago—instead. But the idea of Bakunawa tugged at her. She could use a break; they all could. Maybe Niles would want to come along as well.

When Fletcher rejoined her beside him on the sofa, she turned to him and said, "I like your idea about going someplace warm and tropical, but how would you feel about something a bit more primitive?" Niles shot her a warning glance, suspicious about where she might be going with this.

"Primitive, you say?" Fletcher turned to face her. "Tell me more," he said, intrigued.

"Well, there is this island in the Andaman Sea ..."

"Oh no, no, no, no ... absolutely not, Imogen," Niles interrupted. "You are *not* going to Bakunawa."

"Why not? It's perfect. Remote. No tourists to deal with ..."

"But hostile natives!" Niles barked back at her.

"Dad, they know us," Imogen pleaded. "D'ar is your friend. Just think how relaxing it would be. Think about the weather!"

"When you say *us*, surely you're not thinking that includes me as well?" Niles asked, pointing his index finger first at Imogen and Fletcher and then back at himself. "Because there is no way I'm going to Bakunawa with you, or anywhere else for that matter," he said. "My time traveling days are over, done!" he emphatically stated, sitting back down and crossing his arms in noncompliance.

Imogen understood Niles was frightened of traveling. How could he not be, especially after what he'd been through, but they all needed this for their mental health.

"Oh, come on Dad," she pleaded. "I get that you're scared, but what was it you used to tell me when I was little? To get right back up in the saddle when you fall off the horse? Bakunawa would be the *best* place to go your first time. You've been there before. You know the terrain, what to expect. Your stuff is there. Don't you want to read it? Visit D'ar? I know you do."

"But what about COVID?" Niles asked. I know that none of us has it, but if there's a potential of introducing a virus to the Bakunawans, should we really risk it?"

Imogen had an answer for that. "It's funny you ask because it was before COVID but when the field agents were here, Simon had a discussion with them on that very topic. I guess he had been reading about the 1918 Spanish flu outbreak and he wanted to know if a sick traveler could potentially go back to another time and start an epidemic there."

"And what did they say about that?" Fletcher asked.

"You know how whatever we take with us becomes the period equivalent?"

Fletcher and Niles nodded.

"Well," she continued, "evidently, the same applies to disease, so, for instance, if one of us had COVID and traveled back to say 1918, the virus would present as the Spanish flu, and sure, we could very well die from it. The same for any other contagious disease, but it could present as the flu or perhaps just a common cold if there's nothing going around at that time."

Niles scratched his chin, pondering what she said. "hmmm, interesting ... and Bakunawa?"

Imogen replied. "So, In Bakunawa, where there are no diseases, it would not present at all."

Like an excited puppy, Fletcher interjected, "Well, that's great! It's settled. Make me a time tourist!" Niles frowned and covered his face with his hands. He was torn. On the one hand, yes, it would do them all good to get away. On the other hand, what if something bad happened? How could he ever be confident again that time travel was safe? Only someone who has spent eighteen years reliving two months of their life over and over could know what it mentally does to a person. He was finally starting to feel a little less confused, a bit more like his old self again, and now this was what they were asking him to do. Still,

Imogen was right, you have to face your fear, otherwise it holds power over you.

"Okay, Imogen," he conceded, exasperated, "you guys win. We'll go …" Obviously delighted, Fletcher beamed. "Yay Dad!" Imogen said.

" … but only," he continued " … on one condition, that the photograph is secured in a safe place where no one can tamper with it." The circumstance for which Niles had been trapped was the fault of Teddy, who had destroyed his anchor photograph, the one he had entered to go look for Jade, thus trapping him within that time.

"I know what can happen. I saw the ashes of you and Mom's photos in the trash can. That's why I rented the office space downtown," she reassured him. "The whole purpose of getting it was to ensure that I would be the only one with access to photos, and I would know that they would be completely safe while I traveled."

Fletcher could barely contain his enthusiasm. "It's settled then," he said, standing up and clapping his hands together. "When do we go?"

He immediately noticed the look on Niles' face. He still didn't look so sure, and Imogen had also seemed to retreat, pulling the blanket up tighter around her chest. Like Niles, she too wrestled with her own fears about time travel and the safety of her unborn child. Sensing their apprehension, Fletcher pulled back.

"Well," he offered. "We can go anytime, right? Or not. Or hey, maybe before we go, we can watch this series from New Zealand about a family of brothers who live secretly as Norse Gods. Or ... ooh, there's a couple of UK crime drama limited series that look pretty good, too."

2

The room felt muggy and oppressive. Simon got up and unlatched the large floor-to-ceiling, dual-pane window. A sudden whirling whoosh of incoming air sent the pages of the book he had been reading on the bed fluttering madly. They didn't call Chicago the Windy City for nothing, he guessed.

In a suite perched high up on the forty-third floor, Simon had an amazing view of Lake Michigan and the Chicago skyline. On clear mornings, he liked sitting out on the small balcony observing the variety of boats that traversed the lake's waters. The tower he'd been living in for the past few weeks had all the amenities one could possibly ask for—a five-star restaurant, a four-lane indoor heated pool, a sauna and steam room, a day spa, a fitness center and rec room, a library, even pickleball courts. Yet here, at Daguerreian Society Headquarters, the stunning view and opulent facilities were the only things Simon couldn't complain about.

Thank goodness he had headphones to listen to Pink Floyd and other new music he'd recently discovered. The few people he had engaged with in conversation had been interested in him as a time traveler, but how do you connect with anyone when you have no point of reference, no common ground? Imogen had mostly understood but he still struggled at times to make her understand that coming from an entirely different time shut him out of certain conversations. She frequently assumed everyone got her pop culture references, forgetting that his frame of reference was 1913, not the two-thousands.

Not only that, but he'd barely been here a week when the pandemic shut everything down. He wasn't sure whether it was part of the DS protocol or not, but from that point on he was quarantined, not allowed to leave the building at all. From his sky top window, he could see the city out there, spread out like a beacon of light, but it seemed as much out of reach to him as the moon. Making matters worse, they still had not returned his phone to him, nor allowed him to contact Imogen—something about not wanting his personal life to be a distraction. Although as much as he hated to admit it, part of him felt relieved by their separation. The tension between them at the airport when they were saying their goodbyes was palpable. It was wrong, he knew, but he needed time away from her.

Still, he worried about her, not so much about the time traveling she did, but that she might be sick. People were dying from this virus. And yet he knew that she had Niles—they needed this time together—and Fletcher. The three of them were probably holed up at Imogen's house right now playing games, maybe even barely missing him, he thought sadly.

So far, the tests, which were supposed to answer questions about time travel, had not materialized. Simon understood that he was an anomaly, a serial jumper. So why were they not testing him to find out if he was able to jump from photograph to photograph indefinitely? What were his limits, capabilities? Could he get physically near to himself without running into the weird limbo/time loop state that Imogen and her father, Niles had experienced?

In the reading materials he had been given, there had been mention of areas or time periods that had become inaccessible because too many travelers were going there, but no explanation of why this might be happening. Did they think he might be able to travel to those places? He also hoped to learn more about how the society operated in terms of locating people. Always in the back of his mind was his mother. Where was she? Was she even still alive? The questions burned in his heart like an infinite flame, and her whereabouts were also the primary source of contention between he and Imogen.

Ever since Fletcher had brought it up, that Imogen had never once offered to search for his mother, he had felt growing resentment toward her. Maybe he should have brought it up more often, but it seemed like she always had other priorities. At the very least, she could have offered. Why didn't she? As soon as Simon was finished with testing here, finding his mother would be his top priority.

Meanwhile, the days here had become a confusing blur of being probed, prodded, and tested. Mornings on the treadmill—walking, running fast, running slow, hooked up to a ridiculous number of sensors that recorded everything from his blood pressure, heart rate, body temperature, and oxygen saturation to motion, arterial pressure, sweat gland activity, respiration, and glucose levels. An array of large monitors constantly beeped and booped, sending out streams of data that skittered across the screens creating a sort of perpetual dancing, jitterbug light show. And let us not forget the nifty helmet, also equipped with sensors, that recorded his brain function as he moved. When he wasn't on the treadmill or the stationary bike, throughout the day he was required to wear what they called Smart body sensors that continuously monitored his physiological, behavioral, health, and emotional state.

He had spoken briefly when he first arrived with Agent Metzger, and then Kevin McCord had been tasked with giving him a tour and an orientation, which he immediately passed off to his assistant, Brittany. The once friendly, affable data tech, who had explained everything using a Marvel universe analogy now seemed uncharacteristically prickly and preoccupied.

"You remember Kevin, Simon," Metzger had said, as the other agent approached them. "Kevin McCord." Simon extended his hand to shake, but Kevin ignored it, focusing instead on explaining something to his assistant who followed closely behind him frantically typing notes into her phone. "Oh hey," he finally acknowledged. "Good to see you, Simon. Brittany will show you the ropes. Gotta go." And then he was gone.

He'd seen him around the building a few times after that first encounter, but when he did, Kevin had avoided making eye contact, seemingly always busy or in a hurry to get somewhere else. Until last week. Simon had just finished up his morning session on the treadmill. Sweaty and spent, he pushed open the door and immediately plowed into Kevin who happened to be passing by at that exact moment. Brittany, trailing closely behind rear-ended Kevin, spilling her iced latte down the front of her sweater and partially onto Kevin's back.

"Whoa, hey!" Kevin roared as he backed away from Simon. "Watch it there, buddy."

Simon quickly jumped back. "My apologies," he said, "I was not aware that you were passing outside the door." Kevin turned around and glowered at Brittany, who was frantically dabbing at the spilt coffee on his backside with a napkin. Not only was he late for a meeting, but now he'd have to change his shirt and why did Simon always have to speak like some twentieth century dandy? Oh right, because he was one. Still, annoying. He tried to make a quick exit, but then Simon, seizing the chance to speak to him, reached out and grabbed his arm, pulling him back. "Um, Kevin, may I have a word with you please ... in private?" he asked. Brittany flashed an uneasy smile and scurried off in the direction of the bathroom to get more paper towels, leaving Kevin alone with no choice but to chat with Simon.

"Uh, sure," Kevin said. "Let's go over here," he said, motioning them to a grouping of leather sofas, an office perk intended for those rare employee moments of spontaneous synergy should they arise.

"I'm sorry for banging into you like that," Simon again apologized. "No problem," Kevin said, noticeably looking down at his wristwatch. "Look Simon, I'm late for a meeting, is there something on your mind?" Simon shifted in his seat. "Yes, well yes there is. Frankly, I have been here for several weeks now and other than the technicians who hook me up daily to the sensors, the staff, the servers, and random other people employed here I have had no contact with anyone who can explain exactly *why* I am here." Kevin started to answer, "Look Simon, I don't know what to tell you, I …"

Simon continued undeterred. "Since I have been here, I have not once traveled in time, which I was under the impression was the purpose of my coming here for testing, nor has my phone been returned to me, which means that I have been unable to call Imogen. I very much want to call her!" he said, the timber of his voice trembling with suppressed emotion and frustration. "She deserves to know that I am all right," he added, "the pandemic situation, notwithstanding!"

Kevin extended his arms above his shoulders in mock surrender. "I hear you, I hear you, buddy," he said in the friendliest tone he could muster. "But, as I was about to tell you, I have no control over the powers that be, man. I'm just a lowly employee around here myself."

Something about Kevin's tone and disposition didn't ring true to Simon. He couldn't be sure, of course; he had no evidence, only his gut, but it seemed as though Kevin might be hiding something. "Well then," he said, "perhaps I can have a word with these so-called 'powers that be.'"

3

Never particularly good at hiding his feelings, especially around Imogen—Fletcher had worn them on his sleeve on more than one occasion, most spectacularly when after hiking to the top of the butte, he'd bent down on one knee and proposed to her, which she had gently declined. So far, out of respect for her relationship with Simon, he'd done a fairly good job of suppressing his feelings for her, although he was pretty sure she knew how he felt anyway.

Today, however, his emotions were on full display, but in a different way. He was excited. No doubt about it. They were going somewhere. At last, an adventure! Time travel! The prospect filled him with delicious anticipation. How Imogen and Simon took this miraculous gift so calmly for granted, like it was no big deal, was beyond him. Before they left the house to go to her office downtown, Imogen had briefed them on Bakunawa, the island they would be traveling to.

It was one of several islands of an archipelago located in the Andaman Sea bordering Myanmar and Thailand in the northeastern Indian Ocean, she explained.

Cool! Warm. Tropical. Great. Let's go! Fletcher thought. But ... she had added, inhabiting the island is a tribe of hostile, spear-wielding natives. Oh. Not so great. "Wait ... what? Did you say spear-wielding natives?" Fletcher had echoed. Niles had argued this point for not going when Imogen had first brought it up, but Fletcher either hadn't paid much attention or just figured, like most tropical places, the locals disliked tourists.

Imogen didn't appear concerned. "Yep," she answered. Fletcher was confused. "Um ... And why exactly do we want to go to this particular island? Aren't there like hundreds ... maybe thousands of other, safer islands you could choose? Islands without angry, hostile, armed people living on them?"

Imogen smiled. "Well, yes, we could go anywhere, as you know, but this island is kind of special to me." She looked over at Niles and smiled. "And to Dad." Niles nodded in agreement. Imogen explained that not only was the island stunningly beautiful, remote, and untouched, but both she and her dad had visited it before; they knew the tribal leader, even had a special hut of their own to stay in while they were there. Fletcher was still a bit concerned, but getting away was the main objective—hostile natives or not. And if Imogen and Niles said it would be okay, he trusted their judgment ... mostly.

When it was time to go, Imogen and Niles, their arms snugly interlaced with Fletcher's, stood facing one of the photographs Imogen found in her parents' studio before it burned down of Bakunawa taken remotely by anthropologists at various times over a twenty-year period.

"Ready?" Imogen asked. Both men nodded as Imogen focused on the picture. Within minutes, the space around them began to shift and change; darken, stretch out and twist. It had been a while and Imogen felt herself getting dizzy and feeling a bit queasy, but the sensation passed quickly. Soon, the darkness became a bright light and the trio, arms still folded securely together, found themselves standing on a sandy beachhead under clear blue, cloudless skies. A light breeze wafted gently across their faces, ruffling their hair, rustling the fronds of nearby palm trees; the sound of a boat engine faded in the distance. And almost immediately, they were surrounded by dozens of angry islanders, a myriad of faces contorted in rage; sharp-edged spears pointing directly at the trio, poised to take out the intruders trapped within the center of their circle.

In rising unison, the voices shouted, "Fte uko chea? ftch uko chea toko? ftoko xe chea yequo wkequ? ftoko ij cheak zeuh?" (*Who are you? Why are you here? Where do you come from? Where is your boat?*)

It was all Fletcher could do to keep from freaking out. "Oh my god, Imogen," he whispered, his body rigid with fear. "You weren't kidding about hostiles, were you?"

"I'm afraid not," Imogen said. Yet she remained calm, as did Niles. "Stay still," she whispered back.

Slowly untangling his arm from Fletcher and Imogen, Niles cautiously raised his hands above his head, palms out in a nonthreatening stance and spoke in their native language, "Niles, wkionx (*friend*) of D'ar; Imogen, Jto ij hto xuavthok ew nipoj; (*daughter of Niles*); Fletcher, wkionx of Niles and Imogen."

At first, it seemed his words served only to anger the natives further causing them to become ever more agitated and aggressive as they thrust their spears in the intruder's direction and hurled more enraged, indecipherable invectives at them. Even Imogen seemed a tiny bit frightened, Fletcher noted. Not a good sign. The natives began to inch closer and closer, their loud chants ringing in their ears, so close Fletcher could feel their hot breath on his face. Imogen's grip on his arm tightened and he squeezed his eyes shut, bracing for what horrible thing might come next. Sheesh, all he had wanted was to get away for a nice tropical vacation. But then, he felt Imogen loosen her grip on his arm and Fletcher ventured a peek. Miraculously, the expressions on the faces of some of the natives began to soften as if they recognized the trio. They lowered their spears and slowly backed away. Fletcher watched the ripple of movement as they began to part the way for someone who was pushing up through the crowd from the rear. When this person, an elderly man, finally emerged from the gauntlet of tribespeople, he immediately broke into a broad grin and began waving his arms wildly above his head and shouting excitedly.

"Niles! Im-oo-gen, xuavthok ew nipoj Niles (*Imogen, daughter of Niles*). Niles relaxed at the sight of his old friend D'ar and the two moved toward each other and embraced. D'ar grabbed Imogen and pulled her in for a warm, albeit forceful hug. Fletcher began to relax too until D'ar noticed him standing there and the smile on his face became a fierce glare. "Fte uko chea? (*Who are you?*). Fletcher's eyes flashed on Niles in utter panic, but Niles quickly stepped between them. Gesturing with his hands over his heart he said to D'ar, "Fletcher, wkionx." "Ah!" the tribal leader said nodding. And before Fletcher could react, the tribal leader had him in a tight bear hug, his arms pinned to his side. "Wkionx to Niles, wkionx to D'ar!" he said. Fletcher lifted his hands as far as he could and cautiously patted D'ar, fully relieved that he was *wkionx* and not dinner.

When D'ar finally let go of Fletcher he turned his attention back to his old friend Niles, and the two men strolled away arm in arm, leaving Fletcher and Imogen trailing behind them as they headed off the beach. The excitement over, the other natives retreated, moving off in various other directions. "Whew," Fletcher said, taking a deep breath. "That was a close one." Imogen chuckled. "You were okay the whole time," she said. "We wouldn't have let them impale you ... much."

"Oh, yeah, ha ha, well it's a good thing your 'friend' D'ar was close by."

Following D'ar and Niles they entered a dense, canopied rainforest. On the well-trodden trail, Fletcher marveled at the abundance of flora and fauna—the tall grasses, palms, deciduous trees, and wild orchids and candlewood along the way. Although the plants and scents were not of the same variety, it reminded him of the lush old growth forests in Oregon. It seemed forever ago since he and Imogen had gone hiking together. Up ahead, he could tell that she was breathing in the fresh air and enjoying the beauty of it as much as he was, and notably, no rain!

Even pregnant, Imogen always had a way of moving fast, not always gracefully, but when she was hiking especially there was an almost joyous spring to her step. Then, as if she sensed he was thinking of her, she turned and glanced back over her shoulder at him and smiled. "Catch up slowpoke," she teased, picking up the pace.

Was it so wrong for him to love her? Yes, yes it was. Fletcher knew that, especially after she'd brought Simon back with her, even more so after he and Simon had become good friends, but his feelings for her had not faltered. It was horrible to even think, but if he was honest, these past couple weeks, despite a pandemic and everything else bad going on in the world, had been the best weeks of his life, because he got to spend it with Imogen, admittedly, the love of his life. Sure, she'd always be fond of him, but fondness was just a kind way of forever relegating him to the friend zone. It seemed fated—in this story anyway—that sadly, Fletcher would not ever be getting the girl.

The trail abruptly ended in a small clearing where sunlight spilled downward like wispy waterfalls through several apertures in the canopy above and in the center, the tiny overgrown shelter that Niles and Imogen had individually spent time in. When she entered Imogen found Niles already inside the structure, perched comfortably on the bamboo bed lacing up his black canvas Converse All Stars. He looked up at her and grinned like a kid. "They still fit." Imogen had left everything—his sneakers, reading glasses, notebook—exactly as he had left it, in case he ever returned. At the time, that possibility hadn't seemed remotely attainable, so now, seeing him here reunited with his things was more than touching. On impulse, she reached out and embraced her father for the first time since she'd found him stuck in 1997 and brought him home. It was a breakthrough moment they both felt deeply, until Fletcher entered the enclosure and broke the spell.

"Wow, this is really spectacular," he said as he quickly scanned the inside of the enclosure. From an engineer's perspective, he was quite impressed by the solid design of the walls and interior. He ran his hand along the bamboo wall tracing the neat, clean lines and marveling at the hut's crisscrossed bamboo beams above that created the yurt-like, pitched roof.

"How long has this been here?" he asked, turning back to Niles. Niles squeezed Imogen's shoulder, scratched his chin. "hmmm, hard to say. I'm thinking probably a really long time."

"Incredible," Fletcher said. "For a primitive hut built by a tribe that seemingly exists out of time with no access to the outside world the craftsmanship and symmetry is extraordinary."

"And that's only the beginning of the magic that is Bakunawa," Imogen said, changing the subject. "Wait until the dancing and drumming starts later and they pass around the quuntuhhun!"

"The quuntu-what?"

Niles chuckled, adding, "Yeah, I don't think you'll be thinking much about hut building after you try some of that!" Fletcher shrugged and looked down.

"Cool shoes," he said, noticing Niles change of footwear.

Leaving Fletcher in the hut to sleep off the effects of last night's quuntuhhun, Imogen and Niles found a spot in the clearing to drink D'ar's special tea made from pineapple, mango, coconut, and pomegranate and enjoy the morning coolness and the rays of sunlight that made the place feel so special, like they were seated in a garden in a Claude Monet painting.

"How are you feeling, Imogen?" Niles asked, sitting down cross-legged on a blanket of palm fronds he'd laid out for them. He had not said anything to her before, but secretly worried what effect, if any, time travel might have on her pregnancy. He too was aware that Simon's mother had been pregnant with him when Teddy kidnapped her and dumped her in the past. He had survived, obviously, but time travel could be tricky. It was difficult to know if rules would be consistent in every situation. Imogen joined him on the ground. "I'm okay," she answered.

"Are you sure? No problems with the pregnancy?"

"I don't think so, Dad. I feel good. That feast last night was something else."

"It sure was. Seemed like Fletcher enjoyed himself."

"A little too much," Imogen said, chuckling. "I tried to warn him not to drink so much quuntuhhun, but he wouldn't listen."

"He'll pay for it when he wakes up," Niles said. Both quietly sipped their tea from their carved wooden cups until Imogen broke the silence.

"Dad. Niles?"

Niles looked up from his tea. "Yeah?"

"Um," she began. "You know when I visited Bakunawa by myself, well I probably shouldn't have, but I read your journal and the things you wrote in it about Mom."

Niles shifted uncomfortably and looked away.

"I'm sorry, Dad. You don't have to tell me anything. I haven't wanted to burden you after all you've been through, but I thought you should know."

Niles looked at Imogen and placed his hand on hers.

"It's all right, Imogen," he said. "You're not burdening me. I realize I've been avoiding talking about what happened these past few months. I wanted to, but it just never seemed like the right time."

"Is now the right time, Dad?" Imogen asked.

Niles breathed in deeply and began. "The last time I saw you Imogen was the night before you were supposed to go to the carnival with Jade. Do you remember that?"

Imogen nodded. "I do," she said.

"You two were so excited. Your mom, Francis, not so much. She never trusted that the carnival workers wouldn't forget to tighten a screw on one of the rides or that you'd get food poisoning from eating a deep-fried corn dog gone bad. But we both knew how important it was to you and Jade, a childhood memory in the making. That morning, everything changed when you came back home after finding that Jade was gone. I had never seen you so upset over anything before. We were both worried about you, of course, but for me, seeing you that way was heartbreaking.

We both figured you'd get over it eventually. Kids are resilient that way and we tried to compensate for the loss of your friend by ramping up the fun activities and outings, but when you were still brooding and unhappy after the summer ended and into the school year, I felt like I had to do something, figure out where this girl went at least, give you some closure. That's when I went into your room while you were at school and found the letter she'd sent you.

At first, I was delighted. This meant that you had answers and could probably move on. I read it but something seemed wrong about it. For one thing, it didn't sound like a nine-year-old child had written it, despite the handwriting. All it said was that she had a fun summer and that her mother had gotten a job."

"I remember," Imogen said.

"It just didn't ring true to me." But when I saw the picture, she'd enclosed of her standing in front of a house I checked the postmark and saw that it was in Danbury I started thinking maybe I could find out more. The problem back then, of course, was we didn't have the GPS satellite technology we have now. The town isn't that big, but big enough that I couldn't just drive around and potentially find that particular house. It was a needle in a haystack situation really."

"So you decided to go through the picture."

"Right. And you know what happened to me after that."

Imogen had been waiting years to ask the next question. "Teddy destroyed both anchor photos, yours and Mom's. Where ... and when did Mom go? What was her photo?"

Niles looked down at his lap. His jaw tightened and he pressed his lips together, pausing to gather the strength he needed to tell this story before continuing.

"You said you read my journal, then you know that your mom and I were having problems in our marriage," he began. "The truth is I didn't want your mother to know that I was going to look for your friend." He shook his head. "I don't know why it mattered, but it just felt like something I needed to do on my own without a bunch of explanation. Your mother said something about having some business to attend to somewhere. I didn't press her on what it might be about or where she was going because I was focused on my own damn plans of finding Jade, for you." Niles looked away, ashamed. "I never knew where Francis went or why she went there because ... I ... I didn't ask."

Imogen suddenly realized that she had never seen her father cry before and she didn't like it. He had turned away from her now, his hands pressed against his eyes to hide the tears, but she could see his shoulders trembling as he tried to hold back the tide of emotions.

"Daddy, it's okay," Imogen blurted. She tugged at his shirt in an effort to get him to turn around and face her but didn't have to try hard because he reached out on his own and grabbed hold of her tightly and they held each other like that for a while in a long-suppressed moment of shared pain and sorrow and loss.

When the moment had passed, Niles released his daughter, and looking into her tearful eyes, managed to smile. "Remember when you used to mess around with the loose folds of skin on my elbow at night when I tucked you in?" he said. Through the tears, Imogen laughed out loud at the unexpected memory. "Weirdly, yes," she said. "And the trolls—to this day I still hold my breath when I drive through a stupid tunnel!" Soon they were both laughing as old memories came flooding back. It could never make up for the years they had lost, Imogen thought, but it sure was better to reminisce *with* him here sitting next to her than it ever was without him. They were back together and that was all that mattered.

They sat silently for a few minutes, simply enjoying each other's company and the moment before Imogen asked, "I'm curious, Dad, I know you and D'ar became friends, but how did that happen?" She shuddered to think what might have happened to her the first time she visited if D'ar had not stepped in and recognized her. The Kansas debacle had rattled her so much she'd neglected to do her homework, randomly choosing one of the pictures of the island from the bundle of photos she'd found in her dad's drawer, assuming it was just some nice tourist destination. After returning home she had done some research on Bakunawa. It was the last restricted area in the world where the indigenous natives were protected by the government. She had read a couple of years ago about a man who, on a mission to convert them to Christianity, had rowed up alone in a boat to the island. It did not end well for him.

Niles explained that because they had arrived without a boat, D'ar believed that they had traveled using some sort of magic. He was sort of right. When D'ar saw them disappear into thin air the first time they left, he was convinced of it.

"You know, that after we've used up the photos in the bundle, we can't return here again on the assumption that D'ar might still be alive," Imogen said. "Without his protection, the others might not hesitate to kill us and leave our dead bodies on the beach like they did to that missionary."

Niles nodded in agreement and Imogen noticed a look of sadness on his face again. "What's wrong?" she asked.

"I always hoped that Francis would come home and maybe at some point come back here with me, to this island, read my journals, know that I loved her at least," he said.

"We'll find her, Dad. I promise. I found you, right?" Imogen said, trying to cheer him up. "I'm a private investigator, that's what I do."

"Then you must have, over the years, tried to find something out about her," he said.

Imogen wished she had better news for him. "Yes, I've searched databases, obituaries from newspapers around the world, public records, nothing comes up," she said. "I swear, it's like she vanished off the face of the earth, Dad."

But after she said that something, a memory, popped into her mind.

"There is one thing though ... "

"What?" Niles asked.

I have this fuzzy memory of visiting a different beach once, when I was like four," she said. I had been looking at a picture in Grammy's photo album when it happened. I don't know, maybe it was the first time I time traveled. It was weird, but what I really remember most is that Mom was there. I was standing right next to her, and she spoke to me."

Niles leaned forward, interested. "Really? What did she say?"

"I said hi to her and she asked me what I was doing here?"

"Do you remember anything more specific, Imogen?" Niles probed, "like where this particular beach might be?"

Imogen paused in thought, as she attempted to draw back the curtain on the memory. All of a sudden, something else did occur to her, a different recollection but one that seemed connected to the one she was trying so hard to recall.

"I remember it smelled like salt and sort of fishy," she said. "I had a case a few years ago in San Francisco, 1967," she continued, excitement building in her voice. "And Dad … it smelled just like that … just like Fisherman's Wharf! Oh! And now that I think about it, Teddy mentioned something about San Francisco too. Do you think it could actually be the same place? A clue to where she might have gone?"

A slim smile and something in his eyes that looked like hope lit up Niles' face. "I don't know, Imogen. It might be or it might not, but it sure sounds like a good place to start!"

Just then Fletcher stumbled out from inside the hut, his hair a wild tangle, shielding his eyes from the bright rays of sunlight. "What are you guys doing out here?" he mumbled. "What time is it?" A hilarious question on an island where people essentially existed outside of time.

"You look terrible," Imogen commented, restraining a giggle. Fletcher grunted, turned back around and reentered the hut.

After he was gone, Niles handed Imogen his journal. "What's this?" Imogen asked.

"You wrote something in it, last time you were here, do you remember?"

"No," she said.

"Read it," he said. "It might be illuminating."

Mostly our lives are ordinary. We go through our days moving from one mundane task to another, but every now and then something extraordinary happens, a kiss, or something that makes us realize how wonderful and precious life is. And it becomes an indelible memory that we can go back and retrieve like a little movie reel spinning in our heads that we can replay and rewind and relive for an instant anytime we want to. Is this a memory or a beginning? I'm not sure.

4

Left Bank PARIS, 1930 Montparnasse

Tiffany remembered drifting away, letting go, watching the lights go but then she was awake feeling that strange feeling of emerging from nothing, from a place where no light or dreams exist. Like coming around after being anesthetized when you remember voices in the distance as you fade away, and then an instant has passed, only that instant has been hours, and you find yourself back in the world as abruptly as you left it. Was she alive? Was she cured? Maybe she was dead; she was too frightened to open her eyes. But she did. A dingy room. Gloomy. Curtains drawn. A too soft sofa and a scratchy knitted Afghan covering her legs. From the kitchen, rustling low, whispered conversation that she could not make out.

And then a person bursting into the dim room. "Ah, you are awake!" a woman's voice with a throaty French accent called out. "At last!" she said. "For a while we feared we may have lost you."

As she drew near, Tiffany could make out her shape—tall, lanky, large golden earrings, a purple bandana loosely wrapped around her head like a gypsy cap, wispy black bangs and curls escaping out the sides of it. She turned on a lamp by the sofa, which then illuminated her moon-shaped face, a kind but hard face, the face of an honest person Tiffany supposed she could trust with her life. Plopping down next to her, she drew a cigarette from a slender silver case, lit it, took a drag, and exhaled a puff of smoke shaped like a perfect ring that floated in front of Tiffany's impressed gaze.

"Drag?" she offered.

"No thanks," Tiffany replied. "I don't smoke."

"Too bad for you," the woman said smiling as she said it. "I'm Lili, by the way, and you?"

"Tiffany," she answered. "Tiffany Rose."

Lili blew out another puff of smoke. "Tiffany. Hmm. Like the jewelry or the lamp?" she asked.

Tiffany shrugged. "I'm not sure," she answered, confused. "No one's ever asked me that before, but excuse me … um Lili … where am I?"

Lili patted Tiffany's legs as she got up and headed back to the kitchen. "I imagine you are quite hungry, Miss Tiffany Rose."

A sudden wave of dizziness engulfed her. Tiffany rested her head against the soft satin pillow and closed her eyes. This was all so strange. The last thing she remembered was feeling terribly groggy and disoriented and speaking to a nurse. Was it at the asylum? Yes, that's right. Crestview. It had to be. She had thought they were taking her for another shock treatment. It was confusing. How had she gotten here from there? Was this a dream? As the jumble of baffling questions swirled through her mind, she felt the presence of someone next to her again. She opened her eyes to Lili standing before her offering her a spoon and a bowl of something.

"Here darling," Lili said. "You must eat something." Tiffany drew her slouching body up to a more upright position and took the spoon and bowl from Lili. The enamel bowl ornamented with delicate flowers, was warm in her hands. Felt good. Comforting somehow. She breathed in the aromatic smell of several indistinguishable, but not unpleasant spices in the thick dish, which featured a potpourri of vegetables and what looked like hearty chunks of beef.

"It is Pot-au-Feu," Lili said. "Soup. Is good for you."

Tiffany took a taste and smiled. Mmm. Yes, it was good. Very good, in fact. "Thank you," she said. Lili got up and switched on a floor lamp allowing Tiffany to finally see where she was. The room wasn't terribly large, but the high ceilings gave it the appearance of a much larger space. The Parisian-style apartment featured white walls, tall ceiling-to-floor windows adorned with a set of chic but threadbare red velvet curtains, and old herringbone parquet floors. Though shabby and clearly of a used or found-object nature, the room's art deco-ish bohemian décor was unconventional, unstructured, creative. Layered textiles and textures, rugs, bold colors, plants growing everywhere, gemstones and tassels, it was an amalgamation of human history, with many layers representing a mishmash of other times and other cultures. The bright colors and unusual items made Tiffany feel happy and hopeful. Only someone who had been confined for years behind the drab walls of an insane asylum could fully appreciate the whimsy and sheer fabulousness of this place.

Lili planted herself beside her on the divan. "I will tell you a story now while you eat, no?" she said. Tiffany nodded and Lili began to speak.

"Nikki brought you to us a few nights ago. You were in a coma," she said.

"But where is here?" Tiffany immediately interrupted in between chews.

Lili placed two fingers against Tiffany's lips to shush her. "Here, is Paris, *when* is 1930" she answered, "but stay quiet, darling. I will soon get to that." Tiffany could not believe her ears. Paris! How the heck did she get to Paris? Did she come by boat? How long would that take? No, Lili said it was 1930? How was that possible? It was always difficult keeping track of the time at Crestview, but hadn't it been later? Had she gone back in time? It seemed so, but she couldn't be sure about anything. A million puzzling questions raced at light speed through her head.

"You have questions." Lili seemed to read her mind. "They will be answered, you will understand when I finish." Resigned, Tiffany went back to eating her soup allowing Lili to continue.

"There was a patient uprising at the asylum where you were. Dominique and others rescued you from getting, what do they call it, a lob—something." Lili struggled with the pronunciation. "I ... I don't know ... eh, a brain scramble?"

"Do you mean a lobotomy?" Tiffany asked. Long, long ago, back in school they had read about Rosemary Kennedy, JFK's sister, who had a lobotomy when she was only twenty-three, a procedure that had rendered her unable to walk or talk, permanently disabled, and institutionalized for the remainder of her life.

"Yes, yes, that is it!" Lili confirmed. Completely rattled by the realization that she had come so close to the same fate, Tiffany let the bowl slip from her hands, spilling the remainder of Pot-au-Feu onto her lap.

Lili jumped up and sprinted to the kitchen to grab a towel. She quickly returned and began to mop up the spill from the Afghan while Tiffany apologized profusely. "Oh, I am so, so sorry," she repeated.

"It is fine, Miss Tiffany," Lili assured her. "Do not worry yourself," she said as she wiped up the remaining soup with the towel. Setting the bowl and the Afghan aside, she made Tiffany lean back, readjusting the pillows behind her and grabbing another throw blanket from a nearby chair and tossing it across her lap.

Lili picked up where she left off explaining how bad conditions had become at Crestview. New doctors had arrived at the asylum and put new procedures and practices in place. Electroshock therapy had increased, and they had started using this new experimental therapy—lobotomy. Some patients had shown modest improvement, while others were not so lucky. Fearing they would be next, some of the patients planned to take over the asylum.

"But how could I have not known what was going on?" Tiffany was even more confused now. "And I didn't know anyone named Dominique either!"

"At Crestview, Dominique was not a patient," Lili explained. "She was one of the nurses."

Tiffany tried not to be impatient, but this story was sounding crazier by the minute.

"Nikki left certain doors unlocked, arranged for orderlies to be called elsewhere, and when the time came, the patients rebelled, overtook the staff and doctors. As many as could go escaped, but some were left behind—too sick or incapacitated to leave, I'm afraid."

Tiffany hung her head. She knew who some of those patients might be. They may have been her friends, but she was glad that some of them were able to escape. Yet, still lay the burning question, if she was drugged up, on the precipice of a lobotomy, maybe in a coma, how did she manage to escape Crestview?

Again, Lili seemed to know what she was thinking. "Nikki brought you through a photograph."

The last time Tiffany had traveled through a photograph Teddy Diamond had kidnapped her and dumped her unceremoniously in the year 1885. She was relieved that at least this time she had been asleep and thus spared the trauma of that first unwanted experience with time travel. She should be afraid, but she wasn't. If she'd learned anything in her life it was that you are stronger than you know and that anyone can be a student and anywhere, anytime can be a classroom.

Lili explained to her that Nikki had suspected that Tiffany might be living outside of her time. "Why would she think that?" Tiffany asked.

"She said that you had been at the asylum for many years but did not seem to grow old," Lili answered.

Tiffany didn't know much about the rules of time travel but that made sense. It hadn't taken her very long to realize that time moved differently, perhaps slower in the past. She had been seventeen when Teddy abandoned her, twenty-four when she was committed to Crestview, but sometime around 1913, or so, it had seemed like for some reason, she stopped aging.

"Where is Dominique … Nikki now," Tiffany asked, anxious to meet her liberator.

"After she left you here, she returned to the hospital to try to rescue others." Tiffany revered this Nikki person even more. Not only had she snatched her at the last moment from the clutches of a doctor set on scrambling her brain, but she had gone back to save as many others as she could. "Will she come back? Tiffany asked. Lili shook her head and shrugged. "Are there other time travelers here?" she asked. "Are you …?"

"No, I am not a traveler, as you call it," a flustered Lili exclaimed, holding her hands up in front of Tiffany in a please stop motion. "You have too many questions all at once," she said.

"Oh, I am sorry," Tiffany said, "but can you tell me again what year it is?"

"Nineteen thirty," Lili answered. "You are in Montparnasse in the Latin Quarter of Paris, France. I live here ... with others."

Tiffany wondered who these "others" were. She was about to find out.

Feeling much better with a belly full of hot soup, Lili instructed Tiffany to make herself at home when she was up to it, which meant exploring her new surroundings. Time-wise, Tiffany was still living in about the same era, give or take a few years, as the one she had been snatched from in the US and certainly, this new place was a wonderful improvement over Crestview.

***

Like firecrackers bursting in the night sky, a creative explosion erupted everywhere in the City of Lights in the early thirties. Similar to the early influx to the city in the twenties, impoverished artists, writers, musicians, actors, and young people rejecting the aristocracy flooded the Left Bank seeking new ways to live.

Over the next few weeks, Tiffany discovered she resided in a sort of half-way house for this quirky demographic—*boheme*, a French name for the nomadic. One woman, who Tiffany suspected might be a prostitute although couldn't be certain, never spoke but didn't really need to because, oh yes, she was always nude. Another, who worked in the nearby music hall, spent most of her time walking around the flat on her hands, which was a part of her acrobatic act in the show, Tiffany gathered. There was a painter, a queer fellow who quoted Shakespeare more than he painted. A trio of lesbians, two dressed in loose trousers and fedoras, and a third who mostly wore a flowery ruffled apron over a flimsy chartreuse slip while she cooked fabulously delicious dishes or lounged on the divan exposing her vulva and hairy armpits and legs.

People came and went with regularity. It was not at all unusual to come out in the morning and find some unknown person sleeping on the sofa. Music, mostly American jazz songs by Cab Calloway Duke Ellington, Big Bill Broonzy, or Lead Belly on the radio or via scratchy 78 rpm records played night and day on a dusty Victrola. And at any given time, a cornucopia of smells ranging from cigarettes and sweat to wine and sex and turpentine, or sometimes the fragrant aroma of fresh-baked sourdough bread or spicy, pungent French cuisine, wafted in and out of the space.

The days passed and as much as Tiffany delighted in the goings on at the flat, she felt increasingly useless. Everyone worked here, everyone except her. But she was unsure about what she could do. She had been locked away for so long, she wasn't sure she even had any marketable skills. She couldn't do acrobatics like Genevieve, and she had no cooking skills like Margo. But Lili, she discovered, had a far less unconventional occupation than her eccentric housemates—she worked as a clerk at a bookstore in the sixteenth arrondissement. This was something that interested her, something she could do. She had always loved to read. She read to young Simon whenever she could get her hands on a book and, of course, reading was her only means of escape when she was in the asylum.

One morning, Tiffany joined Lili on the balcony as she sipped a demi-tasse of espresso before work. "Say, do you think they might need any help over at that bookstore where you work? I don't have proficiency, but I love books, and I love to read. Or I can sweep floors, dust shelves," she suggested in earnest.

Lili's weak, dismissive smile was telling. Tiffany sensed she might be pacifying her. "What is it, Lili? She asked."

Lili sighed and set her cup down upon the saucer. "I appreciate that you want to work, darling, but do you think you are, well ..." she hesitated to choose her words carefully before adding, "mentally fit?"

Tiffany understood. "Ah, I see" she responded. "The asylum. You think I'm crazy, right?"

Lili raised her eyebrows without vocalizing her concerns either way. "I'm not crazy, Lili. I assure you. Do you have time for a story?"

Lili glanced at her watch and nodded. "Oui, a short time."

Tiffany sprinted to the kitchen to grab a demi-tass for herself and quickly returned. "All right," she began. "In 1997 ..." Lili's jaw dropped slightly at the mention of a year sixty-seven years in the future, but Tiffany continued. "In 1997, a boy took me through a photograph and left me there alone. It was 1885. I was seventeen and pregnant."

Lili sat in captivated silence while Tiffany replayed her story about saving up to buy a camera and how she took pictures of herself and left them near the place she was abandoned hoping that someone in the future, a time traveler perhaps, might one day find them and come back and rescue her; how Herbert, whom she had thought was a friend, helped her but then had betrayed her. She spoke of women, how in those days, they could be committed for any old reason—laziness, grief, masturbation, excitability, reading too much. It was a convenient way for men to keep opinionated, unruly, or otherwise inconvenient women and girls in line.

"I was a bit too vocal about being from the future," Tiffany confided. "And of course, I sounded irrational and maybe I was a little bit crazy at that point." She spoke of her son.

"My son's name was Simon. He was a good boy. When they had me committed, they took him away and I never saw him again." Thinking of him made Tiffany very sad and she looked away. "He would be a grown man by now," she said, "if he's even alive."

Lili, clearly touched by her story, reached over and patted Tiffany's hand.

"One more thing," Tiffany continued. "The answer to your question, the one about whether I was named for the lamp or the jewelry. It's neither. My mother named me after a pop singer named Tiffany who was discovered singing in a shopping mall in the nineteen eighties."

One week later, Tiffany started her new job at Shakespeare and Company, 12 rue de l'Odéon. More than a bookstore, Shakespeare and Company was an icon. Opening in 1919, by her kind and cheerful American employer Sylvia Beach, the English-language bookshop and lending library had been the center of expatriate life in the twenties, frequented by the century's most influential writers, including Ernest Hemingway, Gertrude Stein, Simone de Beauvoir, and others. Beach had even published author James Joyce's famous, banned in the US novel, *Ulysses*.

Tiffany's job was to sort and reshelve books and other ephemera and keep them dust-free as well. Although Lili commanded a higher paying job—she was in charge of maintaining the logbooks—details on library memberships, renewals, and reimbursements—Tiffany was more than satisfied working silently in the background. The simple act of being busy and useful pleased her in a way that no one outside a mental institution would ever understand.

She loved everything about this warm, welcoming place. She loved the wall-to-wall, row-upon-row of books, the photographs on the walls, the smell of the books and the tactile feel of holding them in her hands. She liked the physicality of climbing up and down the ladder to reshelve books and magazines she had never heard of before. Not only that, but each new day might also bring a surprise visit from a famous person to the store. At any given time, Ernest Hemingway could stroll in, looking for a particular book or to exchange gossip with Sylvia. Famous photographer Man-Ray might drop by to inconspicuously poke around in the photography section.

Lili had even let her borrow a couple of her dresses and accessories to wear to work until she could afford to purchase her own. The routine of getting up, getting dressed, applying makeup, fixing her hair, eating a piece of toast and espresso, brushing her teeth and heading out the door might seem insignificant, but for Tiffany each of these tasks were small triumphs, a gift of routine that was all her own, not dictated by burly hospital orderlies in white uniforms forcing pills down her gullet or binding her in a straightjacket or shoving a metal plate in her mouth and shocking her body until her eyes rolled back in her head and she lost consciousness. Tiffany silently thanked Nikki, the nurse who had whisked her away from that awful place and deposited her into a life that she could never have imagined for herself.

Unfortunately for Tiffany, however, all was not copacetic. There were residual aftereffects from the trauma she had experienced. Because of the shock therapy treatments, she had difficulty sleeping. Quieting her racing thoughts became a nightly struggle. Lying in bed watching the minutes tick by until she would have to eventually arise and go to work only exacerbated the problem. She took to walking the streets at night. Perhaps the night air would clear her mind, and she could come home and sleep, she thought. It was worth a try anyway.

She should have been afraid. She knew there was crime and vice all around her in the city, but for some reason, she was not. Maybe she'd used up all her fear at Crestview and had none left, but after a few nocturnal excursions, Tiffany discovered how very much she enjoyed this special time in this big, beautiful city, shrouded in a silent fog of darkness, rain often reflecting silver on the narrow cobblestone streets, quietly devoid of the humanity of daylight.

Apparently, she soon discovered, there were other sleepless denizens like herself out walking the streets after dark, and after so many nights, an unspoken familiarity began to form as each acknowledged the other; a nod here a small wave in passing there as if they shared a secret that only night people understood. It became a comfort of sorts. The elderly man in the suit and cap stepping gingerly off the curb on Rue de la Harpe, his cane leading the way; the disheveled woman with the smudged lipstick and tussled red braid who emerged nightly from the same half-lit flat above the patisserie on Rue d'Ulm; the young man with the rosy cheeks and jaunty hat, walking his Yorkshire Terrier.

One night as Tiffany started to turn a corner, she stopped short quickly leaping back into the shadows behind the building after observing a strange man she had not seen before. She noticed that he carried a camera with him.

On cue, red braid woman left the flat, came down the steps, and exited through the outside door the way she always did. The man with the camera approached her. The two spoke briefly, she nodded, he backed up and snapped her photograph. He handed her something and she walked away. This became a nightly ritual, though not always at the same place. Sometimes the man was alone, sometimes in the company of a friend—a man wearing a long coat and a fedora. They talked and laughed as the photographer snapped pictures of ordinary people—all of whom were out at night for various reasons. Tiffany began following him to see where he might end up and what he might do—who he might choose to photograph. Night after night, she followed close behind as he frequented brothels and opium dens and night spots. Tiffany had always had an interest in photography. After the years of taking photographs to leave behind for someone in the future to find, she had learned a few camera tricks herself.

This particular night, as she was following the man, he seemed distracted. He turned slightly and looked in her direction and she ducked stealthily behind a facade. The man stopped suddenly then, turned around to face her directly and called out in French, "est-ce que vous me suivez madame? (*Are you following me madam?*) Tiffany emerged slowly from the shadows, embarrassed to be caught. She had picked up enough French to know that she had been exposed. "Oui," she mumbled. The man came closer. "Parles-tu français?" he asked.

Shaking her head, Tiffany replied, "Non … monsieur."

"n'aie pas peur," he said, first in French. "Don't be frightened," he repeated in English.

"I'm not afraid," Tiffany boldly replied.

"That is good," the man said as he drew ever closer. Under the light from the streetlamp, his features came into focus—jet black hair, dark eyes, and thick eyebrows—revealing a man perhaps of Eastern European descent. He extended his hand to Tiffany in a friendly gesture. "I am Gyula Halász. You may call me Brassaï."

Shaking his outstretched hand, she said, "A pleasure to meet you, monsieur Brassaï. I am Tiffany Rose Elliot."

"Are you interested in photography," he inquired, bringing his camera around and holding it up in front of him.

"I am," Tiffany said. "But I would like to learn more."

A sly smile crossed Brassaï's face. Turning slowly on his heels, he extended his arm for Tiffany to take. "Follow me then," he said. And she did.

5

Imogen vacuumed, she rifled through papers, dusted, she tidied up the office, emptied the trash basket, gave the toilet bowl a quick scrub, fidgeted with the photograph sitting on the desk in front of her. She didn't need to go. She certainly didn't need the money.

The trip to Bakunawa had been great, fantastic, had lifted all their spirits. She'd drawn closer to her dad as well as to Fletcher—creating an equal measure of guilt, secret delight, and confusion. She loved their company, but she needed space. Time away by herself, to clear her head. Think. She had hoped that she would hear from Simon, but still not a word. What could he possibly be doing that he couldn't call? She had tried to call his cell phone many times, but it always went straight to voicemail. Maybe the Society had taken his phone, but still, it was strange. And he still did know that she was pregnant.

The last time she visited the nineteen twenties she had been assaulted by a creepy patron in a smoky, illicit speakeasy on New Year's Eve. Nevertheless, she had accepted this job and felt she had to follow through. And besides, it wasn't like it was high risk or anything like some jobs she had undertaken in the past. The client was simply interested in obtaining some land documents. Essentially, all she had to do was visit city hall. She knew that they couldn't make photocopies in the twenties, but they usually kept triplicate copies. A few extra dollars slipped discreetly to the clerk, and she could probably walk out in five minutes with a set that she could then secure in a postal box for future pickup. Easy peasy.

Still, the fact that she hadn't felt good this morning when she woke up, more weird than ill, had given her some pause, but after coffee and a piece of cinnamon toast she felt better. No need to postpone the case. Quick turnaround. She'd be back home in a jiffy.

Things could not have gone any smoother. It was 1924. She had been deposited steps from city hall. Walked in, requested the deed numbers, and ten minutes later, the documents secured, she was headed downtown to the post office.

The marvel of traveling to another time outside of her own was not lost on Imogen, especially on a gorgeous spring day like this one. Delicate white and pink blossoms dotted the line of trees planted along the avenue and the sun felt warm against her skin. Walking, or rather, strolling today felt extraordinarily enjoyable. It reminded her of the first time she ever walked into a photograph back in college. She'd been studying the turn of the twentieth century for one of her history classes and had ended up in 1901 where she ran into her grandmother and her grammy's beau

Andre! It had been a perfect spring day, like today, and coincidently it was also the first time she met a younger version of Simon. At the time she had not an inkling that she would run into him again years later.

Indeed, this was the part of time travel she liked best; when she didn't feel rushed, could take her time, enjoy the weather, people watch. There really was nothing like experiencing a place in a completely different time than your own, scrutinizing the clothes people wore and observing how they behaved, people doing just regular stuff, walking their dogs, socializing in person—and nary a smart phone in sight, she marveled! Even though she knew there were problems and tribulations and injustice in every time period, here, today, things just felt simpler, slower. In her time, she was always on. If her phone beeped, she grabbed for it to check who was pinging her, constantly checked her email, scrolling through social media apps, eyes focused on the moving screen. If anything, the pandemic had been a bit of a wake-up call for her and likely for a lot of other people. What simple joys had we been missing out on? Even though they still had cable and internet service, being forced to stay inside had freed her up for doing other things, hobbies like cooking, talking, reading. It felt like freedom, in a way.

As she made her way down the sidewalk leisurely browsing the art deco furniture and fancy hats and purses and dresses in the storefront windows, she nearly missed it. The gold plaque in front of her. Attached to the towering brick building was a plaque with a name that jumped out at her. THE DANIEL B. COOPER BUILDING, it read in intricate engraved script. Hmm, could it be? she wondered. Nah. Still, it was curious that name should pop up in this time and place. Why not drop in and check, she thought. Couldn't hurt, wouldn't take long. She had nothing but time. After entering through the fancy brass and glass revolving doors, which always had a way of making her feel anxious and on high alert that she might stumble and embarrass herself at any moment, she glanced from the entryway, the building's opulent interior; high, high ceilings, marble floors, rich wood paneling, chandeliers. It reminded her somewhat of the Benson Hotel except on a much larger and grander scale. After looking around a bit, she strolled over to the front desk to casually inquire about the name on the outside plaque.

A smartly dressed woman in a simple, solid color V-neck dress with a matching light jacket, her short brown hair trimmed in the bobbed hairdo, a trendy staple of 1924 style, spoke into the handset of a black rotary dial metal desk phone. As Imogen approached the wood desk, the woman held up her index finger in the universal gesture of one moment please before ending the call shortly thereafter.

"How may I help you," she asked.

"Excuse me, but I was wondering, can you tell me who Daniel B. Cooper is?"

"Ah, Mr. Cooper, yes, the namesake of this building. He is one of our city's most prominent citizens," she said in a proud but animated, slightly flirtatious tone, Imogen thought, before adding, "Quite the philanthropist, patron of the arts, *our* Mr. Cooper."

"Really?" Imogen asked, surprised. If it was the D.B. she was thinking of, that didn't exactly sound like him, but she pressed for more info. "Does he work here? Would there be a possibility that I could meet with him, with Mr. Cooper?"

"Oh no, no, I'm afraid not, the woman said, shaking her head with resolute conviction. "Mister Cooper is a very busy, busy man. But if you'll leave your calling card, we'll make sure he gets it," she finished, her terse tone changed now to that of a protective receptionist shielding her very important boss from unwanted, uninvited, pushy guests like her who might wander in off the street.

Imogen wasn't easily deterred, however. "Would you mind telling him that Imogen Oliver is here to see him?"

"Well, Miss Oliver. I'll be happy to tell him, but I'm quite certain he is much too busy today to see you."

"Please," Imogen pressed, not about to turn around and leave. "I insist."

"Oh well, fine," the exasperated receptionist said as she picked up the phone and dialed. "I am sorry to bother you, Mr. Cooper," she spoke into the receiver. "There is a Miss Imogen Oliver in the lobby to see you." Imogen watched the woman nod, a look of surprise crossing her face.

"Mr. Cooper will see you Miss Oliver, right this way."

Imogen rode the elevator up to the seventh floor and the doors opened into an entire furnished suite, even more luxurious than the plush lobby downstairs. From across the room, D.B., standing dapper in a suit, silk tie, and tweed jacket, rushed over to her, grabbing and squeezing her in a tight bear hug. "Imogen!" He cried. "Is it really you?"

"It's me," she said, equally surprised that it was really, truly him, but a cleaned-up version of the scruffy airline hijacker she'd shared a flask of rum and smoked cigarettes with in front of a fire on a dusty Washington state trail not long ago.

He took her hand and spun her around in a circle, the heels of her pumps doing a little tap dance on the hardwood floors. "You are ravishing, my dear!" he said, admiring her stylish 1920s era outfit.

"I could say the same for you, Mister "I-have-a-fancy-building-named-after-me" Daniel B. Cooper!"

D.B. guffawed. "Oh now, I haven't changed a bit."

"Oh sure, but can you still blow smoke rings?" Imogen playfully inquired.

"Of course!" he said laughing and taking Imogen's arm and gently guiding her to a posh velvet-covered sofa. "Sit right down and tell me what you are doing here Imogen, how are you? I want to hear everything!"

Imogen welcomed the comfort of the ultra-cushy sofa. She was beginning to feel overly fatigued from walking. D.B. pulled a chair up close and sat down facing her. A lot had happened in her life, too much to tell in one sitting, really, and nothing that she thought D.B. might find all that remarkable. She was more interested in his story, how had he gone from fugitive hijacker on the lam to all this?

"I want to know, Mr. Cooper, how you managed to become one of our city's most prominent citizens, quite the philanthropist, patron of the arts, *our* Mr. Cooper'" she said imitating the sing-song voice of the gushing receptionist downstairs.

D.B. chucked. "Oh, you've been talking to Margie ..."

"Margie, is it?" Imogen teased and D.B. appeared to blush a bit.

"But seriously," she said. "How did you do it? You must have figured out time travel, and somehow you parlayed the money into a fortune ..."

D.B. explained how after she had gone, he had hiked back down the mountain and made his way to Portland, where he had laid low for a year or so, working manual labor jobs and practicing deep meditation using old photos he'd picked up at local antique shops.

"And one day, it worked!" he said.

"Remember when we first met on the mountain back in '71 and you told me people were going to know who you are?" Imogen asked out of the blue.

"I certainly do."

"Well, they do ... know you."

D.B. broke into a wide grin and his eyes twinkled with delight as he leaned in closer to her in his chair. "Really? Spill it, sister!"

Imogen couldn't help but laugh at D.B.'s childlike enthusiasm. He truly hadn't changed. A good thing.

"You got your wish," she said. "In the twenty-twenties people are still obsessed with the mystery of the elusive D.B. Cooper."

"Is that so!" D.B. said trying hard not to show how pleased he was.

"Yes, in fact, you've become a conspiracy theory. I read an article online just the other day about this citizen investigator who claims to know who you were ... are."

"And just who do they think I am?" D.B. asked, curious.

"The article said a Boeing subcontractor at a titanium plant named Vince Petersen from Pittsburg, fits the evidence left behind. They're still trying to get a DNA sample from the clip-on tie you were wearing." D.B. sat back and quietly pondered all that she'd told him.

"So?" Imogen said, breaking the silence. "Is that you? Are you Vince Petersen from Pittsburg?"

D.B.'s smile disappeared, replaced now by a seriousness Imogen had not seen before.

He paused before answering with just one word. "No," he said.

"So, what is *online?*" he asked, changing the subject.

Respecting his secrets, Imogen did not press him, instead after giving him a brief overview of the internet before moving on to something else. "You know," she said. "I've always wondered, what does the B in D.B. stand for anyway?"

Cooper chuckled and said, "Nothing. It literally stands for nothing. My middle name doesn't even start with a B. I just liked the sound of it, the way it rolled off your tongue, I guess. But maybe, it stands for badass, eh?"

"I have another question for you," Imogen asked. "Of all the times and places you could have gone, why the twenties? Why did you settle here and now?"

D.B. hesitated, tapped his fingers against his chin thoughtfully. "Hmm, I don't rightly know," he said. "I guess I've always had a bit of fascination with the roaring twenties, the flappers, the bootleg gin, but I'm also cold and calculated as you well know," he said, giving Imogen a sly wink.

"Honestly, I thought it might be the best time to invest and profit from all my hijacking dough. All the way up until 1929 when the stock market crashed the twenties were booming. Figured it would give me a chance to make a killing, and it has—tenfold! And the beauty of it is, I don't have to stay. I can go anywhere, anytime. I know history. I know what's gonna happen. So before the shit hits the fan in NYC in 1929, I won't have to worry about a Depression, I'm out of here, long gone."

"You know you're still a criminal. You stole that money in 1971," Imogen reminded him.

D.B. stood up and said, "Yes, well that's why I'm glad I ran into you Imogen. The two-hundred grand or so I started with is just a drop in the bucket compared to what I have now," he boasted. "I'd like for you to take it back with you."

"And do what with it exactly? Give it back to the airline? Tell 'em D.B. Cooper felt bad, developed a conscience, and now wants to return the money he stole from you?"

"No silly. I know you can't do that," he said. "Keep it for yourself if you want. I certainly owe you for enlightening me about time travel. Or do something good with it. Donate it to a charity, save the Earth, feed a kid, wherever you think it might do the most good." He walked over to his desk and pulled from a drawer an envelope full of cash.

"You know I can't take it with me," Imogen said.

"Oh yes, of course, I know," D.B. acknowledged. He pulled an elegant gold pen from his vest pocket and scribbled an address on a piece of paper and handed it to her.

"I'll call ahead. There will be a safe deposit box there in your name waiting for you to pick it up if you so choose," he said.

She gave him a half smile. "I'll think about it," she said, taking the slip of paper and stashing it in her purse. "I should be going," she said. It's been terrific seeing you again D.B., honestly, really great."

Imogen rose to stand up and immediately felt dizzy and ill. She clutched her abdomen as a sharp burning pain seared through her, taking her breath away and causing her to teeter backward. D.B. reached for her arm to help steady her. "Are you all right, Imogen?" he asked, a look of deep concern registering on his face.

Imogen gasped for breath, "Um, yes ... no ... I don't think so." Another wave of pain shook her, worse than the first, causing her to buckle over. "Oh no, the baby!" she cried out.

"The baby?" D.B. said, stunned. "What baby?"

"I'm sorry, D.B. I have to go," Imogen managed to say between gulps of air. "I have to go home, now."

〰〰〰〰

After the spinning stopped and the tenebrous shadows had receded, Imogen lay on the couch in her office whimpering in unbearable pain. With some effort she had managed to get to the bathroom where she immediately threw up. She felt something wet between her legs. Her hand came away bright red. "Oh god!" she howled into the empty room as an intense feeling of guilt seized her. What was happening? What had she done? Had she killed her and Simon's baby?

Tottering slowly back to the couch she reached for her phone.

It rang twice, then a "Hello?" on the other end.

"Fletcher," Imogen whimpered weakly into the phone.

"Imogen, where are you? What's wrong?"

"I'm at my office. Please come quick."

6

Shirtless, facing the wide mirror over the men's room sink, Kevin turned sideways, first this way and then that way, sucked in his belly. Earlier, his bungling assistant Brittany had spilled coffee down his back forcing him to rinse his shirt out in the sink to keep it from staining. Fortunately, he had a clean replacement that he kept in his employee locker in anticipation of moments like these.

Growing up Kevin was a scrawny kid. Even his sister Jennifer, who was two years younger than him, was bigger. In elementary school, the kids teased him relentlessly. He wasn't good at sports, always the last one to be picked for teams. He didn't necessarily hate how he looked now, but he wasn't thrilled with the current condition of his body either. I should hit the gym more, he thought, shouldn't let myself go, but knowing full well he wouldn't be going anytime soon. Getting up and working out every morning had been part of his daily routine once, that is, before Jackson moved out.

Jackson, who lovingly called him "Kevie;" who packed a special treat, a candy bar, or a brownie or a slice of cake, with his lunch each day; who had indulged his obsession with the Marvel Universe; encouraged him and made him believe that perhaps one day he could be someone important and respected at the Daguerreian Society—a guardian of the universe or time lord—he had joked. Jackson, standing in the foyer with his suitcases waiting for him to come home from his run one morning and announcing, "I'm moving to St. Louis ... and I don't want you to come with me."

Kevin didn't outgrow his scrawniness as he'd hoped, and the relentless cruelty of 7th and 8th graders has no bounds. The taunts weren't only about being a runt, a weakling, there were whispers and rumors that he was gay. Kevin wasn't even sure what "gay" meant. To escape, he withdrew into books, but especially Marvel comics. His heroes, Iron Man, The Hulk, and Captain America, in particular, were everything he wished to be—strong and noble and good.

Kevin carefully unfolded the clean shirt and smoothed out the wrinkles. He wished he had an iron handy, but this would have to do. Remarkably, he couldn't fault Jackson, not for everything anyway. It was true, he carried some baggage from his childhood like most everyone else and he had enough self-awareness to recognize that he was also what some people might call "extra." Although he'd never been formally tested, Jackson had once, toward the end, suggested that Kevin might be more than extra, might even be on the spectrum. For years, Jackson had patiently put up with Kevin's obsessive habits—how the forks and spoons had special places in the dishwasher and must never ever touch; the toilet paper roll that had to be hung a particular way, the constant sorting and arranging and rearranging—clothes folded a certain way and organized in the closet by color by fabric by category; books by genre; his Marvel comics and video game fixation, and his constant need for reassurance.

Kevin understood that his desire for order and routine was a bit of a problem, that it made inhabiting this messy, chaotic world difficult for him, that it drove a wedge between him and the love of his life. Jackson was the buffer that helped him cope with it. And it was the reason why he loved and embraced the Marvel heroes so much. In a world of chaos, they defeated the bad guys and made things right again. As it should be.

Like his heroes, Kevin felt that his mission in life, too, was to sort things out, make things right, and maybe even get some credit for his efforts. And with the current state of the universe, they needed someone as meticulous, dedicated, and laser-focused as Kevin. It was the wild, wild west of time travel out there, anything goes. Not only were people with good intentions trying to change history—attempting to murder Hitler as an infant, for example, but what of time travel in the hands of someone with less than noble ideals. What if someone like Adolf Hitler had been able to time travel? What hell might he have unleashed beyond what he was capable of doing without that knowledge? What of other despots? Stalin, Mussolini, Castro, Pol Pot—or any of today's power-hungry dictators—Kim Jong-Il, Putin—he shuddered to think of it. And what kept him mostly up at night was the danger of someone with COVID traveling back in time and starting another pandemic.

The world was out of order, and it wasn't right. Did they not understand the risks they took, the damage they were doing? The madness of it? All the data pointed to disaster, and he feared it could eventually collapse on itself from the strain. And why was no one else but him sounding the alarm? Because ... thinking about it made him seethe inside. Because they were focused instead ... on Simon.

"Damn Simon," he said aloud to his reflection. "*Perhaps I can have a word with these so-called 'powers that be'*". He sarcastically mimicked Simon's words today in the hallway. Jeez, he couldn't get away from that freak fast enough. Sure, he had "special powers" and all that but from the moment he met him, he knew there was something he did not like about the guy. That Niles and Imogen were fine, nice even, but Simon, Simon, what a smug phony douche he was, pretending to be all proper and dandified like he was more refined, somehow better than everyone else.

So he had special powers and they had brought him to Chicago, and ever since he got here, it had been Simon this, Simon that—Simon the phenom can do this, oh look what Simon did today. Who cares that he was a serial jumper? And to think that Kevin was the one responsible for them finding Simon in the first place. He was the one who first spotted the anomaly and notified the brass. Shit, he didn't expect a medal, but he had expected a little more. They thanked him, sure, even promoted him from lowly data monitoring technician to assistant manager of field collection—got him out of the monitoring room in the basement. And for what it was worth, they had even given him an assistant, Brittany Kane, who was mostly competent, but whom he secretly loathed and he wasn't quite sure why. Frankly, she exuded an ick vibe that was difficult to describe or tolerate. Maybe that she reminded him of certain girls back in high school who, along with their jock boyfriends, made fun of kids like Kevin, the way he talked, his mannerisms. He wasn't out of the closet then and although the bullying was relatively mild, high school had not been a pleasant experience for him. He had no desire to attend their class reunions or revisit anything associated with the small town he grew up in. He visited his mother there from time to time, but never let anyone know that he was in town, even the few peers he did sort of like.

But despite that, what more did he want?

The answer was pretty simple really. He wanted what Simon had, what he no longer had. The ability to travel through time again. For all the scientists employed by the Society, you'd think they could have figured out why he had come down with the time sickness, but no one seemed to care enough to find out.

Only a few short years ago, he had the gift of time travel—the most marvelous, wonderful gift one could ever possess. Talk about escaping into books or comics, time travel was the ultimate escape! Thank goodness he had explored so much of time before it all came crashing down—on any given weekend he might be exploring any one of the twenty arrondissements in 1930s Paris, or smoking Maui Waui in a surfer's shack in Malibu in 1967; tagging along with excavators on an archaeological dig in the Valley of the Kings in the 1920s or venturing near H.H. Holmes murder castle during the Chicago World's Fair in 1893. Witnessing Secretariat win the Kentucky Derby in 1973 or hoisting a hammer and adding to the destruction of the Berlin wall in 1989; looking up at the London rooftop at 3 Savile Row in 1969 as the Beatles performed "Get Back," their last gig together as a band, or attending one of Albert Einstein's theoretical physics lectures at Princeton University in 1940. With time travel, the world was his oyster.

And being hired at the Daguerreian Society was his dream job. Even if it was an entry level job, Kevin was more than thrilled to be part of this grand experiment. Handling the archives of time travelers before him excited him because he was one of them. Perhaps he would one day be part of this vast learning database. But then, the sickness. Everything was fine. He'd spent a divine weekend partying in 1970s San Francisco, at a gay bar called Toad Hall in the Castro. Everything was fantastic until he landed back at his apartment and immediately vomited all over his expensive hand-knotted Persian rug. He chalked it up to being hungover, no big deal—he'd drink lots of fluids, replenish his electrolytes, take a day off kicking back on the couch watching old black and white movies—that'd be it, he'd be up and around in no time.

But then the next time he traveled, it happened again, and again after that and again and again after that—each time worse than before as he became more violently ill upon return. Most time travelers experience a milder form of sickness when they first start entering photographs. It takes several trips for the body to adjust to the rigors of time travel, although it never goes away completely, hence the need for rest following a trip. It followed this pattern for Kevin as well, until suddenly, out of the blue, for no apparent reason, it was happening every single time, and it took days and days to recover. He was missing work. When he began to also get sick upon arrival, not just upon return, he knew that something was seriously wrong. He had confided in his supervisor. The supervisor advised him to abstain from traveling for a while, which he did, for six months, but on his first trip and several after, it was the same, the sickness, but also vomiting up blood. It had become a dire, life-threatening situation. Time travel seemed to be tearing apart his insides. He realized that this was a permanent condition. It had happened to a few other travelers as well, but researching why didn't seem to be a high priority for the Society's scientists and Kevin's repeated inquiries went nowhere. Did they not realize how devastating this was for him? Clearly not.

 The only good thing that came from it was meeting Jackson. Miserable, discouraged, defeated, and forced to travel by regular means, Kevin decided to vacation in Bali, which led him to Jackson, who was alone there on business. They literally bumped into one another in the hotel hallway one night. He had run out of ice and was on his way to fill up his bucket. Jackson, who had finished filling up his bucket in the tiny ice room was leaving the same time Kevin was coming in. In typical Hallmark movie meet-cute, rom-com setup style, they collided causing Jackson to spill his ice; and Kevin, apologizing profusely, helping him—and that was it. They laughed, took their buckets of ice, and retreated together to Kevin's room to share a nightcap. One thing led to another, and they'd ended up talking all night. The rest of the vacation was filled up with dinners and sunsets, romantic midnight walks on the beach, long talks, holding hands, in an accepting environment where no one cared anything about two gay men meeting for the first time and falling in love.

But Jackson was gone now and what was he left with? Nothing and no one. He knew it was silly to dwell on it, but it all seemed so unfair. The angry child in him seethed. If he couldn't travel, why should anyone else get to? A part of him longed to be in charge. If Kevin McCord was in charge, he'd find a cure for the sickness. Things would be better with a meticulous guy like him. Instead of passively monitoring something as huge as time travel, they could be doing big things like deciding who and when people could jump—order from chaos—essentially keeping those forks and spoons separated for the betterment of everyone.

He fastened the last button and had begun to tuck his shirt neatly into his khakis when his phone began to vibrate. A name he did not recognize popped up on caller ID. Normally, he wouldn't answer these types of probable spam calls, but the name, someone identified as Carl Loomis seemed vaguely familiar to him.

"Hello," Kevin said. "Yes, speaking. You say you have what?"

He listened, nodded, a smile beginning to form at the corners of his mouth as the voice on the other end of the call spoke at length.

The call ended and Kevin put the phone back in his pants pocket. He finished tucking in his shirt and while doing so admired the tailored fit in the mirror. A good choice. Pastel blue was his color. Jackson had always said so. His mood brightening, he turned back and smiled at his reflection. He had a good feeling. Things might be about to change for Kevin McCord.

Mimi Pinky leaned in close, her nose practically touching the phone, as Carl called the number. He switched to speaker mode so she could hear but then ended up having to gesture at her more than a few times to keep quiet during the call to the agent.

"Overland parking garage, 7:00 p.m. Got it," Kevin McCord said.

Carl ended the call and shoved the phone into his pocket. "That's it, all set."

Money was always front and center in Mimi's mind. "How much do you think we can get for it?"

Carl shrugged. "Don't know, but I have a feeling this book is important to them."

"It sure doesn't look like much to me," Mimi said with disgust. "Don't know why anyone would pay good money for a stupid old goddamn book filled with gibberish—not that I'm complaining—I'll take what I can get … "

"We," Carl corrected her. "What *we* can get. I'm the one who lifted it, remember?"

"Fine, we," Mimi conceded. "The main thing is we get this McCord fellow over a barrel. This is small potatoes; the real money is the pawn shop. I want what's mine," she said, her face pinched in ugly resentment. "Grandson or no grandson, Simon and that nasty girl of his don't deserve what my Teddy built. I'll see to it."

"yeah, yeah, heard it all before ... " Carl gestured, impatient, his voice trailing off as he wandered into the kitchen to grab another beer from the fridge. When he returned, Mimi had picked up the book, *A Guide to Photographic Time Travel* by George Eastman and was flipping through it. "You know, I am related to this guy," she said sighing heavily. "At least somebody in the family amounted to something."

7

The powers that be, Kevin had said. Who were these powers that be? Simon didn't know. Running into him in the hallway, finally, after three months confinement at HQ, he had thought for an instant that things might change, someone on his side, someone who would listen to him, tell him he could return home, or at the very least, make a phone call to Imogen. But instead, Kevin had been standoffish, had brushed him aside as though he were nothing but a bothersome insect. And then he ran off to the men's room. Simon thought about tagging along after him, but he needed a few minutes to gather his thoughts.

"Simon!" a voice shouted from behind him. "What are you doing out here in the hallway, buddy?" It was Big Marcus, one of the personal trainers that monitored him on the treadmill.

Simon turned around. "Oh, hello Marcus," he said. "I was just on my way back to my room to shower and I bumped into Kev…" Marcus cut him off mid-sentence. "Would you mind coming back in here, please, I need to talk to you," he said placing his massive hand on Simon's shoulder and guiding him back through the doors of the lab.

"What? Why?" Simon protested.

Marcus led him back through the testing room that Simon had become so familiar with over the last few weeks, past the treadmill and the machines that monitored him, and down a long corridor of closed office doors.

"Right this way," Marcus said opening a door at the end and ushering him inside.

"Have a seat," Marcus instructed.

"What's going on? What's this about?" Simon inquired, but Marcus simply smiled and replied, "The doctor will be in shortly," as he closed the door behind him. Inside looked like your typical doctor's office, a desk, bookshelves containing an array of medical texts, several framed university degrees, Stephen C. Hostin written in calligraphy hanging on the wall.

A couple of short raps on the door, and a slender, tallish man with a stubble beard in a white coat breezed into the room. He extended his hand to Simon and introduced himself. "I'm Doctor Hostin," he said. "And you must be Simon." Simon stood up and shook the doctor's hand. "Please, sit," Hostin instructed Simon as he followed suit, taking the leather chair behind the desk facing him. He folded his hands together and spoke. "So, I'm sure you're wondering why you're here today."

Simon was indeed wondering that, but at the same time he was also quite embarrassed. His T-shirt, drenched with sweat from the morning's workout, clung tightly to his body; he was sure he reeked. He shifted in his seat uncomfortably before answering the physician. "Yes, I am curious as to why I'm here, but you see, I've just finished testing today and I could really use a shower …"

"Oh, of course, Simon," the doctor said. "I apologize. Terrible timing," he conceded with so much sincerity in his soothing doctor's voice, it immediately put Simon at ease. "You can hit the showers very soon. I promise I won't keep you long," he assured him. Simon relaxed a bit and leaned back in the chair. "What is this concerning, Doctor Hostin?" he asked.

"Well now," the doctor said, clapping his hands together, "you have been here at the facility now for, what? Several weeks now …?"

"Three months," Simon interrupted. "It's been three months."

"Yes, right, three months." The doctor seemed to have lost a layer of confidence in the presence of Simon, but he took a breath in and pressed on.

"We've asked a lot of you," he began. "And I know it's been difficult for you being away from your loved ones." Simon, tempted to take the opportunity to air his long list of complaints about not having access to his phone among other things, instead remained silent and nodded agreement, allowing the doctor to continue.

"Thank you for your patience, Simon." The doctor hesitated again and then laid it all out, "But I'm afraid you can't go home just yet."

Simon leaned forward in his chair. This wasn't at all what he wanted to hear. "What?"

Hostin raised his hands. "Hear me out, please. No more testing," he said. "We have a task for you."

"A task?" Simon responded incredulously. "What sort of task?"

"We need you to travel to what the scientists here at the Society have labeled the Dead Zones to find out what's going on."

Simon was intrigued and a tiny bit excited that he was going to finally get to travel through time again, but at the same time, dead zones sounded ominous.

Hostin sensed Simon's apprehension. "Bear with me, Simon. I'm going to try to explain to you what we know and why it's important for us to explore these regions. When I'm finished, I'll try to answer as many of your questions as I can. Fair enough?"

Simon nodded. "Of course."

"The Daguerreian Society, as you know, is made up of scientists and technicians who study and monitor time travel. And the original reason for inviting you here, Simon, is because you are an anomaly. But more than that, you are unique. For some reason, for which we are yet to determine, perhaps because you were conceived in your current time, but born in the past, you have an ability to serial jump—in other words, move from one time to another through a photograph without first having to return to your anchor photograph. There is something in your DNA that is different from most people. We are still working on finding what that anomaly is.

"Meanwhile, though it may not seem like it from your perspective, we have learned a great deal from the testing you've undergone here at the facility."

More at ease talking with the doc now, Simon asked, "Do I have a superpower?"

Hostin smiled. "Well, we wouldn't go as far as to call it a superpower, but you do have unusually high stamina, your heart rate is above average, which is always a plus for travel through time. You appear to have a higher natural tolerance versus other people who have experienced side effects from traveling—from vomiting and pain to heart palpitations, even bleeding in some rare cases. But we did notice something unusual. That helmet you were wearing?"

Simon nodded. "Oh yes, the helmet of torture."

That made the doctor laugh. "That's the one," he said. "It measures, among other things, brain function and we discovered that yours is unusually high."

Simon chuckled. He knew he was no dummy, but it was nice to hear that he had a highly functioning brain. "Like Einstein?" he asked.

"Not exactly," Hostin continued. "The brain activity in your temporal lobe is tuned with the universe and highly developed. What this means is that travelers seem to have an uncanny knack for identifying one another. They might not realize it at the time, but they are naturally drawn to each other as if some unseen force of nature has intervened to bring them together. You, Simon, are especially attuned to these and other unexplained phenomena."

Simon took this in. Hmmm, he thought. Was that why he had been so drawn to Imogen the first time he saw her in 1912? Indeed, there was something, some invisible force that seemed to draw him to her. He didn't understand it at the time, but now in hindsight, it may have been the case.

"So where do I fit into this?" Simon asked.

"In a nutshell, as I mentioned, number one: physically the tests show that you can withstand the rigors of time travel without any adverse side effects. Number two: mentally, changes in your DNA, possibly in the womb, affected your brain, which makes you hyper-aware of your surroundings and tuned into the presence of other travelers, as I mentioned. It's not clear yet how this might benefit or enhance you during time travel, but we'll have more of an idea if it comes into play after you visit the dead zones."

"Pardon me, doctor, but I mean, how do you know all this? What precisely are these so-called dead zones and has anyone else attempted to go there?"

"Those are all solid questions, Simon," the doctor said. "We know this because there are certain details that we've been able to track. We know that the universe, for the most part, is self-correcting. In other words, if something has been publicly documented, that history though it can be altered, the outcome cannot be changed—something for which your partner Imogen attempted recently in Kansas."

Simon shifted uncomfortably in his seat at the mention of Imogen. She had been wrong to try to save those girls in Kansas, and had been properly reprimanded by the Society, but he understood why she did it. Who wouldn't want to save someone if they knew what was going to happen? Imogen had been devastated. It was a truly hard lesson.

Hostin continued. "We know something is happening because our data indicates that over the years, a high percentage of travelers have frequented the same areas or time periods attempting to change history—particularly regions in Europe during the 1930s and forties, specifically Germany, Austria, and Poland, places where the existence of Adolf Hitler has been well documented, plus a few other places," he said. "This has put an incredible strain on the universe causing these locations to be closed off entirely, ergo the name, dead zones."

His thoughts returned to Imogen's motivations, and it made sense. Of course, if a traveler had foreknowledge of something terrible that was going to happen in history wouldn't they do everything in their power to go back and try to change it? He had read a great deal about World War II and the atrocities executed during this bloody period in world history. Clearly, people might want to attempt to erase the tyrant from existence, perhaps when he was an infant, or by killing his mother, or via other opportunities to murder him later in his life to prevent him from ever coming to power in Germany and thus, saving millions of lives.

"To answer your earlier question, Simon, nobody has been there ... yet," Hostin said. "While monitoring time travel as we normally would, we have observed travelers still trying to enter these dead zones, but when they attempt it, they are bounced back immediately. We don't know why that is. That's why we need you—someone with your enhanced capabilities—to go there for us and find out the answers ... if you are able."

The doctor folded his hands together in front of him on his desk, paused, and then asked Simon a final question. "What do you say, Simon, are you up for the task?"

8

The squeal of the rental car's tires echoed off the tubular walls as he made the tight turn onto the upper rooftop level of the parking garage where Carl Loomis had instructed they meet. He had not indicated where on the rooftop or what type of car he would be in, but Kevin, smart enough to know that one should never be boxed in, wisely chose a parking space close to the exit in case a quick getaway might be in order. You never knew how these things might go down.

He knew about Eastman's book, Imogen and Simon had told him about it, and how four men had broken into the pawn shop and ransacked the place looking for it specifically. Three of the men had been arrested but one of them got away, with the book presumably, because afterward, it was nowhere to be found. He wasn't sure what was in the book, but it must be important if the Society wanted it so bad. The investigators on the case had hoped that eventually the person who stole it would resurface perhaps looking for a buyer, so Kevin was more than surprised when, of all people, he was the one contacted, not the police, not a higher-ranking official at the Society, him. How incredibly fortuitous was that?

He parked the rental car and waited, his mind drifting. Kevin couldn't help feeling a little excited, this could actually be the once in a lifetime opportunity he'd been waiting for, the chance to take back control of his life, maybe even the world.

The only time he had ever felt any power growing up was when he was playing video games. Immersed in the gaming world, he could choose to be invisible if he wanted or become any number of powerful, confident, indestructible avatars. In that world no one picked on him; no one made threats. It ended when he got caught kissing a boy at seventeen. Kevin's parents took his comics and video games from him. He ran away vowing never to return home. A gamer friend took him in, helped him finish high school, he won college scholarships, and turned his love of computers and gaming into a degree in data technology.

College, a coveted job at the Daguerreian Society, meeting Jackson, living life openly as a gay man, it seemed like his life was complete ... and yet, the words of his parents still echoed in his mind—"You're a sinner, Kevin ... an abomination. People like you don't deserve to exist ... "

Tapping on the driver's side window abruptly pulled Kevin out of his head. Startled, he turned to see a tall figure wearing a dark-colored hoodie, sunglasses, and a baseball cap. As Kevin reached for the door handle to get out of the car, the man shoved his leg up against it, preventing him from opening the door. Kevin was confused until the man opened his sweatshirt revealing a concealed gun lodged in a holster attached to his side. Kevin nodded understanding and the man removed his leg so that he could slowly open the car door and exit the vehicle.

So he had a gun. Not unexpected, but a little alarming still. Kevin would have to handle this delicately. Breaking the awkward silence that ensued between them Carl spoke first. "I have what you want," he said using a deeper timbre than normal.

"Eastman's book?"

"That's right, and a journal and some long scroll paper thing." Carl reached into his backpack and pulled the book out partially for Kevin to see.

"How much are you asking?" Kevin asked. He wanted Carl to throw out the first figure for negotiation.

"Twenty-five grand," Carl answered without hesitation.

The sunglasses made it hard to gauge whether Carl was dangerous or not, and Kevin certainly did not want to offend him, but twenty-five grand was exorbitant. He paused, pursed his lips, and shook his head. "mmm, I'm afraid twenty-five grand is just a little too steep for my pay grade."

Carl wasn't expecting this. "Ain't you guys like the government?" he asked. "I know you guys got money to burn."

Kevin wasn't deterred and he wasn't going to let this man intimidate him. If he had to walk away, he was fully prepared to do it.

"No, we're not government. The Daguerreian Society is privately held," he lied. "I can give you five grand now and another $5,000 in two months. That's it. Take it or leave it."

"Aw come on man," Carl said, whipping off his glasses, all prior bravado falling apart. In a voice that now resembled a whiny teenager, he moaned, "Can't you do better than that? I mean, I didn't go to all the trouble of stealing it for nothin', ya know." Realizing how he sounded, Carl straightened up again and lowered his voice to a more menacing tone. "I goddamn know this book is important to you all," he said. "Twenty grand," that's as low as I'll go.

Kevin waited a moment to respond before clapping his hands together and turning away from Carl. "Well, I guess we're done here then," he said. He turned and reached for the car door handle, but Carl stopped him. On impulse, he pulled the gun.

"Don't be an idiot … Carl, is it? You gonna shoot me right here in the parking garage?" Kevin asked.

"Yes … no … I mean …" Carl stammered. "All right, just give me the five grand now," he demanded.

"Do you really think I'd be stupid enough to bring the cash with me?" Kevin asked.

Carl's attitude changed completely after he placed the gun back in its holster.

"Look," he said," his voice softer, calmer, normal, almost friendly. "I don't give a rat's ass about this book, ya know. I mean, I'd like the dough and all, but I'm mainly doing it for her."

"Her?" Kevin asked.

"Mimi Pinky. I mean yeah, I was all in with those guys at first to ransack that pawn shop and when I saw the book on the floor, I just grabbed it. Mimi thinks we can get a lot for it, she told me to ask for a hundred grand, but I don't care anymore. I just want her to like me, man." Carl hung his head, embarrassed.

"Hey, dude, it's okay. I hear you," Kevin said. "Women make us crazy, right?" He just threw that out there. He was gay. What did he know about women?

Carl snorted. "Yeah, they sure do," he said. "Never thought this one would though. I thought she was a pushover, an easy mark, but turns out, she's not. She's tough on the outside, but she makes me feel, I don't know, cared for, like my ma used to, I guess."

"Listen, Carl. I'll give you the five grand now and the other five grand later, like I promised. I know it's no hundred thousand, but this is a deal between you and me, a transaction. I'll give you a receipt and everything."

He extended his hand. "Deal?"

Carl stepped forward and shook it. "Okay, deal."

Kevin got into his rental car and pulled a pouch from the glove compartment, got out, and handed it to Carl.

Carl's eyes widened at the sight of so much cash all at once. "I thought you said you didn't have it with you?"

Kevin smiled. "I lied."

He started up the engine and opened the driver's side window.

"Hey Carl."

"Yeah?"

"Before you go, can I ask you a question?"

"Sure."

"Why did you choose to contact me and not someone else from the Society?"

Carl was hesitant to reveal too much, but hell, he'd already spilled on everything else, this seemed like a fairly harmless question.

"Well, ya see, I was snooping around Imogen's place after I saw you and that other guy in the suit leave and I found a card in the grass with your name on it."

Kevin remembered he'd meant to give Imogen his card when he and Metzger visited but couldn't recall whether he had or not. He must have dropped it in the yard on the way in or out.

"Cool. Take care Carl. We'll be in touch."

Kevin sat in the car, debating whether to look inside the book now or wait. Before he could do anything, though, he heard a quick honk of a horn, looked over to see Carl rolling by in possibly, aside from the Gremlin, one of the ugliest cars he'd ever seen, a 1987 Buick Grand National. He knew his cars. Matchbox was his jam growing up. Carl gave Kevin a friendly wave as he rolled on by in the beer-bottle brown beast.

Kevin breathed a sigh of relief. That went better than expected. He was out five grand, but there was a reason the Society wanted this book and the best part, they didn't know he had it. And bonus, along with the actual book, Carl had managed to pilfer one of Eastman's journals. He was anxious to find out what secrets both held to time travel.

First, he opened the journal, which shed some light into why he did not wish for the book to fall into the wrong hands. It was exciting to see the fine cursive script written in Eastman's own hand.

In 1906, I stumbled upon a formula for time travel. It involved one entering a deep meditative state. "I shared my discovery with several of my colleagues, fellow scientists, and we agreed that the finding and the existence of the book, A Guide to Photographic Time Travel, should remain a secret.

He went on at length about the Spiritualist movement, which had gained popularity in the late nineteenth century and involved spirit photography. Evidently, many people were leery of photography back then, afraid that taking someone's photograph could actually steal their soul.

If photography itself was suspect, we believed that the public was not ready for something as groundbreaking as time travel.

Closing the journal and setting it aside, Kevin carefully picked up the prize, the hundred-plus year-old cloth-bound book that featured lovely gold stamping on the spine and cover and a small, restrained floral motif, none of which indicated anything about the contents within. Opening it, he read the first page:

Everyone can travel forward in time. We do it at a steady rate of one second per second. Einstein's theory of relativity suggests that we live in a four-dimensional continuum in which space and time are interchangeable. The faster we move through space, the slower we move through time. However, while Einstein's theory attempts to explain time travel to the future, it stops short of how one might move backward in time, to the past.

Now, that question has been answered. Through experimentation with photography, the capability of time travel to the past has been revealed, but there are rules and consequences, which will be outlined in more detail later in the text.

As he flipped through the pages none of it made much sense. Simon had mentioned that it seemed to be just a lot of meditation type mumbo-jumbo, but there had to be more to it than that. Why else would the Society want it?

As he laid it on the passenger seat atop the journal to look through later something fell out of it onto the floor. Kevin reached down to pick up what looked like a rolled up piece of paper, kind of like one of those tiny Chinese handscrolls. He carefully unrolled the one long piece of paper, filled up completely with all manner of undecipherable diagrams and charts and calculations, numbers, and mathematical formulations. Kevin couldn't help but smile as he backed the car out of the space and headed toward the exit. He had no clue what this meant, but he was sure as hell gonna find out!

9

Rolling sluggishly over onto her left side, Imogen kicked the bulky blanket off her and stretched her legs out cat-like as far as they would go. Looked at the clock. 11:15. She was tired, too tired to get up. That, or maybe the thought of getting up in and of itself was tiring. At any rate, after three days of lying in bed, she wasn't sure how she felt about anything. The doctor at the ER had sent her home with a prescription for paracetamol for pain and told her to take it easy for the next few days. That addressed the physical part.

The part they didn't mention, however, was how to cope with the roller-coaster of emotions one experiences following a miscarriage. Along with being tired, but not being able to sleep and having no appetite, intense feelings of shock and sadness and anger rattled around inside her head like balls on a roulette wheel, and maybe the worst of all, irrational guilt. She couldn't shake the question, what if traveling through time had caused the miscarriage? Had she killed her baby? On an intellectual level, she knew probably not—Simon's mother had been pregnant with him when Teddy took her to 1885 and left her there. If Imogen had even remotely thought that time travel might harm the baby, she would have never considered going. Plus, before this trip, she had traveled with Niles and Fletcher to Bakunawa and everything had been fine.

"You heard the doctor," Fletcher reassured her, "there's no treatable cause for miscarriage, and when it happens before twenty weeks it's usually nature's way of dealing with an abnormal embryo." He was right, of course. She understood that her body was going through incredible post-pregnancy hormonal shifts that were likely intensifying her emotions, but that didn't make them feel any less real.

The most frustrating part of it was that Simon didn't know—he didn't know about the miscarriage or even that there had ever been a baby—and she had no way to tell him. Calling his cell phone was a waste of time. Almost certainly he did not have it with him because every time she called it went directly to voicemail. She had tried repeatedly to reach Daguerreian Society headquarters but was never able to speak to a live person, instead callers were subjected to phone tree hell followed by at least an hour of on-hold nineties music before being dropped completely.

Thank goodness for Fletcher. Honestly, she didn't know how she would have gotten through any of this without him, which most certainly added to her guilt. *I lean on him too much*, she thought, *but who else do I have, really?* Damn it, she was at it again. Thinking too much.

Shifting onto her back again, Imogen's hand brushed against her flat tummy and another overwhelming wave of sadness unexpectedly rolled up on her—something that happened all too frequently these days, it seemed. On nights alone in the dark without Simon she had often stroked her belly and thought *we made this*, but now in an instant, it was gone, everything; no baby, no Simon, nothing.

Imogen knew grief but this felt different somehow. It was like grieving in reverse—instead of mourning the loss of someone you knew and loved, you grieve the baby you'll never meet, that you'll never hold in your arms; a child who will never call you mommy or give you kisses or fall asleep on your chest to the sound of your heartbeat; who'll never grow up, never marry or have children of their own. It was all just so incredibly overwhelming and sad, and to stifle the sound of her sorrow Imogen pulled the pillow over her face and wept.

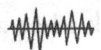

On the fourth day, Imogen woke up to someone speaking her name. Groggy from the sleeping pill she'd taken the night before, or whenever it was, she thought she must be dreaming.

"Go away," she moaned as she pulled the covers over her head and rolled away from the offending entity who was rudely interrupting her sleep.

"Imogen!" Fletcher repeated, louder this time.

"What?!" Imogen answered irritated, this time raising herself up on one elbow. "Jesus, what do you want, Fletcher?"

Fletcher lightly touched her shoulder. "I want you to get up, Imogen." Imogen flopped back down on the bed. "Nooooo."

"Yes," Fletcher said, tugging at her arm and dragging her limp body up to a seated position, her feet dangling off the side of the bed, pajamas twisted and crumpled, a tangled mass of hair sticking to her cheek. The sleeping pill had done its job too well, knocked her out, and now she felt worse than when she hadn't been able to sleep.

"I don't want to get up," she protested.

Fletcher persisted. "Imogen," he stated with authority. "You have been in bed for four days." He could smell her breath, and it was bad. "And honestly," he said. "You smell." Imogen rolled her eyes. "Gee thanks."

"You're welcome," he answered. "So today, you are going to get up and walk to the kitchen and eat some breakfast and after that, a shower."

The thought of breakfast caused Imogen's stomach to lurch. "Ugh," she said. "I can't even."

"Yes, you can, and you will." Despite her arms being as floppy as a couple of boiled noodles, Fletcher managed to haul her up to a standing position. He helped her into her robe and slippers and led her to the kitchen table where fresh orange juice, an Asiago bagel with cream cheese, and a hazelnut latte with whipped cream awaited.

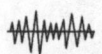

The warm pool at the community center was Imogen's new sanctuary, her happy Zen place. Fletcher had encouraged her to go to the gym, but right now the thought of working out, getting sweaty around a lot of other intense, sweaty people, the racket of weights hitting the floor, treadmills and bikes humming, feet pumping, loud music blaring did not seem appealing. Rolling out of bed early and heading to the pool, however, provided minimal effort and maximum return.

Bending her knees and raising her arms up out of the water she arched her back. It felt good to stretch, and when the early morning rays of the sun spilled through the wide glass windows across the blue pool it felt like you were swimming through a shimmering magical doorway. For just a little while Imogen felt transported, calm, unburdened.

Gliding effortlessly through the water, her arms and calf muscles buoyant, she moved without strain as she paddled, her arms moving gracefully from side to side like a gazelle. Water felt like life. Other than the shower, the pool was the only other place she didn't feel distracted, where she could think, or not think. But Fletcher was on her mind today, a conversation they had shared last week when he had forced her to get out of bed had been playing on repeat in her head.

Sitting across from him at the kitchen table in her robe, her hair a nasty mess, and "stinky" as he had so bluntly put it, for the first time since the miscarriage she had been able to laugh.

"How's the bagel?" he asked.

"Bagelicious."

Fletcher snickered. "Oh bagelicious, is it? hmmm. Someone must be feeling better."

"I do actually," she said, "a little."

"What do you feel like for dinner?"

"You know," she said, "now that my appetite is back, pasta sounds kind of good."

"What's the most relaxing type of pasta? *Spa*-ghetti. What do you call a fake noodle? An *im*pasta. Get it?"

"Stop it!" Imogen pleaded, smiling. "So cheesy, but thank you for making me breakfast."

"It was my pleasure, plus I couldn't have you starving on my watch."

"On your watch, huh? Are you watching me?"

"Yeah, I guess I am. Someone has to."

Imogen looked up at him from her plate and asked him, "Why are you being so nice to me?"

Without hesitating, Fletcher answered simply, "Because I love you." All corny jokes aside, his face now was that of serious sincerity.

Imogen, for once, was speechless. No snappy comebacks came to mind. Awkwardly, she picked up her bagel and took a bite, and then Fletcher smiled and a few minutes later, they moved on to other topics. But it had stuck with her. Of course, she knew that Fletcher loved her. She loved him, too. They'd been friends since college. And it wasn't necessarily unusual for him to say it. It was the *way* he said it. Different. Like love, love. Real love. Not just friend love. And it terrified her because you can't just leave the L-word hanging out there once it's been dropped. Somebody on one of those wise reality TV shows had once said something actually profound: If you sweep things under the rug, it will create a lump that you'll eventually trip over.

The tips of her fingers were starting to wrinkle up. She'd been in the pool for well over an hour now. Getting out of the pool she hated, her body so heavy with the weight of wet, and chilled by the sudden cold but then it was only a short walk to the giant hot tub in the far corner which you stepped up to and then down into and then "ahhhh" the word that escaped everyone's lips upon entering the blissfully hot bath of rising steam and eddies swirling around you and various jets that massaged your lower extremities. If there was a heaven, Imogen was certain, the hot tub was it.

Still, as much as the pool and the hot tub made starting the day infinitely better, going home afterward was a bit of a letdown. Sure, Imogen felt better now physically, but mentally not so much. She still felt sort of like dead inside. Depressed, likely, but she wasn't sure how to pull herself out of it just yet, despite Fletcher's unexpected declaration of love.

People came and went, mostly regulars, older people seeking the healing properties of the warm pool and hot tub after surgery or therapy for their achy joints. It was as much social gathering as a daily ritual for most of them. Imogen was relaxing against one of the jets enjoying the warmth when Nancy Hall, a retired nurse, got in. Imogen knew practically everything about Nancy and her husband Rudy, her three grown kids, her four grandchildren, one of whom would be starting at the university this fall, that she played the French horn, where they had stayed recently in their travel trailer, and that she was an avid romance reader.

"Hi Imogen," Nan called out warmly as she sat down beside her on the ledge. "How are you feeling?" Imogen had confided in her about the miscarriage. Nancy had offered her some great advice for physical healing, and she appreciated that she asked now about how she was feeling.

"Much better, thanks," Imogen said. "How about you? Planning any big RV adventures?"

"Not too many. Pandemic is still with us, so a lot of the state parks are still closed."

"Oh, that's right. That's a bummer."

"Yeah, it is, but we've gotten to spend a lot of extra time with the grandkids, so that's been fun. I've also caught up on my reading, that's for sure!" Nancy said, laughing.

"What have you been reading?" Imogen knew asking this question was an invitation to a lengthy conversation with Nan, but the hot tub was relaxing, and she sort of welcomed a distraction from her own swirling thoughts concerning Simon and Fletcher.

Nan's face lit up with enthusiasm at an opportunity to discuss books. "So, I discovered this new author recently. Well, she's not exactly new. Her books are older, but she's written something like thirty-seven romance novels. I've read three so far, and I AM HOOKED," Nancy gushed. "Have you ever heard of her, Loretta Ross?"

The name didn't register at first, but slowly it dawned on Imogen. Of course. Loretta. 1946. Kansas.

Love on the Kansas Prairie. The cover featured a freight train barreling down the tracks against the flat, dusty landscape of the Kansas prairie. The tagline read: *Can Hudson and Violet, two passionate star-crossed teenagers find lasting love on the windswept Kansas prairie? Or will tragedy and heartbreak derail their love forever?* It had been real-life Harry and Vivian's story and Imogen and Loretta had both been there to witness it.

Loretta Ross was another time traveler. She was managing the hotel Imogen stayed at when she went back to try to find out what happened to an elderly man's first love. Despite Imogen's efforts to change history, it ended in tragedy, just like it was supposed to. She didn't know about Loretta until she returned home and picked up her mail:

Dear Imogen. I hope you don't mind, but when you were here, I copied down the PO box number from the package you were mailing so that I could contact you. I could be wrong about you, but I thought I'd take a chance anyway. If you're ever in 1973, look me up. Your friend, Loretta Ross

" ... They're romance novels but kind of historical fiction too, and soooo descriptive ... "

Lost in her own thoughts, Imogen had practically forgotten that Nancy was still talking.

" ... It's mind blowing, every detail," she said. "It almost feels like she went back in time and lived the story herself!"

Imogen smiled. *Well, yeah,* she thought, *they were written by a time traveler!*

Nancy continued. "Right now, I'm reading *Winter of the Midnight Sun*, it's about a teenage Inuit couple who fall in love against their parent's wishes in the Alaskan bush, but I have another one of hers in my bag. You can borrow it if you want," she offered enthusiastically.

Imogen wasn't terribly enthralled by romance novels, but knowing what she did about Loretta, that the stories weren't entirely fictionalized accounts, changed things.

In the women's locker room after both had changed out of their swimsuits, Nancy pulled a worn paperback from her bag and handed it to Imogen.

She Left Her Heart in San Francisco. On the cover, the Golden Gate Bridge in the background, a park filled with hippies, and two young girls in sandals and floppy hats seated together on a blanket in the foreground with the tagline: *In the swinging City by the Bay theirs was a different kind of love.*

"Let me know what you think!" Nancy said cheerfully as she turned and headed for the exit, waving and calling back over her shoulder, "Have a great day Imogen, see you next Thursday."

10

Historians uncovered approximately forty-two assassination plots on Adolf Hitler's life. The true number cannot be accurately determined due to an unknown number of undocumented cases.

Simon had always wanted to visit Europe. In fact, it had been a virtual stickpin on a map travel destination on Imogen's "bucket list," as she called it. He didn't, however, expect to be here now, alone, without her, under such unpredictable circumstances.

But here he was in Austria, and it did not disappoint. It was exactly as he pictured it—lush, green, mountainous, stunning—an ideal destination for any intrepid tourist. Getting here had been different than what he was used to. Because it was a dead zone, he was unable to take the direct route through one photograph. He entered through a recent photo first and then worked his way back through time, jumping through similar location photos taken in different decades—the early two-thousands, nineties, eighties, seventies … finally arriving here in October 1889.

Here was Braunau am Inn, a sleepy town located along the lower Inn River on the border with the German state of Bavaria. He wasn't sure what to expect upon arrival, but so far, the town appeared ordinary—neat, clean, filled with old-world charm, medieval churches, and architecture dating back to the Middle Ages. Why was he here? Braunau am Inn's claim to fame—the birthplace of Adolf Hitler.

A focal point of his mission into the dead zones, Hitler was obviously a popular target for assassination. From food poisoning, bombs and snipers to poisoned letters— many had tried to take him out; none succeeded. Those attempts, which occurred in his later years when he became a dangerous demagogue, were documented; however, data gathered at the Daguerreian Society showed that heightened activity centered around this particular time and place—when he was an infant. Never mind, the ethical problems of killing an infant or a child for something he hasn't yet done or even murdering an innocent victim, for instance his mother before he was born, for whatever reason, many people with the ability to time travel felt compelled to right a horrible wrong that this man had wrought upon humanity, and if that meant traveling to his birthplace and killing him, stopping him, no matter his age, no matter the cost, then so be it.

Simon began to walk this route, as many others before him had. His destination: the Pommer Inn at Salzburger Vorstadt 15, a gasthaus with a restaurant on the ground floor and rented flats and rooms above, and home of Alois and Klara Hitler and their infant son Adolf.

He wasn't sure where to find the address and thought about asking directions until he stopped, turned, and started heading east after feeling a peculiar sensation of being pulled in that direction by invisible forces. With each step, he felt an odd presence of others. It felt like the time when he first met Imogen, how he was drawn to her, although this felt much stronger, as though there were *many* others. As he followed his impulse, his mind wandered. It was not lost on Simon that he and the dictator were nearly the same age. Simon was in fact older, having been born in 1885; Hitler in 1889. It was hard to fathom that he had shared the same timeline with a monster, although neither knew at this point in time what lie ahead, what one would become. But at this moment, the Society's objective to monitor time travel became abundantly clear. Not everyone who travels has good intentions. What if someone like Hitler had been able to time travel? And what of future wannabe dictators? Simon understood the assignment.

He walked down several more streets, always heading east. People sat on porches; children played in the street. Merchants sold their wares. The weather was warm and pleasant for October. The leaves on the trees were beginning to turn golden yellow and orange, crinkle up, a slight breeze gathered them up and sent them dancing down the brick street. As Simon rounded another corner, however, he knew he was getting close to something because the sensations intensified, uncomfortably so. His ears began to buzz with a high-pitched hum. The touch of his skin felt clammy and tingly. He was dizzy and with each step he took the ground below him felt dangerously unstable. An odd sense of static vibration beneath the surface drew him closer, and when he turned onto Salzburger Vorstadt and the Pommer Inn came into view, he knew he had reached his destination, the epicenter of activity.

Simon stopped and stared in awe. All around the perimeter of the building hundreds of blurry phantom beings popped in and out at lightning speed. They zipped in—some stood still for an instant before zooming back out; others were mere flashes that appeared and then almost immediately disappeared. Fletcher had introduced Simon to video games on the computer. The way the people were behaving here appeared to be similar to the character animation glitches he'd encountered while playing *Mass Effect: Andromeda*. It was otherworldly, a little disturbing, and dizzying to watch. The closer Simon got to the building, the more frenetic it became as people glitched in and out at a furious nonstop pace. Were all these people coming here to murder the child? he wondered. Certainly, they could have visited Hitler's birthplace at any other time if they were only sightseeing, so it would seem so.

The apparitions were transparent, and as Simon drew closer, they whizzed through him and around him, ghost-like, as if he wasn't there. He was close enough to reach out and touch them, to see what they were wearing, the expressions on their faces, but they were oblivious to his presence. If their clothes were any indication, each seemed to be in different stages of time travel—some were in contemporary dress, while others wore clothing apropos to other eras. It was fascinating to observe the transitions the universe provided for what was needed in real time.

Simon stood still for a moment and glanced above at the upper floors of the Pommer building, wondering in which flat the Hitlers resided and whether baby Adolf was being tended to up there right now, also aware that the sweet, innocent child in the baby picture of Hitler that circulated widely on the internet would grow up to become a tyrant—so terrible, so destructive; that his actions would bring death and despair to a world that would never be the same again. The feeling of being close to or in the same proximity of history was always awe-inspiring to Simon, no matter what it was, even when it was encountering the bad, horrible parts, circumstances of war and protest, death and destruction, frailty and sadness, illness and poverty, even Hitler. He felt a keen sense of empathy and reverence for history. Anyone who time-traveled had to notice the patterns of things, how history repeated itself, and the importance of paying attention to and learning from it, lest we repeat it as historians warn.

As he was thinking these thoughts, like bees, ghostly phantoms whizzed by his head, and he felt the ground beneath his feet shift and begin to vibrate and move violently. Although there was nothing visible, he sensed that what was happening was below the surface. Although there were specific spots now that had become completely inaccessible, the scientists feared that as these zones became more crowded and overrun by tourists, they would bleed out, both temporally and physically, into neighboring regions, effectively shutting them down as well and closing them off permanently. Perhaps this was what they meant.

The Society's theory was also that these regions or dead zones that were frequently visited could only accommodate a certain amount of people at one time.

Although most of the activity was primarily clustered around Germany in the 1930s and 1940s others were cropping up in other locations as well: Los Angeles at the time of the Sharon Tate murders, tragedies of the Civil Rights era. Clearly, there would be interest in, for example, visiting Dallas in 1963 and preventing Lee Harvey Oswald from shooting John F. Kennedy from the window of the School Book Depository, or delaying Abraham Lincoln from attending Ford Theater on a certain April night in 1865. The list of events that might naturally draw people to them was endless—9/11, the Kent State shootings, the murder of Martin Luther King, and those were only events that had occurred here within the United States.

Numerous events around the world were also potential targets, for instance, the sinking of the Titanic, nuclear and environmental disasters that could have been prevented, the list was long. Indeed, the sheer magnitude of catastrophes times the number of people who wanted to change history made this a potential disaster in the making.

Simon was no scientist, but as the only person in the world capable of accessing these dead zone areas the momentous task set before him was to find answers to the scientist's questions: Why were travelers bouncing back? Why do some stay longer than others? When they bounce do they return home, or to some other limbo state? What photos are they using? One of the rules of time travel was that a photograph could only be used by a person to travel through a single time. Did that also apply to a photograph posted, say, on the internet that was being used repeatedly? Was there a limit to how many people could enter it? If so, how many? So many questions swirled in Simon's mind, and for a moment he didn't notice that a small earthquake was brewing under his feet; the ground beneath him was beginning to swell and distort, causing him to feel dizzy and disoriented, a not at all pleasant feeling at all.

Quickly, he spun around and hurried away from the pulsating earth, back to the safety of the street, where he could see that the ground there was flat and stable still. Simon stood a moment longer observing the feverish traffic of fast-moving travelers. There were half a dozen people obliviously milling about on the street, going about their everyday lives. A horse-drawn carriage passed behind him, the wooden wheels creaking; the horse's hooves clip-clopping along on the stone street. No one seemed to notice anything out of the ordinary.

Reaching down he picked up the brown leather suitcase he'd left sitting on the street. The first thing he had done upon arrival was to check inside. He was relieved to find that although the suitcase had changed into an 1880s iteration, the contents were somehow unchanged and intact—special equipment from the Society to test and monitor the scientist's theories and bring back the data before the universe collapses and ends time travel for good.

11

June 2, 1901

With the release of the wildly popular Brownie #1 camera and rolled film in 1889, his company had grown exponentially. But even with all his successes, George's youthful passion that started it all, his first love, always returned to the simple act of making pictures, which now involved using the camera and film of his own invention. In his private time, he was often seen roaming the grounds of his estate snapping off pictures with his Brownie #2; of flora and fauna, of his two playful dogs, trees, anything that caught his attention. And he especially enjoyed returning to his darkroom to develop the film himself, not that it occurred to him—widespread developing and printing services were still in the future.

This darkroom, equipped with everything he needed and more, was a grand improvement over his previous one back in the early 1870s when he was first experimenting with dry glass plates, which was little more than the size of a broom closet really. He could scarcely afford the necessary chemicals then, let alone adequate space on his meager bank clerk salary.

Today, pulling the black apron up over his head and cinching it up tight, he entered the large room where he prepared the three vats of chemicals: developer, stop bath, and fixer. He closed the door and, in the darkness, he carefully removed the film and rolled it onto a reel before flipping the light switch on. Bathed in a surreal pool of red light and surrounded by quiet solitude, the space was a welcome respite from his busy life.

Watching the images slowly materializing from nothing onto the photo paper like magic never grew old. Each individual memory slowly coming into view. As he moved through each print, one photo emerging from the developer bath was muddy and blurry. It appeared to be one taken of his dog Rex but was juxtaposed with the stem of a long-stemmed delphinium from the garden which ran straight up through the center. Likely he had neglected to advance the film between shots, thus creating a double exposure, a fairly common photography mistake, but as more of the image came into view, suddenly, George began to feel quite strange. Something was happening and he wasn't sure what. The walls around him seemed to expand and contract and fold inward. He felt a prickly sensation on his skin, pitch darkness, then an extraordinarily bright flash of light. Suddenly, feeling very exhausted and ill, he slumped against the table to quell the dizziness and try to understand what had just happened. Deciding to stop for the day, he placed the remaining film in a light-resistant cylinder and left the darkroom. His head suddenly pulsating with pain, he took to his bed for a nap. George shrugged off the strange white flash of before, attributing it to prolonged exposure to the pungent metallic-like odor of the photographic chemicals.

A month later, he was back in the darkroom again, developing the rest of the film and studying the emerging images. After focusing intently on one image in particular, he again began to feel odd, as he recalled he had previously, the walls folding in, the prickly sensation, the darkness but then gradually sunlight, no bright flash like before, and he realized he was physically no longer in his darkroom, but standing on the lawn under clear blue skies, the same as in the photograph. As his eyes adjusted to the light he glanced across the way and recognized his mother, and he distinctly recalled this event that had already happened. After excusing himself to visit the inside lavatory, he handed the camera over to her to hold. She must have taken this photograph of the Delphiniumin the garden. But if he had left the scene, how was it that he was here now? His mother turned and upon seeing him, raised her hand and waved. He started to wave in return, but felt his body being strangely pulled away and sucked back into the darkroom. Had he really been there just now, in the picture? Had he nodded off and been dreaming? It seemed so real. He felt his stomach churning and he had to sit down for a few minutes before exiting the darkroom to find his mother.

He found her lounging in the shade near the garden. "There you are, Mother!" he called.

"What is it, dear?" she asked, looking up from the newspaper she was reading.

"Do you remember when I was taking photographs here in the garden a month or so ago?"

"Well, I'm not sure," she answered. "That seems quite long ago."

"The reason I ask," he continued, "is within the batch of photographs I am developing in my darkroom I came across one that I don't recall taking. It is a close-up of one of the delphiniums in the garden. I believe you may have taken the picture."

"Delphiniums, hmmm," she said, scratching her chin and searching her memory. "Wait! Oh yes, I do remember! I took the picture and then I remember thinking how queer it was when I saw you wave at me from across the lawn, and then when I looked again, I saw you walking toward me from a completely different direction."

"Aha!" George thought. What was he experiencing, if not time travel, through a photograph? And what if … what if one is not allowed to encounter oneself and that is why he was pulled so abruptly back to the darkroom. He turned briskly to go.

"Where are you off to, George?" his mother inquired.

"Experiments, experiments to conduct," he murmured under his breath, his voice trailing as he turned around and dashed toward the house.

<hr />

Ever since he took possession of Eastman's book, journal, and the scroll from Carl in the parking garage Kevin had devoted every spare moment to trying to decipher the Einstein-level scribbles, to no avail. At one point, he'd even enlisted a physicist friend to help, but even he couldn't make sense of it. Apparently, early twentieth century science was murky and unverifiable, speculation at best, modern-day woo at its worst. At some point, Eastman had clearly stumbled upon a formula for time travel, but his calculations and charts and drawings and endless lists of possible chemical combinations did not sufficiently provide a logical explanation for it.

It was frustrating reading, to say the least and for Kevin, understanding it felt urgent; like time was running out. Already things were going awry. Granted, Kevin wasn't privy to the inner workings of the Society … yet, but he had ears, and he listened. There was chatter that something unusual was happening in Europe. He'd overheard the term "dead zones" bandied about. He wasn't sure what it meant, whether something was happening to the universe as he feared, but he certainly wanted to find out. Likewise, even Eastman had seemed troubled by the consequences of too much time travel. In his journal, he wrote:

We did not know how having this knowledge might change the world. If everyone could time travel, would it rip the universe apart? Could items that might have been removed from circulation in the past, what we named the "misery index," cause a ripple effect with catastrophic results in the future? We agreed that the phenomenon requires more study.

Short of some epiphany, or aha moment, chips falling magically into place, the planets aligning, or a lightbulb exploding in his head, Kevin was at a loss.

Notwithstanding, history did have its share of Eureka moments: Sir Isaac Newton in 1666 observed an apple falling to the ground to develop his theory of universal gravitation. Frederich August Kekule von Stradonitz' dream of a snake seizing hold of its own tail inspired the benzene molecule. In 1907, Albert Einstein's thought experiment on whether a man that falls freely would not feel his weight led to the theory of relativity. Heck, Paul McCartney's classic hit song "Yesterday" came to him when he awoke one morning to the tune playing in his head in 1964.

It could happen, he supposed. In fact, he had felt excited and encouraged this morning after opening the news app on his phone and scanning the science category. The headline from the *Washington Post* read: Time is not a flat circle. In a major discovery, scientists find it's more like a choppy sea.

He eagerly clicked the link to read the story:

In a major discovery, scientists this week say they've found that space-time churns like a choppy sea, a mind-bending finding suggests that everything around us is constantly being roiled by low-frequency gravitational waves.

The claim that telescopes across the planet have seen signs of a "gravitational wave background" has sent a thrill through the astrophysics community, which has been buzzing for days in anticipation of the papers that were unveiled late Wednesday.

"We've been on a mission for the last 15 years to find a low-pitch hum of gravitational waves resounding throughout the universe and washing through our galaxy to warp space-time in a measurable way," NANOGrav chair Stephen Taylor of Vanderbilt University said at a news briefing Tuesday.

"Hmmm ... Interesting," Kevin said aloud. "Low-frequency gravitational waves ... choppy seas ..."

Although neither he nor the Society acknowledged it, Kevin was a self-taught expert on time travel. Kevin couldn't help dreaming about one day getting a shot, the higher ups actually listening to his ideas. Despite being relegated to the basement, for years he was knee-deep in the Society's research. He knew all the rules—that you enter a state of limbo if you run into yourself, that you cannot bring items back from the past and that it is imperative that your anchor photograph stay intact. He understood the science of tracking travelers, and that the universe is sensitive to vibrations between photograph and viewer. Could these gravitational waves have something to do with dead time zones? Without knowing exactly what was happening it was difficult to make any sort of a connection or form a hypothesis.

⋘⋙

After work that night, Kevin tossed his keys on the kitchen table, set his laptop down, slipped off his work shoes, and plopped onto the sofa. Man, it had been one long-ass day. He was tired but mostly grumpy from dealing with interns all day. Sure, some of them were great—so eager to please, so ready to take his job at their first opportunity. And Brittany, his assistant. That girl. What a mess. She was the worst, not to mention supremely weird. She wore old lady clothes, and she smelled like cat piss.

Reflexively, he reached for the remote and switched on the cable news for background noise before rummaging through the freezer for a burrito bowl to toss in the microwave for a quick, easy meal. When it was done, he poured himself a glass of wine, sat down with his meal on the coffee table, and stared at the TV. He hated coming home to an empty house. Nothing sadder than eating alone in front of the TV. The news was depressing. He switched channels, *The Bachelor* was on. He felt shitty. Watching the nasty pettiness made him feel a little less shitty, but the truth was, he hated his life. He was miserable. He missed Jackson. *Maybe I should get a dog, or a cat,* he thought.

He turned off the television and ate in silence, each chew amplified in his head, wondering if life would ever get any better. As he was contemplating his dreary existence, he noticed it, his guitar, sitting over in the corner gathering dust. He hadn't picked it up and played anything in ages, at least since before Jackson left. Hmmm, maybe what he needed to feel better was a little creative outlet. Maybe. And who knows, a hit song could magically pop into his head, like it did for Paul McCartney, and he'd be rich and famous. *Yeah, right.*

Tossing his half-eaten microwave meal into the trash, he grabbed a dish towel from the kitchen and used it to dust off the guitar. It wasn't anything fancy, your standard Yamaha F310 acoustic guitar, more sentimental value than anything. He'd mentioned to Jackson one time that he took lessons as a kid. He picked up on that and surprised Kevin with it one year for his birthday. He was able to pluck out a few tunes from memory, but Jackson encouraged him to learn, so they'd gone out together and purchased chord books. He practiced consistently for a while, but like most hobbies, it quickly fell by the wayside, and of course, after Jackson left, he lost all desire to play anyway—why expose himself to yet another painful reminder of their failed relationship?

It felt good in his hands. Sturdy, substantial. He strummed the strings with his fingers, which hurt a little bit, the callouses he'd built up playing now long gone. He managed to play "Greensleeves," the one and only song he could play all the way through by ear. It was out of tune, and he was rusty for sure, but it wasn't terrible. He found a pick lying on the floor where the guitar had been, opened up the guitar tuning app he still had on his phone, and began plucking individual strings while turning the tuning pegs to raise and lower pitch.

Getting excited now, he got up and grabbed one of the chord books off the bookshelf and laid it out on the coffee table in front of him and began to strum. Starting with "Stand by Me" he moved through his repertoire: the Beatles' "Love Me Do", "Smoke on the Water," and "Yesterday," obviously; "A Horse with No Name", both Elvises: Presley's "Love Me Tender" and Costello's "My Aim is True," and then, of course, the Ramones' upbeat "Blitzkrieg Bop." Soon, he felt himself loosening up, his shoulders relaxed, his mind floating on a wave of tranquility, lost in the music and the pleasant sounds echoing off the walls of the condo. The act of making music—first playing each single note followed by a series of chords vibrating through his fingers—felt immensely freeing and for a brief while, he felt the creative juices kicking in, along with an incredible joyful sense of existing outside of his own head for a change, in the wonderful way writers and artists and musicians become so immersed in their art they lose all track of time. It was magnificent and exhilarating and needed.

He finished off the set with "House of the Rising Sun" pausing to listen to the final note as it continued to reverberate within the quiet space, and then … lightning struck. There it was, plain as day. He couldn't believe it, the Aha moment he was hoping for: Vibrations! Choppy seas! Time is not flat! Music is analogous. A string that is under tension will vibrate at a certain frequency. Hitting two or more notes together creates resonance when the two vibrations combine.

Could that not also apply to double exposure in photography, a common mistake made by photographers who failed to wind the camera forward before taking their next shot? he wondered. One photo equals a note. Two photos mashed together, a chord. Kevin was on a roll. He knew he was onto something here and his mind rushed feverishly from one thought experiment to the next.

Therefore, if frequency is the period between waves, he posited, how much of an interval do you need to find the right resonance to create the "time chord" that turns time travel on and off? Had Eastman stumbled upon the magic chord, the two perfect high points in the wave to open up time travel in the universe without realizing it? Perhaps if Kevin could find the right frequency, he could turn time travel off, the way Eastman had turned it on. Was double exposure the missing puzzle piece? And might it also be the key to these dead time zones he'd heard of?

"That's it!" he said out loud. "It has to be." Kevin was excited but also a little giddy. In the moment, no doubt brought on by this evening's inspired music combined with his epiphany, the R.E.M. tune "What's the Frequency, Kenneth?" burst into his brain like an exploding candle and he couldn't help giggling. The wheels were turning in his head about how to test his theory. He knew what he had to do. It wouldn't be nice. It wouldn't be pretty, but it had to be done. But who first to test it on? He paced back and forth before stopping abruptly in the center of the room answering himself, "Well, interns, of course ... and Brittany."

12

Imogen pulled the paperback Nancy had given to her from her backpack and turned it over in her hands. *She Left Her Heart in San Francisco.* In comparison to Loretta's earlier work, the cover looked different than her earlier romance novels, more contemporary, edgier. And that tagline: *In the swinging City by the Bay theirs was a different kind of love.* Scanning the pages as she flipped through it her eyes landed on one word, "lesbian." *Oh wow,* Imogen thought. Loretta really was pushing the envelope with this one for sure. Back then, writing about the San Francisco late sixties' counterculture scene, let alone lesbian lovers, would have probably been risqué. *Well, this should be interesting,* she thought as she sat down and began reading the first chapter:

Disheartened and tired, Liz stood in front of the Capris Motel observing the red neon Vacancy sign as it blinked on off on off, considering whether to go in. Even in the dark she could see that the motel was rundown and a little dicey. Not quite as neat and clean as it appeared on the postcard Mary had sent her. But it was late. She was exhausted. The suitcase she'd carried all the way from the bus station downtown felt much heavier now than the one she'd carefully packed back home in Modesto. Sighing, she entered the dimly lit office, which smelled of Pine-Sol with just a hint of ashtray and vomit. A handwritten sign at the desk read: Ring bell for service. She pressed it and immediately regretted it; a piercing and unpleasant trill vibrated throughout the cramped room, but it worked because in shuffled the night clerk. One long, out of place piece of stringy, greasy hair hung in front of his dirty, dust-speckled wire-rimmed glasses; Creepy didn't do him justice. In big bold letters his name tag read ERNEST. Liz immediately felt uneasy. "Um, I have a reservation."

"What's your name?" Ernest asked without looking up. She told him her name and he shuffled some papers around pretending to search through a long list of reservations that she was sure did not exist, before finally replying, "Ah, Elizabeth Parker. He turned around and pulled a key attached to a plastic pink octagon key ring with a giant number embossed on it from the pegboard behind him and slapped it down on the desk in front of her. "Here's yer key," he said. "Room 27. You might need to jigger it in the keyhole. There's a jacuzzi tub in your room, but it don't work. Management pulled the plug on it. I'll show you where to park around the back but I ain't responsible if somebody messes with it." He grinned at her. He was missing a front tooth.

"Um, that's okay," Liz said quickly taking the key and backing away. "I'll find it myself."

Imogen was hooked. Several hours later, she finished reading the final chapter, closed the book, and set it down beside her. Not only was Loretta an excellent writer, but the story was fabulous ... and strangely, familiar. I have to go, she said out loud.

"Are you in here on the computer, Niles?" Niles turned around to Fletcher standing in the doorway of Imogen's office.

Startled, Niles stopped typing. "Um, yeah," he answered. "Did you need to use it? Imogen is in her room reading, I think. She said it was okay if I got on for a bit."

"Oh yeah, sure, of course," Fletcher said. "I didn't mean to sound like I was quizzing you. I just hadn't seen anyone around this morning; wondered what you were all up to."

Niles turned back to the screen. "What are you doing?" Fletcher asked, smiling, curious. "Writing a novel? Texting a girlfriend?"

Responding to Fletcher's probing questions, Niles fidgeted uncomfortably in his chair. The internet was a relatively new thing in 1997 when he had traveled back to find Imogen's friend Jade and had gotten stuck in a time loop that held him captive for twenty-two years. He had a lot of catching up to do—mostly just playing games, but also browsing news sites, marveling at the profusion of information available at one's fingertips, and mostly being totally blown away by how much cameras had evolved since he was a photographer using his Pentax 67 and developing film in the darkroom. Indeed, the digital cameras of today were nothing short of amazing—there were mirrorless cameras, powerful macro and micro lenses, and one camera that boasted a whopping 576 megapixels! Even the cameras installed in cell phones were as powerful as the professional models! He couldn't wait to get his hands on one and start shooting again. He missed getting out in nature, hiking, shooting waterfalls, chasing the golden hour. But shooting with Imogen and his wife Francis he missed the most.

Fletcher drew closer and Niles flinched a little. "I don't mean to disturb you Niles, but I was wondering if I might talk to you. Do you have a minute?"

Niles minimized the email tab that had been up on the screen and twisted around in his seat to face him.

"Sure, what's up?"

Fletcher pulled a chair over and sat down next to Niles. He wasn't sure where to start and the words came out jerky and uneven. "I'm ... I'm just ... uh, well, I need someone to talk to about something," he said. "I used to talk to Simon. We were good friends, but even if he was here to talk to, I couldn't really talk to him about this."

"What is it, Fletcher?" Niles said, growing impatient for Fletcher to get to it.

"It's about Imogen," he blurted. "I feel a little strange talking to you about your daughter, but it well, it concerns her ... and the way I feel about her."

Niles nodded understanding. He was aware that Fletcher and Imogen had dated in college but had decided to stay friends.

"I ... you see, I have feelings for her still. I shouldn't, I know. She's with Simon and I would never do anything to get between them ... but with Simon away and the pandemic and all we've grown closer these past few months, and then, you know, the miscarriage." He hesitated before continuing, "and a while back, Jade, Imogen's friend told me that she said she still has feelings for me too, and that she regrets how things ended between us."

"Have you told *her* how you feel?" Niles asked.

Fletcher stared down at his hands for a moment before answering. "Yes. She'd been in bed for three days and I made her get up and eat something. She asked me why I was being so nice to her, and I just blurted it right out, told her, because I love her."

"And what did she say?"

"Nothing. I changed the subject before it got awkward."

Niles was at a bit of a loss. He'd spent the past few months getting to know Fletcher. He barely knew Simon. He, of course, just wanted what was best for his daughter.

"Here's my advice, Fletcher," he began. "Be patient. For now. I'm not a religious person, but I do believe the universe has a natural way of guiding people toward the path that's meant for them, to the people they're supposed to be with. Simon will come back eventually. We don't know what he's going through at the Daguerreian Society. He may come back changed. Imogen has certainly changed—she's been through a hugely traumatic event. Their relationship may change as well. In the meantime, be her friend, support her like you always have, and wait and see what happens."

Fletcher smiled and said, "Thank you, Niles. You are a wise man."

Niles humbly waved him away. "Nah, not really. Just gotten older and learned a few things along the way perhaps."

"I forget that you're older," Fletcher noted. "You look so young. It's hard to believe you're Imogen's dad sometimes."

It was true. During the twenty-two years he had been gone, since 1997 when Imogen was nine, time moved slower, rendering his appearance that of the man in his late thirties.

"Well, thanks for the advice." Fletcher started to get up, but Niles had something on his mind as well.

"Speaking of Jade," he said. Fletcher sat back down.

"What about Jade?"

Niles brought up the tab he'd minimized earlier, an email he had been composing before Fletcher came in the room. Fletcher leaned in and read the recipient's name. Jade.

"You're conversing with Jade, Imogen's Jade?" Fletcher asked, trying not to sound as surprised as he really was.

"Is that weird?" Niles asked.

"Uh, well, a little ... I don't know," Fletcher replied. "What exactly is going on with you two?"

Fletcher knew the backstory, how Niles had gone looking for Jade after she'd abruptly moved away without telling Imogen when they were children. When Teddy had destroyed the photograph he'd gone through he got stuck in a time loop, but not before he had grown close to Jade and her mother and was instrumental in helping them escape Jade's abusive father.

Niles sighed deeply before telling Fletcher how for about the last month or so they had been regularly emailing each other and chatting online.

"We were friends online and she sent me a text one day. She was curious about the time I was there, when she was a child. We started chatting about things that were going on, masks, COVID, Black Lives Matter protests, and well, I don't know, things just clicked. And I think there's something there, a spark maybe."

Fletcher raised his eyebrows. "Aren't you like old enough to be her father?"

Niles nodded and launched into a stumbling reply. "Yeah, yes, uh, yeah ... Technically, I am. I know it's bizarre."

"She feels the same? About this spark?" Fletcher asked.

"I think so. I mean we've been talking, and you know, chronologically, yes, I am older than she is, but like we talked about before ... look at me. I look the same as I did in 1997 and she grew up and well, she caught up with me."

And then for a minute, things got uncomfortably weird. "But you never had any type of feelings toward her back then when she was a little girl, right?" Fletcher queried.

Niles was visibly mortified by his question. "Oh, heavens no! Of course not," he sputtered. "I would never have ... "

Fletcher felt embarrassed then for even bringing it up and started to backtrack. "Oh, I ... I wouldn't think so," he stumbled. "I wasn't accusing you, just asking, you know."

"It's okay," Niles said. "I realize how strange it must seem. Jade knows it's strange. I can't explain it. We can't explain it. In all honesty, I'm both terrified and thrilled," he admitted.

"It's probably none of my business, but what about your wife?" Fletcher pressed.

Niles pressed his lips together and looked down, embarrassed with this line of questioning, too. Fletcher was about to tell him that it was okay, he didn't need to justify anything to him when Niles offered, "My wife, Francis, and I have been apart for many years now." His face seemed pained as though he didn't want to go on, but he continued anyway. "I don't know where she is, what's become of her, if she's alive or dead. Imogen seems to want to try to find her—it seems like a long shot, but I hope she does. I do want to know what happened to Francis, but it's complicated. We were having problems in our marriage before we were pulled apart … and I've lost so much time already. I feel like maybe it's time for me to move on."

Fletcher couldn't say that he truly understood, but far be it for him to judge how someone else felt.

"Please, don't say anything to Imogen just yet."

"Don't tell Imogen what?" Imogen said as she appeared in the doorway catching Fletcher and Niles, mired in some deep conversation, reminiscent of the times she would come home to find Fletcher and Simon doing the same thing, poring over blueprints together on the kitchen table or looking at charts and schematics on the computer.

Niles nervously closed the email tab again and Fletcher greeted her. "Imogen! How was the reading?" Imogen smiled, but she was very suspicious. What were these two plotting? Niles piped up, "Darn, you always sneak up on us. I was just looking at cakes to order for your birthday, too.

"My birthday?" Imogen said delighted as she walked over to the computer screen. "Let's see. Show me. Can I pick?" Niles blocked her hands from the keyboard.

"No, you can't pick. Now get out of here, you." Imogen grumbled, pivoted on her heel, and left the room.

Fletcher met Niles hand in a high five. "Good save, Niles!"

Imogen blew out all but one of the thirty-two candles on the delicious, but expensive Triple Chocolate Obsession cake Niles felt compelled to order for Imogen's birthday. Niles and Fletcher clapped and yelled "yays" in unison while Imogen tried to look happier than she felt about turning thirty-two. It wasn't the number so much. She didn't feel old or anything but considering everything that had happened recently—the pandemic, Simon being gone, the miscarriage—celebrating felt forced even if it was with the two best people she knew.

"How's that obsession cake? Are you obsessed?" Fletcher teased as she took a bite of it.

"It's quite delish," Imogen conceded. "You guys really shouldn't have spent so much. I know how much these patisserie cakes cost; they are not cheap."

Fletcher brushed off her comment. "Aw, you're worth it."

"And it's not like you turn thirty-two every day," Niles added, patting her shoulder with affection.

"I know, Dad," she said. "I appreciate it, I really do … it's just …" she stopped herself before saying more.

"You just what? What's wrong, Imogen?" Fletcher asked.

Imogen sighed before continuing. "Nothing's wrong, I just need to do something, that's all."

"What do you want to do, Imogen?" Niles asked.

Imogen put her fork down on the plate and turned in her chair to face them both. "Okay, so I read this novel the other day," she began. "It was written by a woman author. Her name is Loretta Ross. I met her when I was in Kansas. She's a time traveler and well, I think this book might be based on Mom's real-life story."

"What?" Niles reacted, surprised. "You're kidding. Why do you think this?"

She gave them an abbreviated version of the plot: A woman comes to San Francisco 1967 to room with her girlfriend. They unexpectedly become lovers until one day when the jealous boyfriend that she left behind shows up and tries to murder her.

"And which character do you think is Francis?" Niles asked.

"I'm not sure," Imogen acknowledged. "It's a story. She's a writer. She took liberties I'm sure, but I know that she time travels to collect fodder for her books. That's what she was doing in Kansas when I met her. And," she continued, "Teddy did mention San Francisco. I know it's not much to go on, but I feel like it's worth a shot to at least talk to Loretta and see if she might know something. Travelers seem to gravitate toward one another."

Niles appeared visibly distressed. Hunched over his plate of uneaten cake, he fidgeted with his fork. "What's wrong, Dad," Imogen asked.

He looked away. "It's just ... I have a hard time imagining that Francis was a lesbian ... not that there's anything wrong with that," he quickly added. "But it just doesn't seem like her. She was always so, I don't know, buttoned up tight, I guess you could say. She didn't show her feelings very much and maybe that's why, I didn't know."

Imogen nodded agreement. She remembered how painful it felt the times when her mother had pushed her away. She may have been the same way with Niles.

"I want you to find out though," he said. "I do. I need closure, I think we both do. We need to find out what happened to your mother."

"Okay Dad. It's settled then. I'll go."

Fletcher, who had been quietly listening throughout the conversation, looked over at Imogen and asked, "So, when are you going?"

"I don't know, soon, I guess," she answered.

"But you're still recovering. Do you think it's a good idea? Shouldn't you maybe wait."

Imogen rolled her eyes. She loved Fletcher and appreciated his concern, but sometimes it felt a little stifling. "I feel fine. I'm going."

"Then I'm going with you," Fletcher stated.

"That's not necessary," she said, shaking her head No. "Really, I'll be okay."

Fletcher couldn't hide his distress. "Come on, Gen, you don't know what you'll find there. San Francisco? Nineteen sixties? It could be all kinds of crazy. And even if you feel fine physically, you don't know what you'll learn about your mom. You'll need someone there to support you … you know, emotionally."

"First of all, I'm not going back to the nineteen sixties, it's 1973, and second, I don't need …" Fletcher interrupted her before she could finish. "Let me be a time tourist with you, Imogen, just one more time … please?"

Always a sucker for Fletcher's pleading puppy dog eyes, Imogen shrugged and relented. "Okay, all right, you can come along … but you have to promise to let me handle things. Be cool. Follow my lead."

"I can be cool," he said, beaming now. "I'll be way totally cool ... er groovy, isn't that what the kids used to say back then. I'll be groovy. Ooh, and I'll bet we'll get some far-out clothes to wear too ..."

Fletcher was still musing about all the groovy things when Imogen got up and left the room.

13

After traveling through the bump bumpety bump, jolting, jarring cavernous roller-coaster ride through time, the abrupt emergence of sunlight was so bright and blinding that both travelers had to quickly shield their eyes. But even before their eyes could properly focus on anything, other senses kicked in, the sound of hundreds of seagulls squawking above them; a long blast of a horn from a distant fishing boat; water lapping against the dock and buoys bumping up against the pier; sea lions barking, and the robust salty fragrance of seawater near the wharf immediately assaulting their anterior naris. And almost immediately upon arriving, Imogen felt Fletcher's arm go limp in hers and he crumpled to the ground. On her own two wobbly legs, she guided him to a bench nearby, where he sat with his head between his knees waiting for the intense bout of nausea to pass.

The return address on the envelope Loretta sent from 1973 was for a house listed in Pacifica, but her map app had shown that the house was no longer there. Deciding it might be easier to rent a car in the city, they decided to enter a photograph near Fisherman's Wharf and then drive the twelve miles or so down the coast to Pacifica.

After sitting on the bench for a while, Fletcher was feeling better. "It smells fishy here," he said. It was nice to be away from COVID, to be able to go out without having to wear a face mask. The air of normalcy here felt good and freeing, people walking, strolling, eating ice cream cones, a street musician in a bright red scarf, sandals, and a top hat strummed tunes on his guitar for tips. There were still hippies around, but by 1973 the pier seemed to be outnumbered by tourists.

As they walked, Fletcher turned to her and asked, "What should we do first?"

"What do you mean, what should we do first?" Imogen answered wryly, immune to his enthusiasm.

"Let's go see *all* the things!" he said. "Look, over there's the wax museum and Ripley's Believe It or Not and Alcatraz; we could ride a cable car, eat at DiMaggio's, we *have* to go there!"

The Doors' song "Riders on the Storm" blasted from inside of a funky record shop plastered with band posters out to the sidewalk. Fletcher stopped to peek inside the store, the interior bathed in groovy black light. "Imogen, look at all the vinyl! he gasped. Imogen tugged on his shirt, pulling him away from the store and guiding him back to the sidewalk.

"Oh, come on Imogen, lighten up, why not?" Fletcher whined.

"This is precisely why I didn't want to bring you," she said. "You never stick to the program. We're here for a reason. You'd never make a good time traveler."

"Why are you such a buzzkill Imogen? Don't you ever do anything fun? You used to be fun," he said. That stung, but Imogen continued to walk as Fletcher went on and on.

"I mean, you're in another friggin' time for crissake! How can you not want to explore and see what's happening. Look at us," he said, glancing first at himself and then back at her. "How groovy are we?"

"Well, not quite as groovy as you thought, right? It is 1973," she said. Fletcher was wearing a T-shirt, jeans, and a pair of high-top Converse. Imogen had on a cotton print dress and leather sandals.

Imogen stopped and placed her hands on her hips and gave him a look of exasperation, but she couldn't help breaking into a smile at his pleading eyes and pouty lower lip. It was too easy to get caught up in Fletcher's childish delight. It's what had drawn her to him back in college. And she had to admit that it was pretty nice having a traveling companion, better than being by herself.

He was right, she'd forgotten how it felt when time travel was all brand-new. How awestricken she had been at the thought of actually visiting another time other than her own and witnessing events that she'd only read about in history books. These past few years she had taken it for granted, but seeing Fletcher so excited made her realize what a gift it was. Why not humor him, she thought. Let him enjoy himself. Allow herself to enjoy the moment, too. For weeks and weeks, she had been miserable and sullen, and then losing the baby had been almost more than she could bear. Maybe he was right, a distraction, a little fun was exactly what she needed. She didn't want to draw comparisons between Fletcher and Simon, but the fact remained, Fletcher was here with her now. Simon was not.

"I tell you what," she said, linking her arm through his. We'll go see the sights, but we have to watch the time so we can rent a car and get where we need to be, okay?" Fletcher beamed, bouncing on one foot like an excited kid in a toy store.

For the next couple of hours they explored the wharf, stopped to listen to music, people watched, enjoying the sunshine. They went to the wax museum, which was sort of cool except Imogen and Fletcher hadn't heard of some of the wax figures they had in residence, like Norman Rockwell and Anton LaVey, a famous satanist located in the underground Chamber of Horrors, although his wax figure was pretty cool. Ripley's Believe It or Not Odditorium was as amazingly cheesy as one might expect it to be, but so much fun—wacky exhibits and curiosities like shrunken heads, the Fiji mermaid, a camel bladder vase, a mummified hand, weird artwork, two-headed turtles. By the time they emerged from inside the museum they were both giggling. Imogen drew the line on the Alcatraz tour, however; it would have taken too long for the tour and the boat ride to and from the island.

"What's next boss?" Fletcher asked, poking her ribs playfully.

"We need to rent a car. Look for a phone booth," she instructed. They spotted one just past the penny arcade.

Fletcher watched with amazement as Imogen handily flipped through the yellow pages in the big, bulky hanging phone book. He'd seen a few remnants of phone booths when he was a kid but had never actually used one. Imogen deposited the money in the slot and arranged everything.

"You're like a time tourist pro," he said, impressed.

Imogen smiled. "Comes with the territory." The car rental place was just a few blocks away.

"Before we go, can I do just one more thing?" Fletcher asked.

Still basking in the moment, Imogen surrendered. "Sure," she said.

Fletcher rushed over to a souvenir machine, pulled some change from his pocket and picked a penny from his palm to use to smash it and emboss the Golden Gate Bridge on it. He watched as the mechanical machine went through its grinding motions and deposited the flattened penny into the slot below.

"You can't take it with you, you know," Imogen noted.

Fletcher sighed and pushed it into his jeans pocket. "I know." Smiling, he took her arm. "Ready to go?"

〰〰〰

The bright yellow Datsun 510 they rented came with a fistful of S&H Green stamps. "What are those?" Fletcher asked. "Got me," Imogen said, tossing them aside as they hopped in the rental car and headed west toward the ocean. Fletcher was impressed that she knew how to drive stick. "Wow, I didn't know you could drive a stick shift."

133

"Of course, don't you?" she asked. Fletcher shook his head. "Nope."

"Really? I'm a little shocked," she said laughing. "A country boy like you?!"

Without the aid of GPS to guide them Fletcher had picked up a map at the gas station and had it unfolded in front of him on the dash. "I'll stick to navigating," he said. "Where are we going, by the way? This seems out of the way. Shouldn't we be heading south on Hwy 1?"

Imogen had turned off on Geary Blvd heading west. "I want to make a detour at Sutro Baths, er ... what's left of them anyway."

"What's that?"

"It used to be a big saltwater swimming pool complex until it burned down in 1966." Geary turned into Point Lobos and Imogen followed it to the entrance of the Lands End parking lot. Parking the car, she got out and motioned for Fletcher to follow. "C'mon."

"Where are we going now?"

Imogen started down a set of sandy stairs that weaved down the hill to the site. A clear blue sky, the Pacific Ocean, and Seal Rock created a panoramic postcard-like view. The ruins didn't seem like much to Fletcher, just a collection of saltwater pools, crumbling walls, and rusting pieces of iron. To Imogen, who had been at the Cliff House on that day in June 1966 and smelled the burning timbers, watched them crack as the structure burned to the ground, and wondered if she'd get out of there alive, it felt a little surreal being back. Loretta had also written about this day in her book.

As they walked around the ruins, exploring the weird structures, looking into the pools, and walking through a tunnel that went through the cliff and led to a beach, Imogen told him why she had been there. She'd taken a case to find a woman's sister who had run away with her boyfriend and never came home. She tracked them to the Cliff House on the same day the fire broke out suspiciously at Sutro Baths.

"Do you think the fire might be somehow connected to your mom?" Fletcher asked as they started back up the stairs to the car.

"Maybe," Imogen said. "I think the only way to find out is to speak to the author."

After leaving Sutro, they got back in the car and headed south on the Upper Great Highway, past Ocean Beach and over to 35 before getting back on Hwy 1 and heading toward Pacifica. It was dusk when Imogen spotted a small beach motel. The blinking red vacancy sign reminded her of the opening chapter of Loretta's book causing her to wonder if Ernest the creepy desk clerk might also be inside. He wasn't, of course. Instead, a lovely, perfectly normal elderly woman rented them a room for the night.

As they were entering the room, Imogen turned back to Fletcher and said, "We can get up and find Loretta's house in the morning." But when she turned around, she stopped abruptly. The room had only one queen-size bed.

Imogen bit her lip and looked over at Fletcher, who also seemed uncomfortable. "Uh, what do you think, should we get another room?" he asked.

Imogen set her suitcase down and sat down on the edge of the bed and decided not to be awkward with her best friend. What the heck, they'd practically been living together during the pandemic. What difference would sharing a bed for one night together make?

"Nah," she said. "Let's just make the best of it. You stay on your side; I'll stay on mine, deal?"

"Deal!" Fletcher said, relieved that Imogen wasn't making a big deal of it.

"I'm beat anyway. It's been a long day." He looked over at Imogen who was fiddling with some weird antennae attached to the TV.

"Me too," she said. "I had fun today, Fletch. "I didn't think I needed fun, but I guess I really did." She turned around and smiled at him, and he smiled back.

"I had fun, too," he said. "With you."

When Imogen opened her eyes, bright sunlight was spilling through the motel room's thin curtains and Fletcher was big-spooning her.

Oh god, oh shit, her mind raced. His arm was draped loosely over her waist and his body was nestled up as close to hers as two bodies could be. For a second, she panicked, wondering if they had done anything besides falling asleep last night. A wave of conflicting emotions flooded her mind—mortification, desire, guilt. She laid silent and still until the initial panic subsided, but then her next thoughts scared her even more because … it felt good. Very good.

There it was. Having someone close to her wrapping themselves around her body like this, holding her, was nice. It had been so long since she'd been touched. She'd forgotten what it was like. She lay there for a minute longer, prolonging the pleasant before trying to unobtrusively slip out from under his arm and out of bed without waking him, but no good, Fletcher woke up. Realizing what was happening, he flew over to his side and leaped out of bed.

"I'm so sorry, Gen," he apologized profusely. "I didn't mean to ... I didn't ..."

"It's okay, Fletcher" Imogen assured him. "Don't worry about it. It's all good. We're good."

"Are you sure? I mean we didn't do anything, I don't think. Did we?"

"It's fine, Fletcher. We didn't." Imogen would never tell him how much she didn't mind. "I'm gonna go hop in the shower now," she said. "Why don't you go see if you can go find us some coffee."

※※※※※

Except for a narrow sidewalk, sand came practically all the way up to the doorstep, a true beach bungalow. It was a little rundown; the paint was peeling on the exterior, but it was funky and welcoming. Several wind chimes tinkled a series of both light and somber notes in response to a gentle ocean breeze; a bevy of hanging plants in handmade macrame holders, and a wicker chair hung from one of the posts. A soft, lilting melody wafted from inside. Imogen recognized the song playing on the stereo: "Will You Still Love Me," Tapestry, Carole King.

She stepped onto the small porch, knocked on the screen door and waited. Peering through the screen door, she could make out the small living quarters decorated in signature seventies orange, harvest gold, and avocado green—a lava lamp, a beanbag chair in one corner, a couch covered with a patchwork quilt, a few pillows scattered about, orange shag carpet. A cigarette burned away unattended in the glass ashtray. Imogen knocked again, this time a bit harder. Someone entered the space from another room in the house, stopping first to turn down the stereo, and then she appeared at the door. A young woman, dressed in a flowery peasant top and a loose flowing skirt, pushed open the door to see who was there. Her curly brown hair was piled wildly atop her head and tied up with a bright orange silk scarf. She looked different than the Loretta she remembered from Kansas, but the freckles and blue eyes were the same.

"Loretta?" Imogen asked.

"Imogen Oliver?" Excited, Loretta pushed the door open all the way and immediately reached out and drew Imogen in for a hug. "It's so wonderful to see you!" she gushed. "So I'm guessing you must have received my letter!"

"I did," Imogen said. "And I was quite surprised to learn that you are a traveler, too."

Oblivious to Fletcher standing on the porch, Loretta placed an arm around Imogen's shoulder and the two of them walked past him and into the house. "We have a lot of catching up to do, don't we?"

The last time they had seen one another had been in Kansas, 1946—seventy-four years ago in actual time, but only a short time ago for them. Although they had both been there at the same time, each had come from different points in time—Imogen from 2019 and Loretta from, 1973, this year. And although they were born forty years apart, weirdly, in this time scenario, Imogen who had recently turned thirty-two was older than Loretta, who was only 25.

Talking about time, made Fletcher's head spin. Despite being completely ignored on the porch by both women he'd followed them into the house and Imogen finally got around to introducing him to Loretta, who seemed lovely, but for the past ten minutes they had been discussing time travel, certainly a fascinating topic, but even being an engineer it was easy to be confused by the math. While they caught up though he marveled at the funky seventy's décor. It felt like he'd entered a time capsule. The orange shag carpet was pretty fab; he noticed there was even a rake sitting in the corner next to the fireplace, for fluffing, as needed. Everything was super boho. The space was cluttered with stuff and more stuff, books, record albums, plants. Somehow though, it worked. Arbitrary chaos.

He was checking out her vast collection of record albums when he smelled something familiar. Loretta had lit up a joint.

"You guys smoke?" she asked as she took a drag and offered up the fat, rolled up joint. Imogen and Fletcher looked at each other and grinned. "Sure," they said in unison.

After taking a hit and handing it back to Loretta, Fletcher casually mentioned, "Marijuana is legal in Oregon."

"What?!" Loretta's jaw dropped along with the joint which fell to the floor and which she quickly retrieved before it could burn the carpet. "Oh my, that's so crazy," she said. "What else is legal in 2020?"

Imogen recoiled a bit at her question, remembering the agents from the Daguerreian Society reprimanding her for giving away too much information about the future.

"Next you'll be telling me that gay marriage is legal too?" Loretta continued. "Is it?" she asked.

Imogen wasn't aware of Loretta's sexual proclivities but wasn't terribly surprised by it either. People have always been gay, no matter what the time period. Just look at their friend Herbert from 1913.

Disregarding their dire warnings about blabbing, Imogen couldn't help herself. "Well," Imogen stated, "the good news is that same-sex marriage is in fact legal, for now, but there are people who want to overturn that decision, along with Roe v. Wade. We're in the middle of a pandemic; the country is divided, protesters in the streets. Books are being banned in schools. You can't even say the word 'gay' in Florida anymore."

Loretta snickered at that. "pffft, Florida, some things never change," she said.

Loretta pondered all the new information Imogen had revealed to her. "Well geez, I thought the sixties were turbulent, but that we'd pretty much settled everything. The twenty-first century sounds pretty awful."

Imogen and Fletcher nodded agreement.

"I'm surprised about Roe v. Wade though," she said. "You know, it was just passed this year. It makes me sad for my daughter."

A daughter. Loretta had never said anything to her about having a child.

Responding to Imogen's confused look, Loretta confessed that she had gotten pregnant at seventeen. "It was before abortion was legal. I had a child out of wedlock, a daughter. At the time, I wasn't ready to take care of a baby, so I allowed the father to take her. Since then, I have lived outside her life, although I do get to see her from time to time. There is a stigma for women that doesn't exist for men when it comes to child custody." Loretta looked stricken and paused to regain her composure before continuing, "I spoke of this arrangement to an acquaintance once. This woman, who was a horrible mother—she partied all the time, did drugs, but when I told her, her shitty response was, 'Well, I could *never* leave *my* kids,' as if leaving them so they might have a better shot at life is somehow worse than bringing them up in a house full of drunks and druggies."

"I'm sorry to say that in the future that stigma still exists," Imogen said. "We are more progressive when it comes to some things than we are for others, I'm afraid."

The serious tone of the conversation hung in the room like a dark cloud as they all sat silently, each preoccupied with their own thoughts about things, each a little stoned, until Loretta let out a big sigh and finally got around to asking, "So ... what brings you two here?"

The question brought Imogen back to the nature of their visit: Loretta's book *She Left Her Heart in San Francisco*. Considering the news that Loretta was a lesbian, Imogen couldn't help wondering how much of the book was autobiographical and how much truly was fiction.

"We're here about your book?"

"My book?" Loretta cocked her head to the side, eyebrows raised. "What book?" She seemed genuinely puzzled by Imogen's question.

"Your book, you know, *She Left Her Heart in San Francisco?*"

Loretta frowned. "Honestly, I don't know what you're talking about, Imogen," she offered in response. "I'm writing a book *now*. It's why I traveled to Kansas, to 1946 for research, but I'm not even close to finishing it yet. In fact, I'm barely through the first chapter."

"Oh," was all that escaped from Imogen's mouth when she realized her error. Fletcher was right, doing the math for time travel was sometimes tricky and she'd just made a major flub. Right now, in 1973, twenty-five-year-old Loretta Ross hadn't written that book yet, or any other book for that matter. *Love on the Kansas Prairie,* her first, wouldn't be published for a few more years still, in 1976. And the San Francisco book, her thirty-seventh novel, was her last one before she died of cancer at age sixty-six in 2014.

As a time traveler herself, Loretta immediately recognized what was happening. Imogen had inadvertently revealed information about her life in the future.

"I'm sorry," was all Imogen could manage. "I … I … didn't mean to … it just came out … oh christ, I'm a friggin' idiot," she berated herself.

Loretta stopped her right there. "It's okay," she said. "We both know this is the danger in meeting someone from your future. And it's so tempting to want to entertain the idea of knowing what's ahead, but I'm pretty sure I don't want to know. However … *She Left Her Heart in San Francisco*, huh, I do like the sound of that title. Maybe I'll use it." She flashed a wry smile in Fletcher and Imogen's direction.

The tension in the room eased a bit. "So I'm assuming you read this book, this novel that I haven't written yet, correct?"

Imogen nodded. Loretta considered this for a second before responding, "I don't really see how I can help you, Imogen. How can I tell you anything about something that hasn't happened yet?"

Imogen was more than disappointed. How did she miss this? What if the story was purely fiction after all and had absolutely nothing to do with her mother's disappearance?

She looked over at Loretta and shook her head, "I apologize, Loretta. This was a mistake. It was great seeing you again, it truly was, but I shouldn't have come here. I mixed everything up and made a mess of things … like I always do," she said, shaking her head disgusted. But Loretta wasn't ready to drop it just yet.

"Wait a sec, Imogen," she said. "Let's talk about this. You don't have to tell me everything but why don't you just give me a brief synopsis of this future San Francisco book."

"Are you sure you want to know?" Imogen asked.

"Sure," Loretta agreed, "tell me."

"All right," Imogen said, hesitant about giving too much away. Choosing her words carefully, she began, "Well in the book, a young woman comes to San Francisco to move in with her girl friend and they become lovers, but when her abusive boyfriend shows up looking for her …" Imogen trailed off "… some bad things happen."

Imogen noticed Loretta's expression had suddenly shifted from smiling to serious.

"Loretta? What is it?"

"I know the ending," Loretta said. She got up from the couch and said, "Wait here, I'll be right back." Vanishing into a bedroom she returned a few minutes later carrying a medium-sized cardboard box that she placed on the coffee table in front of Imogen. "I think this could be who the character in the story might be based on," Loretta said.

Written on a piece of masking tape across the top in bold black letters was a single name: **FRANCIS**.

"May I?" Imogen asked before opening it.

"Of course," Loretta said.

Imogen opened the flaps, peered in, and gasped. Inside … her mother's journal and a silk box of memories.

"Oh my god, it's true," Imogen said as she lifted the contents from the box.

"What's true? What is it? Did you know Francis?" Loretta asked, puzzled by Imogen's strong reaction to the contents. Was it merely curiosity or something else?

Imogen's stunned expression convinced her it was something else.

"Francis is my mother," Imogen replied.

"Your mother?" Loretta gasped. She wasn't expecting that at all.

"Was it you in the book? Were you Francis' lover?" Imogen asked bluntly.

Loretta was taken aback by the direct question, especially not knowing who the characters were in this book that she hadn't yet written made it hard to answer; however, she did know what happened seven years ago to the real live Francis.

"No, Imogen. It wasn't me," she said. "It was Sylvie." Loretta explained that her roommate Sylvia had met Francis at a gala at Imogen Cunningham's home in The City.

"Imogen Cunningham, the famous photographer?" Imogen asked, stunned.

"I noticed right away when I met you that you shared her name," Loretta noted.

"I wonder if that's why she was here," Imogen said. "Maybe she came here to look her up."

Loretta told them that in addition to being internationally recognized for her photography, Imogen Cunningham was a Bay Area personality and traveled in artistic circles that not only included photographers, but also artists and writers and other creative types.

"We needed a roommate, so Sylvie invited Francis to move in and share the rent."

"So she didn't come up from Modesto then?" Imogen asked.

Loretta shook her head. "No, I have no idea where that came from, the fictional part, I suppose."

Curious about the contents of her journal, Imogen opened it and turned to Loretta, "Do you mind if I read a bit of it before we go on?"

"Of course, Imogen," she said. "Take all the time you need. I'll tell you the rest whenever you're ready, just let me know." Taking Fletcher by the arm, Loretta guided him from the room. "So, what's your poison?" she asked as they disappeared into the kitchen.

The leather-bound diary with the words TRAVEL JOURNAL embossed in gold on the front was frayed, and a loop where a pen was supposed to go had come apart. Imogen opened it to a random page and was greeted by her mother's neat cursive handwriting.

July 1971: I met some lovely people today in Eugene, Oregon who live and travel together in a bus commune. They invited me out to some kind of renaissance faire this weekend and I am excited to go.

Over the next hour, Imogen dove into her mother's deepest, most private thoughts and was surprised that in retrospect she had no clue any of this was going on with her. She was a child at the time, but still, Francis did not easily give away her secrets. Francis wrote about being unhappy and bored, how she loved Niles and Imogen, but something was missing. She had made a conscious decision to use her ability to time travel as a means of sampling other lifestyles. Was she searching for one that she could permanently disappear into? Imogen wondered.

As she read, Imogen learned that she first came to visit San Francisco to look up Imogen Cunningham, the famous photographer who was Imogen's namesake. Francis, also a photographer, met Ms. Cunningham at a gallery event and they struck up a conversation about aperture. She invited her to her studio, and they quickly became friends. She introduced her to her circle of friends—artists, writers, other photographers, one of whom was a painter named Sylvia Mack—Sylvie.

August 1965: I met the most wonderful person today at Imogen C's gala. Her name is Sylvie Mack and she is an exceptionally visionary painter. She's like no one I've ever met before. She looks and dresses differently. Her hair is short, short. She wears loose trousers and no makeup. She is beautiful and natural. She talks faster than I can think. Her laugh is contagious. All I want to do is be around Sylvie.

In an earlier entry Francis mentioned Teddy, how Niles had hired a teenager from the neighborhood to work part-time in the studio. One day she caught him rolling up a joint in the stockroom and they'd smoked it together. She wasn't particularly fond of Teddy but sneaking a joint had made her feel young again, reckless. From then on it was obvious that sixteen-year-old Teddy had a major crush on her. At first, she was flattered, but quickly realized it had been a mistake encouraging him. When she tried to extricate herself from the situation, he started getting creepy. She caught him spying on her. It made her extremely uncomfortable.

Imogen looked up from reading when Loretta and Fletcher came bustling into the room. She hadn't realized how immersed she'd been.

Fletcher sat down next to her on the couch. "Is it okay for us to come back now?"

Imogen nodded and closing the journal she asked Loretta, "Where did you live? Was it here at this house?"

"No, not here," Loretta said. "Back then, in 1965 we were living at 48th and Geary."

"Where is that exactly?" Imogen asked.

"Over by Lands End," Loretta said. "Near the Cliff house and Sutro Baths before it burned down in 1966."

"I was there," Imogen blurted.

"You were there?" Loretta asked, puzzled. "Where?"

"At the Cliff House, the day Sutro Baths caught fire." She paused and asked, "Was my mother there too, that day, at Sutro?"

Loretta shifted uncomfortably in her seat but knew that eventually Imogen would want to hear this part of the story. She had no idea what she'd written in that future book she said she'd one day write but suspected that it had something to do with what happened the day of the fire.

"I don't know what story I wrote, but I can tell you what happened here, to Francis. Are you sure you want to hear it?" she asked.

Imogen nodded. "Yes, I need to know."

Fletcher scooted closer to Imogen on the sofa, took her hand in his; was surprised that she let him. He had a feeling that things might get rough and more than anything he wanted to be there for her.

Loretta made herself comfortable too. Folding her legs up cross-legged on the chair she began:

"Francis moved in with us around 1964, I think it was. We were roommates and then she and Sylvie became a little more than roommates. Francis would come and go. Sylvie knew that we were time travelers, and that Francis had another life somewhere else in a different time and place, but she didn't seem to care. Francis always came back, and Sylvie always welcomed her home with open arms."

"In those days, the beach community was tight-knit, we didn't lock our doors or worry about strangers much, so when the guy standing on my porch asked if Francis was here, I figured he must be some new friend of hers. He seemed normal, harmless; he was young, a teenager, probably, but around that time it wasn't unusual. A lot of kids were showing up to check out the scene in San Francisco, so I didn't think anything of it.

I called out to Francis in the other part of the house. She had only been back for a couple of days after being away for a month or so and Sylvie was making plans for them. While he waited, I noticed that he fidgeted a lot, didn't know what to do with his arms, kept folding and unfolding them. A few minutes later, Francis and Sylvie came out of the bedroom holding hands and laughing, that is, until she saw this kid and stopped dead in her tracks. She looked scared and she said, "Teddy! What are *you* doing here?" Sensing her alarm at the situation, Sylvie chimes in, 'Who is this, Francis? Do you know him?'

In a flash, the guy's whole demeanor shifted from nervous kid to angry teenager, and he says, 'She knows me,' and starts threatening her saying, 'So this is where you go. Does your husband know? I bet he doesn't.' He gets really close to her face and starts yelling, 'When I get back, I'm going to tell him everything, that when you leave, you come here to do sick, unnatural things with your girlfriend.' So Sylvie jumps between them and Teddy knocks Sylvie down. She tripped on the rug and fell hard. That's when Francis ran for the door. Hopping on the beach cruiser, she pedaled away as fast as she could go in the direction of Lands End. The guy didn't hesitate. He ran out the door and started chasing after her up the street on foot."

At the first mention of Teddy, Imogen had tensed up, gripping Fletcher's hand harder.

"Sylvie and I followed," Loretta continued, "but between the time it took for me to help Sylvie, who had injured her knee, when we got there Sutro was an inferno. We saw the bike lying in the sand and we tried to find Francis, we searched everywhere; we called out to her, but the flames were hot, and the smoke was too thick to get any closer. We could hear the sirens everywhere. Helpless to do anything, all we could do was come home and hope that Francis somehow managed to get away from him and out of harm's way, but we feared the worst."

Imogen, who had been quietly listening to Loretta's story, let go of Fletcher's hand and began to cry. She looked up at Loretta and through tears whispered, "I saw him."

"Saw who?" Loretta asked.

"Teddy. I was at the Cliff House the day of the fire and I saw someone walking on the beach away from the baths.

It was him. I'm sure of it now. He must have set the fire to cover up what he'd done."

Loretta shook her head in disgust as though the memory was fresh. "He disappeared, this Teddy guy. When it was all over, Sylvie and I suspected he was another time traveler and had probably followed her here from wherever she came from." She paused, hesitant to continue knowing how Imogen's mind must be reeling, trying to grasp what terrible thing Teddy might have done to her mother before he probably set the place on fire. "We knew we couldn't report a disappearing man or a murdered woman from another time, or that we suspected he had torched the place.

Sylvie reported Francis missing. Several weeks later they found charred remains at the site, but they couldn't identify them. Sylvie and I assumed it was Francis."

Imogen continued to sob, and Loretta handed her a tissue.

Loretta waited a moment to let Imogen get control of her emotions before concluding, "After Francis died, Sylvie disappeared. It's been seven years now and still nothing. I have no idea where she went off to. After that, I decided to move down the coast here to Pacifica where rent was cheaper. I put Francis' stuff in a box, and I guess, according to you," she said, "One day I write a book about what went down that day."

Fletcher put his arm around Imogen and pulled her to him for a hug. She melted into him. "I'm so sorry, Gen," he consoled, gently rubbing her back. "I know this wasn't the news you expected to hear about your mother."

Imogen was noticeably shaken. It was one thing to learn that her mother had come to such a horrific end, but to also find out that Teddy was responsible for her death was incomprehensible. Again, Teddy. Did his cruelty know no bounds? First raping Tiffany, Simon's mother, getting her pregnant and dumping her in the distant past; attempting to kill Imogen and murdering her cat. After he murdered Francis, he must have come back, destroyed her photographic portal to cover up what he'd done, and then decided to trap Niles too so that no one would ever find out. Later on, when he realized that Imogen was also a time traveler it must have triggered him. How much did she know? How long before she figured it all out? And what might her mother have gone through before he killed her? Could she have even been alive after he set the fire? Imogen did not even want to think about what she had suffered at his hands.

"I'm awfully sorry too," Loretta said, "that I had to be the one to tell you this story. When we were in Kansas together, I had no idea that we shared a mutual connection with your mother."

Imogen wiped her eyes and gradually regained her composure. It was a shock, certainly, but the reality was her mother had been gone from her life for a very long time and already, just knowing the truth felt like a huge relief, a burden lifted, the closure she was seeking. She could at least go home and tell her dad what happened to his wife so that he could move on to the next chapter in his life as well.

"It's okay, Loretta. I needed to know," she said between sniffles. "It's that closure thing that everyone wants and needs." She filled in the gaps of their story; how her parents had disappeared when she was nine and that they had found out a few years ago that Teddy was responsible for trapping them; how they had found and rescued Niles a few months ago but still did not know where or when Francis had been trapped.

"When I read your book, I knew it was the missing piece of the puzzle," Imogen said. "The story, though different, had so many similarities that resonated along with the fact that I'd been there the day Sutro Baths caught fire. It's fascinating how the universe works," she mused. "Had we not met by coincidence in Kansas I might never have picked up your book and read it."

Loretta thought about that for a minute before saying, "I'm curious about how this book I write in the future will be received." Imogen smiled at her question, responding, "I'm not going to tell, but let's just say, all your books have been well received."

"*All* my books!? So you're saying I'm going to write more than one book?" Loretta asked, excited by the prospect of a successful career as an author.

"That's *all* I'm gonna say," Imogen said, shaking her head.

"Okay, that's fair. I don't really want to know," she said before pondering out loud, "I do wonder sometimes though about how we can even time travel," Loretta continued. "I mean, why us?"

Fletcher piped up with "Yeah, that's always puzzled me, too. Who gets to? Who doesn't? How does that even work?"

"I guess we'll never know," Imogen added, "or… maybe Simon will come back with all the answers."

"Right," Fletcher said, looking away, trying extra hard not to show his disappointment at being reminded of Simon and also grappling with the inevitable; that this grand adventure with Imogen would soon be coming to an end.

14

Ever since his big epiphany while playing the guitar last night that REM song, "What's the Frequency, Kenneth?" had been playing on repeat in his head. Normally, ear bugs were annoying, but Kevin didn't care today as he pulled his chair away, whistled a bar, and sat down at his desk at Daguerreian Society headquarters. After weeks of poring over Eastman's calculations in his goddamn useless book which, by the way, had set him back five grand of his own savings, he finally had a solid lead, a place to start, and it felt damn good. He was anxious to begin testing his double exposure theory, but he needed to prepare.

The first thing he did after logging in to his computer was open up a template for a company interoffice memo. This not only needed to look official, but the project had to somehow be kept on the down-low as well. That could prove tricky, but Kevin thought he might know a way. It would be easy to "spoof" the sender of the message to show a senior management team, or group. The recipients list would be blind so that no one would be able to view who else had also received the highly sensitive official looking memo.

It wasn't unusual for the Society, who operated on a strict, "need-to-know" policy, to conduct studies, like clinical trials, using interns and low-level staffers who were encouraged not to discuss projects even among themselves. To test his theory, he required in-house volunteers who were also verified time travelers.

He would need a name for the subject line—something that sounded official yet also piqued the interest of young volunteers. Hmmm, he thought, drumming his fingers on the desk next to his keyboard. I got it! Project What's the Frequency? Perfect. The song was from way back in the nineties, possibly before some of his subjects were even born, but even so, had likely heard this one at some time or another. The hope was to grab their attention without giving away the underlying danger of the trials—the potentially lethal outcome of sending them blindly into double-exposed photographs.

In the body of the text, Kevin outlined the purpose and parameters of the study: To send time travelers into certain photographs to monitor the frequencies encountered. He referenced the recent mind-bending scientific discovery that time is not a flat circle, that space-time churns like a choppy sea suggesting that everything around us is constantly being affected by low-frequency gravitational waves that can be measured. The goal of the study, he stated, was twofold: first, to understand how time travel was possible by measuring the frequency, or the interval between waves, and second, to study why some individuals become violently ill, while others do not. He did not reveal the true objective, however, which was to pinpoint the precise resonance to create the "time chord" that turns time travel on and off.

There was much to prepare. He would need the volunteers to sign NDAs, of course, as well as a release form stating that they were aware of possible risks. Most travelers knew that no photograph is perfect and to avoid blurry photographs because of the unknowns; if a photo was too blurry entering it was impossible anyway. Double exposed photos were even riskier, but Kevin planned to withhold that bit of information. Satisfied that he'd included everything and set the right tone, he was ready to press SEND when his assistant Brittany suddenly invaded his workspace. Approaching from behind, she shouted out "Boo!" Startled, Kevin quickly minimized his screen. How long had she been creeping around behind him? How much had she seen?

Fuming at her childish prank, he whipped around in his desk chair and faced her. "What the hell do you want, Brittany?" he said, annoyed. Brittany's smile faded as she handed him his favorite drink order from Starbucks. "I ... I just thought I'd pick you up your favorite, a Breve with an extra shot, the way you like it?" she stammered. Leave it to Brittany, to make him feel uncomfortable, guilty, *and* grateful all at the same time.

"Um, okay, thanks," Kevin said, accepting the cup from her and then turning back around to face his monitor. Her signature scent of cat urine, aassaulted his senses. She was still there. "What?!" he said sharply, turning back around to look at her.

"I just noticed that you were working on an official email. Are we doing something exciting?" she probed. Although he was angry and wanted to take her to task for snooping over his shoulder, he also didn't want to set off any alarm bells. Forcing a smile he said, "Well yes, we are doing something kind of interesting. Can you keep a secret?"

"Can I?" she said excitedly. Brittany was giddy at being privy to the Society's inner workings.

Early Saturday morning, Kevin reluctantly picked Brittany up and they drove to an empty field on the outskirts of Chicago to take photographs for Kevin's frequency experiment. He wasn't terribly thrilled about inviting Brittany along. Initially, he had planned to do this alone, but she was his assistant, and he actually could use some assistance, but mostly, if she felt included in the process, she was less likely to blab about it to anyone else.

According to what Eastman had written in his journal, Kevin hypothesized that the interval of the double-exposed photo that turned time travel on was probably less than 10 minutes but more than 30 seconds (estimated time for Eastman's mother to pick up the camera, walk over to the flowers, forgetting to advance the film, and snapping the second photo).

Using a special custom, Society-approved camera capable of creating double-exposure output, Kevin's scientific method to narrow it down was to shoot a series of 20 double-exposed photos within that 30 second to ten-minute range.

"Are you ready?" Kevin asked Brittany who was standing by with a clipboard and stopwatch.

"Ready," she said. Focusing on a stand of trees in the distance, Kevin snapped the first picture and Brittany began timing. At the 30-second mark, Kevin snapped a second photo. These two photos would merge as a double-exposed image in which the interval or frequency between the two could be later measured. Kevin snapped the next photos with a one-minute interval; the next had a 1½-minute interval, then two minutes, and so on up to ten minutes. Obviously, the shorter the interval, the clearer the picture. In the thirty-second photo, the field, trees, cows were fairly clear but as the interval became longer, the photos began to become murky from the long exposure time. The final image was so clearly double exposed it seemed unlikely anyone would even be able to enter it, but dangerous, if they did.

On the way back to the city, Kevin pulled into a Starbucks. As much as he disliked Brittany most of the time, he did appreciate having her there to help him with timing the intervals. Treating her to an iced hazelnut mocha was the very least he could do.

"So, when do we begin the experiments," she asked eagerly as they sat drinking their coffees across from each other at the table.

He hadn't thought that far ahead, but it occurred to him that having Brittany assist was completely out of the question. What if something went wrong? She'd be a witness. He had a better idea.

"Actually, there's a better way for you to assist me," he said.

Brittany leaned in closer. "How? She asked. "Whatever you need me to do, I'll do." Her being this close made Kevin uncomfortable, but he didn't want her to feel in any way suspicious.

"Well, what would you think about being a volunteer?"

Brittany wrinkled up her nose and pulled back away from him. "A volunteer?" she asked. "I thought I was your assistant. Shouldn't I be there to *assist* you? I mean, it just makes sense, you know.

"I know, but here's the thing..." He leaned into her this time, a ploy to butter her up. "You were hired because you were our brightest candidate, Brittany. But not only that, you're an expert traveler. You always return the most comprehensive data. What else? Oh, you don't get sick at all." Kevin could see that it was working. Brittany was trying not to smile, but the compliments were too much for her to resist.

"Really? The brightest? An expert?" There was no containing her excitement for the praise—something Kevin had not acknowledged even once in the time she'd been his assistant.

"Sure!" he said. "You're the best," he lied. How many times had she spilled coffee on important research notes, not to mention, on him, or bungled data reports? Lots. She didn't get sick, ever. That part was true. "So, what do you say?" Will you volunteer? Be a part of this important research, part of the team?"

Brittany violently shook her head, "Yes, yes, of course, I will," she said as she jumped forward knocking her coffee cup over, sending a streaming river of latte across the table and directly onto Kevin's neatly pressed Khakis.

Kevin leapt from his chair, hands in the air. He started to curse but stopped himself. "Godda ... " Grabbing a wad of napkins he began dabbing at his crotch. "I'm sorrryyy, so sorry," Brittany wailed.

"It's fine. It's okay," he reassured her, straining to remain calm. "Let's just get out of here."

Crushed, Brittany followed him to the door and on the way out, whimpered, "So, can I still be a volunteer?"

<hr>

Kevin woke up feeling better than he had in weeks. Finally, today had arrived, the day he could begin his research, despite the Brittany glitch he himself had created. Agreeing to let her participate in the study had thrown a monkey wrench into things—everyone knows you can't run into yourself when you time travel. The only solution really was for him to drive out to the spot in the country again where they'd taken the original double-exposed photos and recreate a few of the intervals, one of which she would enter.

But other than that, over the past weeks, Kevin had assembled a pool of volunteers willing to participate in his research project. With the exception of Brittany, he felt a tad guilty about sending in a couple of the interns that he'd spoken to briefly over the phone during the selection process. Connor reminded him a little too much of his ex, Jackson; and Malorie and Lewis seemed like nice kids too, but they mostly knew what they signed up for when they volunteered. Hopefully, all of them would come back unscathed. Entering a double exposure was always a risk but Kevin reminded himself it was for science.

Kevin arrived at his office early. Hung up his coat, logged into his computer, made sure everything looked routine. He had arranged lab space for the day. He had set up a staggered schedule over two days for volunteers to come in for one-hour sessions: ten the first day and ten the second.

Lewis, a likeable twenty-three-year-old University of Chicago history student who was interning at the Society for one term was the first scheduled volunteer to arrive right on time at 8 a.m. sharp, eager to participate in a real-time, time travel study. Lewis was interested in studying and preserving historical architecture and had secured the internship at the Society primarily because of his ability to time travel. Kevin opened the door to the lab to Lewis who immediately extended his hand to greet him.

"It's a pleasure to meet you Mister McCord," Lewis said, vigorously shaking Kevin's hand.

"Please, call me Kevin," he said, extricating himself from the intern's grasp and gesturing for Lewis to have a seat.

Rather than holding a group meeting to outline the scope of the study and what their role was in it the plan was to sit down with each volunteer individually. While volunteers might know who else was participating, Kevin did not want them to compare notes or discuss the details with one another, if possible.

"So Lewis," Kevin began. "I understand you are majoring in history."

"Yes, sir," Lewis replied eagerly.

"Fascinating," Kevin said, pretending to engage the young man in small talk to put him at ease before launching into the details. Kevin chuckled. "Well, unfortunately," he said, "this study has nothing to do with history." Lewis laughed too.

"The scope of the study was outlined in the initial email we sent out, but in a nutshell, in lieu of this exciting new scientific data about time being affected by low-frequency gravitational waves ..."

"That is so cool!" Lewis interrupted. "I read that, and I was like, wow!"

"Uh, yes, well, we were thrilled by it as well," Kevin continued. "But as I was saying, our goal is to use this new information to measure the interval between waves, which will help us better understand the dynamics of time travel." He didn't feel it was necessary to mention the sickness part. That was something that he would be able to gauge visually.

"Your task, Lewis, is to time travel through a provided photograph, take note of your surroundings, return, and describe the experience," he explained. "If you do not return in a few minutes, a Society-issued beacon will automatically retrieve you."

The "beacon," jokingly nicknamed the "retrieve-anator 3000" was a prototype device the Society had been developing to retrieve travelers, like Niles, for instance, who might become stuck in a time loop. Though still in the R&D phase, they had achieved some limited success with it. Kevin had no idea whether it would work properly for his volunteers or not, but it didn't matter. His primary goal was to reassure them that if anything were to go sideways, they could be quickly brought back.

Of course, the duration of time they spent in the photograph little mattered because time moved at a slower rate in a photograph than present time. Thus, a returning traveler who had spent an hour in a photograph would in present time have only been gone for a minute or so, if not instantaneously.

"That's it. Are you ready, Lewis?"

"Let's do it!" Lewis answered enthusiastically.

Kevin pulled out the first photograph labeled 30 seconds—a double-exposed photo that comprised two shots taken at a thirty second interval—and placed it on the table in front of Lewis. "Anytime you're ready, Lewis."

Lewis picked up the photo of the field and began to concentrate on it. He disappeared and almost instantaneously, returned collapsing in a chair. "How do you feel?" Kevin asked.

"A little queasy," Lewis admitted, gripping his stomach and bending forward in the chair.

"And what did you observe?"

Lewis grappled with speaking and dealing with the upset he felt in his stomach at the same time. "A field, grass, a few trees, some black cows grazing in the distance," he managed to say. "Just like it was in the photo."

"Nothing unusual then?" Kevin probed.

Lewis shook his head, no. He looked a little pale.

Kevin pointed to an adjoining room where he'd set up a cot for volunteers should they need to recuperate after traveling during the experiment. "Why don't you go in the room there and lie down until you feel better."

After about fifteen minutes, Lewis got up and stated that he was feeling better. Kevin thanked him and sent him on his way.

Malorie, the second volunteer of the ten scheduled for today arrived at 9 o'clock. Malorie was new to the Society, and eager to learn everything about time travel. They chatted for a few minutes, and Kevin repeated the instructions he'd given Lewis earlier. Using the scientific method to narrow down the frequency within the estimated time that Eastman had indicated, Malorie's photograph was one that was shot at a ten-minute interval. It was risky sending her into a photograph that was so unpredictable. It could go either way. Kevin said a silent prayer. Thoughts and prayers. He did not say those words with malice. This wasn't who he was.

But he placed the photograph on the table and advised Malorie to concentrate. She focused and he watched as the minutes passed. Frustrating mounting, she looked at Kevin with disappointment in her eyes. "I ... I don't know what's wrong ... why didn't it work?" Kevin sighed with relief. He liked this girl, didn't want to use her as a sacrificial lamb. It was clear that the photograph was clearly too double-exposed for anyone to enter it. He thanked Malorie, reassured her that he appreciated her participation.

Katelyn, the third volunteer, arrived at 10:00 and was able to successfully travel through the photograph taken at a one-minute interval, although she too was sick on return. Kevin noted that in comparison to Lewis' complaints of slight queasiness, she felt much sicker. He sent her into the recovery room to rest and she was on her way within about a half hours' time. The 11 o'clock volunteer, an intern by the name of Edward attempted to enter the photograph marked with a 9 ½ minute interval and like Malorie was ultimately unsuccessful.

Kevin took a lunch break at noon and ate a turkey sandwich at his desk. So far, so good, he thought. No one had died; that was a good sign. The only pattern appeared to be the increased intensity of sickness among subjects entering the photos with shorter intervals.

After lunch, Mackenzie arrived and entered the 1½ minute interval photo. Kevin became concerned when after several minutes she had still not returned. He was just about ready to activate the beacon when she came back and was violently ill. Kevin quickly grabbed a nearby wastebasket to catch the streaming vomit and asked, "Are you alright?" Mackenzie sputtered, coughed, grasped her stomach, and then slowly slumped limply down onto the tile floor. Kevin helped her up and into the recovery room, laying her down on the cot. He brought her a glass of water, which seemed to help a little.

Kevin considered calling the next volunteer and canceling, but despite how ill she was on initial arrival, the recovery time was relatively short, and Mackenzie said she was feeling good enough to leave.

Something odd happened with the photograph taken at a nine-minute interval. Charlie, the fifth volunteer that day was unable to successfully enter the photo despite his efforts at deep concentration—this had been the case with the other two who had not been able to enter photos taken at the longer intervals of ten and 9 ½ minutes. However, Kevin noticed that immediately after focusing on the photo, Charlie suddenly became very sick, and Kevin had to grab the trash can a second time. This was new. Even though the subject was unable to enter the photo, was he somehow absorbing the photograph's vibrations, its frequency? Was that what made him feel sick?

Luckily, Charlie's bout of discomfort dissipated quickly, and he was able to leave.

As he waited for his 3 o'clock, Kevin felt optimistic. Even with the projectile vomit scenarios things had gone surprisingly well. He could only hope that as his bracketing experiment continued, he would find that one magic frequency, that resonating chord that had set time travel in motion more than a hundred years ago.

Expecting another intern wearing a hoodie, jeans, and flip-flops, Kevin was pleasantly surprised when Connor, a grad student pursuing quantum physics at the university, and older than the previous volunteers, breezed into his lab space at three. His hair undercut on the sides with longer, looser hair on top, he was stylishly dressed in slacks, a gray button-up cardigan, leather penny-loafers, no socks. He had a sexy small earring in his nostril. Within the brief few minutes that they chatted Kevin knew he was attracted to him. And Kevin felt certain Connor was sending back nonverbal messages through his gaze, posture, and smile.

Since Jackson had gone Kevin hadn't even remotely felt a spark of interest in anyone. Jackson had gutted him, seized everything in him, leaving him feeling sad and empty and dead inside. It had been the perfect motivation to drive his anger and frustration at the Society, the universe, everyone, but now, this tiny flash of attraction threatened to soften his stern resolve. It also forced another emotion—culpability—what if something should happen to this lovely specimen? Kevin would be responsible. A split-second decision must be made—did he send this beautiful man home or proceed with his mission, even knowing the danger it entailed to his subjects?

At 3:45, Connor got up from his chair and started toward the door. "It was a pleasure meeting you today, Mister McCord ... um ... Kevin, I mean." Kevin grasped Connor's shoulder and gave it a gentle squeeze. "Likewise," he said, smiling. "It's a shame that I wasn't able to help you with your study. I was looking forward to it actually."

"Next time," Kevin said. "I have your number. I'll give you a call."

"Before next time ... I hope," Connor responded, a sly grin forming as he reluctantly closed the lab door behind him.

Promptly at 4:00, Brittany bounced excitedly into the lab. "I'm here, Mister McCord," she called out.

Kevin was in the bathroom trying to contain his feelings of arousal. How he wished that he hadn't had to rush Connor out, but the last thing he needed was

Brittany peppering another volunteer with any of a million questions the nosy girl likely had. Sighing, he came out of the bathroom and greeted Brittany with a courtesy smile. I should have been an actor, he thought.

"Which photo will I be going into?" she asked. He couldn't help but notice that she looked different today. Normally, she came to work in jeans, sneakers, and a baggy sweater, but today she was wearing a pink sundress and sandals. She was also wearing lip gloss, and instead of twisting her hair up into her usual messy bun, it hung long and loose on her shoulders, held by a simple purple clip. You would never have known that Brittany was actually reasonably attractive. He wanted to ask her what the occasion was but thought better of it. Best to get right to it.

"Okay," he said clasping his hands together and offering her a seat at the table. He pulled out the photograph and placed it in front of her. Brittany smiled. "Ah, the two-minute one," she said.

"Whenever you're ready Brittany," Kevin said.

"You're sure this is safe, right?" she asked nervously.

"Of course," he lied.

She offered up a weak smile and looked down at the photograph in front of her. She quickly vanished and Kevin waited anxiously for her to return. A minute passed, five minutes, ten. Kevin was sweating. He paced. He watched the constant movement of the second hand on the wall clock. What the hell could she possibly be doing in there? Was she petting cows? Hugging trees? After fourteen minutes had passed, he readied the beacon to retrieve her. The second hand reached fifteen minutes, and Kevin activated it, but he wasn't prepared for what happened next.

With a roar and a loud thud, a screaming shell of a bloody, mangled, and torn *thing* landed on the tile floor in front of him. Even horror master Stephen King, in his wildest, worst nightmares, would never have been capable of conjuring up such a hellish, grotesque scene. At first, Kevin wasn't sure that it was even her, but the swatches of pink fabric from what was left of her shredded sundress convinced him otherwise. One arm was a stump, the other, along with one leg were completely missing. Still attached though to the foot of the only remaining limb to have come through intact—one blood-smeared brown sandal. Small clumps of hair, one piece held by a purple clip framed the distorted and severely compressed head. The face was an indistinguishable blob of tissue; the sound of the screams originating from a spot where a mouth should have been. Kevin tried to look away but could not. He placed his hands over his ears to block the unbearable noise coming from it. Within a second or two, the screams began to dissipate, became a whimper, and then finally, stopped completely.

Brittany Kane was dead.

In that instant, a thought flashed across Kevin's mind, not of what had happened to her, but that it could have been Connor lying there on the floor. By sending him home, ostensibly he'd saved his life. As that thought drifted away, slowly the shock and panic of what had happened began to set in, and yet, despite that, his pragmatic side took over. What to do with the body? Kevin glanced up at the clock, quarter to five. Anxiety turned into action. He rushed into the recovery room and pulling the blanket and sheets from the cot he ran back into the lab and spread the blanket out on the floor next to what was left of Brittany. Using the sheets as a shield from having to touch her, he rolled her over onto the blanket, using it then to pull her across the floor and into the recovery room. He found some sponges and towels, plastic gloves, a bucket, and bleach in the storage cabinet and rushed back to attend to the mess on the floor. He was grateful that the lab's floor was tiled and not carpeted like some of the other spaces in the building. He feverishly mopped up the mess, wringing out the sponge many times until the water in the bucket turned bright red. A few times when he came across pieces of skin and tissue, he had to stop for a moment to stave off the dry heaves that overtook him.

He was wiping up the last bit of it when there was a knock on the lab door. He looked up at the clock. "Shit!" he said. It was the next volunteer. "Just a minute, be right there," he called out as he made a final swipe and ran the bucket over to the sink, dumped out the water, and hastily hid it under the sink.

His mind raced. What to do? He could send him away, make up something, reschedule maybe, but why? he thought. The volunteer was here. Why stop the experiment now? He could deal with Brittany later. It would only take a few minutes. If the kid got sick, he'd have him rest in the chair in here.

Kevin wiped his sweaty palms across the front of his shirt and opened the door. "Hello, come in, come in," he said, his voice sounding squeaky and high pitched, a bit too friendly, perhaps a tad guilty.

"Is everything all right, Mister McCord?" Joel Young, the next volunteer asked, as he entered and shook his hand.

"Oh yes, of course," Kevin said, inviting the volunteer to sit down. It was really all he could do to keep it together. *You can do this, just keep going, you can do this.* The few minutes he spent explaining the study to Joel helped calm him a bit as he placed the next photograph labeled 8½ minute interval on the table in front of Joel.

Because the subjects had not even been able to enter the photographs at longer intervals, Kevin anticipated that this time would yield the same result. He would be wrong. After concentrating on the image, Joel disappeared into it. Kevin waited and watched the clock, hoping for a positive outcome. *Please just come back sick,* he begged the universe. And then, with a whoosh, Joel's dead body made a thumping sound as it skidded across the floor where just minutes before Brittany had lain.

"Oh my god!" Kevin wailed inside the soundless room.

Two dead bodies. Mercifully, Joel had come back dead but fully intact. No missing limbs, not even any blood. But after he'd finished moving the body into the other room alongside Brittany Kevin now sat in the chair cradling his shaking head in his hands. This was insanity. He should stop. Of course, he should stop. The bodies were piling up. His rational, still semi-sane side was telling him to give up on this foolish scheme, stop this madness; but another side reminded him of why he was doing this experiment at all—to make time travel safer, to find answers to the time sickness, to stop whatever was happening in the dead time zones ... *to make them respect him* ... yes that too, but damn it he knew he was close.

But how could he go on?

Something was changing to make the subjects sicker each interval. How could he quit now? He'd worked so hard. Plus, there were two more volunteers coming in today. Two more bracketed intervals to try. If he could just get through this last round, there was a chance one of them might be the right frequency ...

By the time the next volunteer arrived, Kevin had pulled himself sufficiently together, convincing himself that this was being done to further science and that was all that truly mattered. If sacrifices had to be made, then so be it. He ushered the young intern in, gave her his five-minute spiel, and then laid the 2½ minute interval, double-exposed photograph on the table, as he had done with all the previous subjects.

He smiled at the girl and said, "Whenever you're ready."

Megan placed both hands on the table, leaned forward to look at the photograph in front of her, and began to concentrate deeply on it. Kevin watched as like a puff of smoke, she evaporated before his eyes. He waited then, calmly watching the second hand on the wall clock tick-tick-tick out the seconds. And then, like a huge machine grinding to a halt, at precisely two- and one-half minutes after Megan entered the photo, the universe hiccupped, and time travel ceased.

15

Megan Parker stood frozen in place too afraid to move. Minutes before, she had been seated in a lab at the Daguerreian Society HQ concentrating deeply on the photograph in front of her. The next thing she knew, she was here, wherever *here* was. She couldn't tell if it was her eyes that were blurry or if everything around her was. This place of nothing resembled a thick fog bank. She could make out only a few tenebrous shapes in the distance. Nothing moved. And it was quiet, mind-numbing, insane-inducing quiet. Mr. McCord had assured her that if she didn't return in a short while some sort of beacon would be able to bring her back. After entering the photo, she had felt a weird jerking sensation that might have been the beacon. If that was the case, why was she still here?

She was scared, more than scared, terrified, but she must.keep.it.together. *Just stay still, close your eyes, Megan, don't think about it,* she whispered to herself. *They'll pull you back soon. It's probably just a temporary glitch. The Society wouldn't let anything happen to an intern, would they?*

She repeated the words as long as she could, until she understood the truth. *They aren't coming ...* her final words before she screamed into the void.

Angus Hunter, a Florida man, had two families—one in his current lifetime and another in 1956. In his regular life, he tolerated his wife Anne, a high-powered businesswoman and their two spoiled daughters, but found solace in the arms of Murial, a traditional wife and mother of the fifties who catered to Angus' every need and whim. On this day, however, Murial had sassed him, which angered Angus greatly. He had been drinking and unfortunately, he hit her just a little too hard this time. She tumbled against the stone hearth and hit her head. One of the children got away and ran next door to the neighbors who called the police.

Angus, attempting to flee back through his anchor photograph in the future, panicked when he discovered that for some reason, he was unable to return. The blaring police sirens getting closer, he sprinted from the house. Jumping a neighbor's fence and cutting across several other people's property he found his path blocked by a swamp. He slowly waded in.

Emiliano Romero was an adrenaline junky. He lived for risk. If the young Spaniard wasn't whitewater rafting or jumping out of planes, canyoning, mountain biking, or scuba diving he was engaging in other dangerous, intense extreme activities like base jumping, surfing, paragliding, or chasing the adrenaline high into the past by way of time travel. In the seventies he rode motorcycles with Evil Knievel; he rode over Niagara Falls in a barrel in 1901. The beauty of time travel was that if anything started to go sideways, he could always take himself back. Today, November 1, 2011, he was in Praia do Norte, Nazare, Portugal, preparing to ride a 78-foot monster wave. He knew that Garrett McNamara would set the world record, but Emiliano wasn't here to compete. He was here to surf, or at least give it his best shot.

He paddled out to get closer to the peak of the wave. He could see it rising up, higher and higher. It was massive. Emiliano was both excited and petrified. As the wall of water rose up behind him, he felt himself being propelled up with it. The adrenaline rush was immediate and awesome and then he felt something else, a jolt, a thump that caused him to lose his balance. He wiped out inside the enormous wave; his board disappeared beneath the current; tossing, turning, churning his body tumbled as though in a washing machine cycle. Running out of breath he tried to propel himself to the surface, but the water crashed around him pushing him farther down. In a panic, he focused his thoughts on the anchor photo at home. Nothing. Emiliano felt a split second of disbelief before he hit the coral reef and lost consciousness.

As Thomas Mayfield, a stocky, middle-aged confirmed bachelor stood in front of the mirror adjusting his button-up vest and bow tie, he felt something; a small jolt and then a trembling vibration that he shrugged off. Mayfield had found the love of his life, Miss Emily Thorn, who lived nearly 100 years before he had even been born, and today was the lucky day he would join her. Excited, the wedding ring tucked securely in his pocket, he concentrated on the antique photograph in front of him. Nothing happened. As the hours passed, he became ever more distraught.

In 1878 London, antique collector Maeve Stewart spent a leisurely day frequenting the shops along the cobblestoned streets. She'd purchased a few items—a porcelain vase, a lovely delicate tea set, embroidered doilies, which she had packaged and delivered to the bank vault for later future retrieval. She looked forward to selling them in her store. As she departed the building, she felt something.

It felt like the world had wobbled for an instant. Puzzled, Maeve looked around to see if anyone else had noticed it. A horse-drawn carriage rambled by. A merchant continued sweeping the dust off the sidewalk in front of his store. Maeve dismissed it from her mind until later in her rented hotel room when she tried to return home to Minnesota, and try as she might, she could not. What would become of her Persian cat Mister Whiskers? Maeve wondered.

Evie Aaronson knew it was risky to be Jewish in Germany, even in early 1933, but how could a time traveler resist the temptation of experiencing history firsthand? For her dissertation, she had come to Berlin conducting interviews with ordinary Germans on their feelings about socialism. Wrapping up the final interview she decided to enjoy one last black coffee at the Romanisches Café where she had spent a good deal of time enjoying the company of other intellectuals and students. Seated comfortably at her table, she picked up her cup to take a sip when she felt something. The earth jerked in a way that it felt when you slammed on your brakes in the car. Evie glanced around, but no one else but her seemed to notice. No coffee cups rattled against plates. Nobody looked up. An hour later, the Nazi's came.

At exactly 6:13 p.m. US Central Time, time travel came to an abrupt halt and travelers across the globe found themselves in circumstances ranging from the mundane to the disastrous—many who were in the process of entering a photograph found themselves bouncing back, while those trying to return to their anchors were unable to get home. Millions were trapped in the past—some were cognizant of it, while scores of others were unaware until they tried to return home and found they could not. And none of them had a clue about what had happened.

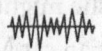

-⋎⋎⋎⋏⋎⋏⋎⋏-

Imogen stood at the edge of one of the decaying Sutro Bath ruins—a wondrous natural juxtaposition of beauty and light and darkness and death—something her photographer mother would surely have appreciated. Gazing out at the ocean's horizon for a bit, she listened to the breaking waves, and the distant sound of hundreds of barking seals that lounged out on the rock with the heart-shaped formation inside it. There weren't a lot of people around at this hour. She had gotten up, told Fletcher she was going for a drive, and left the house early. She hoped her goodbyes to Francis would be serene but the ruins around her were a grim reminder of that painful day, fifty-five years ago, when Teddy chased her mother to this place and brutally ended her life.

Oh sure, she might have the closure she was seeking, but along with it, unresolved anger at Teddy, the person responsible for causing so much devastation in her life and the lives of the people she loved. How could one ruthless, wicked person cause so much pain? First Tiffany, Simon's mother—kidnapping her and dumping her in the past, then later doing the same thing to Imogen's parents, burning their anchor photos, making Imogen think she was an orphan and trapping Niles in a time loop for twenty-two years; murdering her mother. And then, coming after her as an adult with harmful intent.

And it wasn't just Teddy she began to slowly realize. All of this was the dark side of time travel. For her, it had started out innocently enough. She had wanted to help people but had she though? Helped them? Really? Or had she done more harm than good?

She thought that helping Harry Tabor find his long-lost love would give him peace, but once she was there and met Vivian Littlefield, she had tried to save her, yet she died anyway. She'd tried to bring Adam and his son together, but that didn't work out either. It was a thrill meeting the celebrated Zelda Fitzgerald, but was it worth it seeing this real-live person in such pain? Likewise, she thought she brought closure to the family of Nadja, the runaway hippie girl, but had she? Maybe it's better that people don't always know what happened in the past. Perhaps some secrets should stay secret. When is not knowing the truth the better answer?

Learning the truth about her mother didn't ease her pain either and it wasn't over yet. Soon she would have to return home and break her father's heart—tell him the awful, gruesome truth of what happened to his wife. Would it be better if he didn't know? In a way, Imogen wished she didn't know. And then there was Simon. He didn't even know she was pregnant. Fletcher had said that miscarriage is nature's way of dealing with an abnormal embryo, but how could she be sure that time travel hadn't been the cause? So many questions; so much guilt; so much anguish. All Imogen knew in this moment was that everything hurt like hell.

At this once grand pleasure palace, amid the ruins, where ring-necked ducks now made their home, and vibrant orange California poppies and golden yellow native Dune Tansy and calla lilies grew wild next to the trail, Imogen looked up at a clear, blue San Francisco sky, blew a last kiss to the mother she loved but never really knew, and tossed the wildflowers she'd picked along the trail into one of the silent, stagnant pools.

~~~

Loretta, knees tucked under her in the chair, and Fletcher sat facing each other at the small kitchen table, drinking coffee, nibbling on buttered toast, not saying much of anything. Imogen had said she wanted to be alone and had driven away in the car early this morning. Fletcher figured she was heading for Sutro. He didn't ask to go with her. Ever since Loretta had told them what happened to Francis, the mood, rightly so, had been somber.

"How long do you think she'll be gone?" Fletcher threw out attempting small talk.

Loretta shrugged, took a sip from her cup. "I imagine for a while. That was an awful lot to take in all at once."

Fletcher nodded. "Yeah, it was."

"She said her mother had disappeared when she was nine. Was she close to her before that?" Loretta asked.

"No, I mean, according to Imogen, her mother was sort of closed off I guess you could say; didn't show her a lot of affection. I know this is hard for her, but I think she mostly needed closure."

"Yeah," Loretta acknowledged. "How about you two? What's your story?"

Fletcher flinched a little at the question, but it was a fair one. "It's complicated," he said, sighing.

Loretta adjusted her legs in the seat and leaned in. "Complicated how?"

"Imogen and I used to date back in college," he said. "I proposed to her a few years back. She turned me down."

"Ah," Loretta said, leaning back against the chair rest again. "You still love her though. I can tell."

Fletcher sighed again. "It's that obvious, huh?"

"Yeah, pretty much," Loretta said. "Have you told her? Does she know?"

"Yes."

"And ... what did she say?"

"Nothing," he said. "I know she feels something, but we don't know if Simon will ever come back or not. I don't really know what to do."

"Simon? Her boyfriend I take it."

"And my best friend."

Loretta tilted her head sideways and rolled her eyes at him. "Sheesh, what a pickle you two are in." Fletcher nodded agreement.

"Well, I don't know the situation," she continued, "but in the short time you two have been here, I see how she looks at you, how she gravitates to you for support." I believe two people can move on. They can love other people, but real love never truly goes away."

"Hmm, sounds like a true romance story," he said skeptical of her reasoning. "What do you think I should do?"

"Love her," Loretta asserted. "Don't give up."

A few minutes later, Imogen walked through the door. She plopped down on the couch and covered her face with her hands.

Fletcher got up from the table and joined her. "You okay?" he asked. She looked up at him. Her eyes were red and puffy from crying.

"No," she said, her voice breaking. "I don't think I'm okay at all."

Loretta got up from the table to put the dirty cups and plates in the sink. "I'll leave you two alone," she said as she left the room.

Fletcher put his arm around her, and she nestled next to him, almost like a child seeking comfort. In that moment, he understood fully what Loretta saw. Imogen did rely on him for emotional support. She kind of always had, even when Simon was around.

"I just want to go home," she said.

Fletcher squeezed her and replied, "Let's go then."

<hr />

"Thank you for having us," Imogen said, giving Loretta a quick hug.

"I wish it had been under better circumstances," Loretta said. "I know this wasn't the news you were hoping to hear about Francis, your mom."

"No, it wasn't," Imogen said, "but at least now I know, and I think dad and I will be able to move on with our lives."

Loretta gave Fletcher a quick hug. "Take good care of her, huh?"

"I will," Fletcher said smiling. "Thanks for everything."

"You betcha! You're welcome back anytime for a visit, oh and be sure to talk up that future book I'm going to write!"

Imogen laughed. "Of course, we will, you are a talented writer!" she said before turning to face Fletcher. "Okay, are you ready?"

Fletcher locked arms with Imogen. She closed her eyes and concentrated on the photographic portal sitting in the place she'd left it at her office forty-seven years from here.

After a few minutes of deep concentration, Imogen opened her eyes. They were still standing in Loretta's living room.

"I don't know what's wrong," she said. "Why aren't we leaving?" she asked Loretta who was as bewildered as she was.

"I don't know."

"I'll try again," Imogen said. "Maybe I wasn't focusing hard enough." She knew she'd been distracted by everything that had happened on this trip. She closed her eyes again and began to concentrate harder. Still, nothing happened.

"Something's wrong," Loretta said. "Maybe I should try." She left the room and returned a moment later carrying one of the photographs that she didn't use from 1946 Kansas. Placing it on the coffee table, she closed her eyes and began to focus deeply on it as Imogen and Fletcher looked on. Minutes passed and Loretta didn't go anywhere either.

Imogen's eyes widened as the seriousness of their situation began to set in. "What the fuck?" her voice cracking with fear. "What's happening?"

"I don't know," Loretta said. "We'll try again later, but I think you two are stuck here for the time being."

16

The field equipment didn't look like much; a simple hand-held device with several dials and a cord attached to a flat round, saucer-like gadget similar to a metal detector but smaller. The only instructions Simon had been given was to scan the areas where vibrations were occurring. He'd been walking around the Pommer Inn in Austria for a while now and with each step the ground became ever more unstable; he had to be careful where he walked because of the cracks that were forming beneath his feet.

All around him the phantom travelers continued to zoom in and zoom out. Some would fly in and immediately fly out; others appeared, stopped in place, paused for a moment, and then disappeared. Disturbing was the only way to describe it. He'd never visited a haunted house before, but this was certainly how he imagined one to be. Confident that he'd made a complete sweep of the area, he turned off the device and was preparing to step out of the zone of activity when something strange occurred. The ground beneath him suddenly stopped vibrating and the travelers that had been zooming in and out became still and motionless, as if they were playing some cosmic game of red light/green light. He stood still, surveying the zone. He watched, stunned, as the ghost travelers faded away and were gone. Nothing moved. Strangely, the only thing that did not completely shut down at that moment was the humming sound. Simon could still hear it, but it was different, changed. A moment ago, it was high-pitched, a steady unbroken stream of sound, but now the pitch of the hum was lower and sluggish, as though it too was reacting to whatever just happened.

The only logical thing he could reckon was that somehow time travel had ceased. And if that was the case, the magnitude of his obligation came into sharp focus. Linked in time between the past and the present, Simon was born of time travel—DNA tests had shown that his cells were altered. And even though most of his time at the Daguerreian Society had been spent on the treadmill hooked up to monitors, there had been times when they had allowed him in a controlled lab setting to travel to test his abilities. There he learned how to take his skills to another level. They already knew that he was capable of jumping from one time period to another without having to first return to an anchor photograph in his own time, but he had another "superpower" as they called it—the capability of traveling any place without a photograph by merely thinking it, provided he had been there before. This meant that even though time travel had somehow been halted, he was quite possibly the only living being in the universe that could still travel through time. More disturbing was the realization that anyone who had been traveling right now or anyone who was currently in the past, likely was trapped there, and what if Imogen was one of those travelers? He needed to get back to headquarters.

When Simon arrived, the Daguerreian Society was in the throes of utter chaos. Some instruments had completely shut down. A cacophony of blaring alarms bounced off the walls throughout the entire facility as panicked employees, hands covering their ears to block the ear-piercing screeching, rushed frantically through the halls, seeking guidance, for someone, anyone to tell them what was happening.

Simon hurried through the crowd, heading in the direction of the gym. He spotted Marcus and Dr. Hostin talking outside in the hallway as people ran past. He rushed over to speak to them. "Marcus, Dr. Hostin, what's happened?"

Hostin, a look of relief on his face, reached out and grasped Simon by the shoulder. "Simon, am I glad to see you! You made it back before everything shut down!"

"No, I … I was in Austria," he explained, " … when whatever this is, happened …"

Marcus was bewildered. "You traveled *after* the shutdown?" he asked.

"So it is true?" You *can* free-range travel. I wasn't sure I believed it was possible. That is remarkable," Hostin shouted to be heard above the noise. "We'll need you to set this right, Simon," he said gripping Simon's arm again and pulling him in the direction of the lab. But Simon withdrew from him. "Wait? Tell me what happened first. I'm worried about my girlfriend Imogen. If it's what I think it is, she might be trapped somewhere."

"I'm sorry, Simon, we don't have time to worry about that right now," Hostin said. "We have work to do." He snapped his fingers and pointed at Marcus, who stepped forward with the intention of strong-arming Simon into submission. Seizing him tightly around the chest, he forced him forward toward the open lab doorway.

"I need to find out what happened to Imogen," Simon roared as he tried unsuccessfully to wriggle out of Marcus' clutches. It was no use, Marcus lifted weights; his biceps were as wide as Simon's thighs. He almost had him pressed through the door and inside the lab, when unexpectedly, the alarms abruptly stopped. Everything went eerily quiet. Everyone stopped in their tracks, looking around at each other in confusion when the loudspeaker crackled, and a voice began to speak.

"Hello. May I have your attention, please. Everything is under control. I repeat, everything is under control. We are working on the problem. Return to your workstations until further notice."

Marcus loosened his grip on Simon. Seizing the opportunity to escape, Simon squirmed from his clutches and bolted down the hallway. Marcus started to go after him, but Dr. Hostin, stopped him. "Let him go, Marcus. We'll catch up with him later, once we know more."

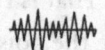

Simon didn't need a photograph to go home. He could plainly see it in his mind's eye. In an instant, he was there. His street, familiar surroundings, porch, elm tree. Home. It seemed like forever ago that he had boarded the plane for Chicago. He couldn't wait to see Imogen, to hold her, smell her, smother her with kisses, feel her soft skin, and touch her hair. Excited, he sprinted up the steps onto the wooden porch. The door was locked. No surprise, Imogen always kept it locked. You never know when a stranger might try to break in, she always said.

He knocked but there was no answer. Rummaging through the bushes he felt around in the dirt for the fake rock with the key inside. Unlocking the door he entered the foyer. Imogen's boots and crocks were lined up against the wall, a couple of jackets hung on wooden pegs. He glanced over into the pottery bowl where she always tossed her keys when she came in. They were there as well as her car, which was parked in the driveway outside.

"Imogen!" he called out. No answer. He entered the living room. No one was there. He looked around the room for a note and found nothing. This was unusual and worrisome. It was all he could do to tamp down the fear that she might have been traveling when everything stopped and was now stuck in some other time and place, maybe frightened that she couldn't return. He did a quick check of the kitchen, the laundry room, the bathroom, the bedroom—all the same, quiet and vacant.

But when he peeked into the office, he spotted Imogen's phone lying on the desk. This was not a good sign. Imogen never went anywhere without her phone unless she was traveling. He picked it up. It still had about 15% battery. He decided to try Fletcher's number. Surely, he would know where she was; he had promised to look after her while Simon was gone. But when he heard Fletcher's upbeat Adekunle Gold "Yoyo" ringtone coming from the direction of the kitchen, he dropped Imogen's phone on the bed and followed the sound. Fletcher's phone was vibrating on the counter.

"What the … ?" he said out loud. Fletcher couldn't time travel, so what the heck? Had the two of them gone off together? His mind leapt from one inference to another. What was going on while he was away? He sat down and tried to gather his thoughts. Why would they travel together? Where would they go? He knew how much Fletcher loved time travel. He had begged Simon to take him that time they went back to visit Herbert. Maybe they'd gotten bored, and Imogen suggested they get away. The pandemic had shut everything down. They couldn't be faulted for wanting to enjoy some different scenery. That must be it, he reasoned, but still, his mind raced with irrational thoughts that perhaps Imogen and Fletcher had rekindled their relationship. But no … no! he told himself, trying to shake off negative thoughts.

"Niles!" he said aloud. Niles would know where they were. Of course, he would. Niles answered his phone on the third ring.

"Oh thank goodness," Simon said relieved.

"Who is this?" Niles asked.

"Niles, it's me, Simon!" he said.

Niles was surprised to hear Simon's voice. "Simon! Where are you? Are you still in Chicago? Is something wrong?"

"Yes, no, maybe," Simon's answers were all over the place. He stopped and took a deep breath. "Niles, listen, I'm at home but Imogen isn't here. Do you know where she is?"

There was a longish pause at the other end. "Niles? Are you there?" Simon asked.

After Fletcher had confessed his love for Imogen, Niles was hesitant to blab to Simon that they were together. Niles cleared his throat. "She's in San Francisco," he finally answered.

"San Francisco? Where? More importantly, *when?*" Simon asked. "Is she time traveling?"

"Yeah," Niles responded. "She is."

"Oh no," Simon moaned, clapping his hand to his forehead.

"Why? What's going on?" Niles asked.

"I don't have time to explain all of it right now, but the universe has collapsed or something. Time travel has completely come to a halt, which means that anybody who was traveling when it happened, is likely trapped wherever they are."

"You're kidding!" Niles said, stunned.

"Where's Fletcher?" Simon asked. "I can't reach him either."

Time to come clean, Niles thought. "Fletcher is with Imogen," he blurted.

Simon was taken aback. "Why? And why San Francisco? Is she on a case?"

"Look, Simon, I know you're worried. I am too now, if what you say is true, but it wasn't a case; It was personal, for me ... and for Imogen."

"I don't follow," Simon said, confused and a little frustrated now.

"She went there to follow up on a clue about her mother, about Francis."

"Oh, I understand." The topic of their mothers was a sore spot between them, but none of that mattered right now. "Do you know what year she traveled to?" he asked.

Niles answer was vague at best. "I'm sorry, Simon. I don't recall, the seventies, maybe. In her travels, she met some woman, a writer who had written a book with characters and a premise that Imogen thought was similar to Francis' story. Fletcher wanted to tag along. That's all I really know Simon, I'm sorry I don't have more concrete information for you."

"So, where did you say you are again, Niles?" Simon asked, changing the subject.

Silent pause on the other end before Niles answered, "Um, well, I didn't say, but I'm not at home. I'm in Detroit."

"Detroit, Michigan?"

"Uh ... yeah."

"What are you doing in Detroit, Niles?"

"It's sort of a long story," he said. "I'm here visiting Jade."

"Imogen's friend Jade?" Simon asked, surprised.

"That's right."

Simon was confused by everything—why Imogen and Fletcher were together in San Francisco, that Niles was visiting Jade in Michigan. None of it made any sense but he didn't have time for the details.

"Should I come home?" Niles asked.

"No. No need. I'll keep you posted," Simon said, abruptly disconnecting from the call.

17

After his call ended with Niles, Simon sat down on the sofa to ponder his next move. As much as he wanted to go straight to San Francisco to look for Imogen, he wouldn't even know where to begin. No, if she tried to return and was unable to, like every other traveler in the world, she would be frightened, but Niles had said that Fletcher had gone with her. Why? He wasn't sure, but it eased his mind at least knowing that she wasn't alone ... as long as he didn't console her too much.

He should probably return to headquarters and see how he could be of help. Hostin seemed to think he was needed anyway. Simon was just about to set his course when there was a knock at the front door. Who could that be? he wondered. When he opened the door, Mimi Pinky was standing on his porch—the last person he wanted to see right now. Even though she was his biological grandmother there was no love lost between them. Ever since their meeting at the attorney's office back in September for the reading of Teddy's will, they had all pretty much kept their distance from each other.

She looked terrible, worse than usual. Her hair was a bee's nest. She was wearing her signature floral housecoat and furry slippers. Looked like the same outfit he'd seen her in the last time he was home, six months ago, but she wasn't wearing any makeup, and her eyes were red and bloodshot like she'd either been smoking marijuana or crying. Being ever the busybody, she explained that she hadn't seen anyone at their house lately and became concerned when she saw movement inside and wanted to come check.

"Why are you really here, Mimi? What is it that you want?" Simon asked sharply. And then, her face contorted, and she unexpectedly broke into tears, wracking sobs that shook her misshapen body. Simon felt bad but still repulsed by her in every way possible.

Without inviting her in, instead coming out to her on the porch, he asked, "What's wrong?"

"It's that goddamn motherfuckin' Carl," Mimi Pinky blubbered. "I hate him. I hate him more than anything."

Simon really didn't have time for this nonsense, but his polite upbringing compelled him to ask anyway. "What did Carl do?"

"HE LEFT ME!" Mimi wailed. "And … he ran off with the money we got paid for that stupid, worthless ridiculous, goddamn book!" She pulled a wadded-up tissue from the pocket of her dirty housecoat and blew her nose into it.

Simon had not thought about Carl Loomis for a while. He was Mimi's sketchy boyfriend, a real rough character, as Simon recalled. He'd shown up with Mimi at the lawyer's office for the reading of Teddy's will, but now come to think of it, Simon had also suspected he may have been involved in ransacking the pawn shop and attacking him and Fletcher ... one of them had gotten away with Eastman's book ... it was making a lot of sense now.

The book she was talking about was *The Photographer's Guide to Time Travel*, the rare book written by George Eastman that they were after. He and Fletcher had found it and some of his journals and browsed through them. Mimi was right, it did just seem like a lot of woo and gibberish and conjecture. When he had gone back and visited Eastman, the man that he found out was his great grandfather, he had told him that he'd given the book to Teddy for safekeeping. Apparently, there was something important within its pages, but Simon had no idea what it might be. Important enough, though, that someone had hired a band of criminals, Carl possibly included, to break into Teddy's shop and steal it.

"So this book," Teddy ventured, "you said you and Carl sold it to someone?"

Either mistaking Simon's interest as kindness or simply motivated by her rage at Carl Loomis, Mimi felt comfortable enough to spill her guts.

"Yeah, his name was Kevin something er other," she said as she dug deep into her other housecoat pocket where all manner of random things she'd stashed there began spilling out—a thimble, a beer cap, a cigarette butt, paperclip, tissue ... Finally, she retrieved a crumpled-up wad of paper. "McCord," she said, handing it over for Simon to look. It was a handwritten receipt of sorts signed Kevin McCord for payment of $5,000 for *A Guide to Photographic Time Travel*, by George Eastman.

Simon did indeed recognize the name—Kevin accompanied Agent Metzger when they had paid a visit to their house after Imogen had rescued her father, Niles from the time loop he had been caught in. Ostensibly, they had dropped by to explain the Society's function as passive monitors of the universe and time travel, and to make Imogen aware that she had been on their radar for a while—the result of several missteps—and particularly that she had been overstepping her bounds, unnecessarily interfering in people's lives to the detriment of the universe. The key purpose of the visit, however, turned out to be that they wanted to invite Simon to headquarters to test his "unique" abilities, they said.

It was curious, for sure, but Simon wasn't exactly sure what Mimi thought he could do about it, and besides he was sort of in a hurry right now.

He handed the receipt back to her and started backing up, "It's regrettable that this happened to you, Mimi, but I really need to be going." As he turned to open the door, she grabbed hold of his sleeve. "Please," she said. She was a sight, her pleading eyes were red and bloodshot from crying, and Simon, for an instant, actually felt a little sorry for her.

"I don't ..." he began, but she interrupted him.

Look, I know there's no love lost between us," she admitted. Simon was surprised. He didn't recognize this Mimi, her voice, usually high-pitched and shrill, was different somehow, low and serious, so sad and dare he say it, sincere? It had to be a trick. She hated Imogen and she hated him, equally with a passion. But something prompted him to listen, to let her speak.

"I hate to admit it, but you were right to hate Teddy," she began. "What he did to your ma was wrong. I know somethin' about being young and alone, tryin' to survive. My life was not like this once," she said, gesturing with her hand at herself. "Believe it or not, I come from a good family, a rich one too. But I ran away with a boy when I was sixteen and my parents would have nothing to do with me after that."

She lowered her chin and stared down at her feet. When she looked back up at Simon, a tear rolled down her cheek. "I didn't realize how much he hated me until that day in the lawyer's office. The things I did to that boy scarred him for life, twisted him all up. Now he's gone and it's my fault. I'm ashamed and lonely and I don't have anybody now. I don't expect you to care. I know you'll never claim me as kin. I wouldn't if I were you, but for what it's worth, I'm sorry. I'm sorry for everything."

Simon hadn't noticed the folder she had been holding until she held it out for him to take.

"Here," she said.

"What ... what is this?" he asked.

"I made a copy of that book and the fancy rolled up paper that was hidden inside it, too," Mimi said. "I don't know why but Carl said that this Kevin fella wanted it real bad, said something about ending time travel and he mentioned your name, too."

"Me? Why?" Simon asked, confused.

Mimi shook her head. "I dunno. But when I saw you over here, I wanted to give it to you ... "

"Mimi, have you seen Imogen around lately?"

"No, not for a while, but with COVID and all, haven't seen much of anybody lately."

Simon wasn't sure if the book was important or not, but if it was and anyone could decipher it, the experts at the Daguerreian Society could.

"I must go, but thank you, Mimi," he said as he lightly patted her shoulder, probably the first time he'd ever been this close to the woman who was his grandmother.

"You're welcome, Simon." For the first time ever, Mimi's smile seemed genuine as she turned around and shuffled back home to her house across the street.

18

Even though the alarms had stopped blasting, Daguerreian Society employees continued to mull about outside their offices and in the hallways, speaking in hushed whispers, speculating about what was going on. When Simon arrived back at headquarters, he immediately went in search of field director Frank Metzger and found him sitting in his office at his desk, staring at a blank computer screen, a puzzled look on his face. He glanced up when Simon came to his door.

"Simon! Come in, come in," he said, waving him over to a nearby chair. "I've barely seen you since you got here. What do you make of all this?"

Simon wasted no time getting to the point. "I think that agent friend of yours, Kevin McCord, might be responsible for shutting down time travel," he said as he dropped the photocopy of Eastman's book on the desk in front of him. After plucking his reading glasses from his shirt pocket and putting them on, Metzger leaned in for a closer look at the title: *The Photographic Guide to Time Travel.*

"Where did you get this? I heard it had been stolen," Metzger said.

"It was stolen from us that night at the pawn shop, by a fellow by the name of Carl Loomis," Simon explained. "And then, he evidently sold it to McCord, according to Loomis' girlfriend, Mimi Pinky who happens to also be my grandmother …" Metzger gave him a questioning look. "… Long story," Simon continued.

Metzger confirmed what Simon had just told him. "You are correct about Kevin," he said, "but whether or not he obtained the information from this book, that I don't know, but somehow he figured out how to shut down time travel, serious business when you consider the danger it puts our travelers out there in."

"What do you think he wants?" Simon asked.

Metzger sighed, stood up, and walked over to look out the window. "It's not completely clear, but as I understand it, he has told the shareholders that he holds the key to time travel; he's in charge now and will not be turning it back on until they meet certain demands."

"Which are?" Simon asked.

"He says he wants the scientists to fix the time sickness problem."

"I don't understand," Simon said. "Why would he shut it all down over this one issue and trap hundreds of thousands of travelers? It seems like there has to be more to it than that."

"Kevin was hired because he could time travel," Metzger explained. "My guess is that it has to do with the fact that he no longer can. Do you remember how he put everything in comic book terms when he was explaining time travel to you?"

"Sure, yeah."

"Like the comics, time travel was an escape for him, and when he became too sick to travel, I suspect he was likely pretty upset. And I heard recently that his partner had dumped him."

"You worked closely with him. Why would he do something like this?" Simon asked.

"We weren't best friends or anything, but when you spend long hours working with someone, you do get to know someone on a more personal level," Metzger said. "I do know that he was a good partner, he liked orderliness, was always very thorough about his reporting, but also overly particular about things, to the point of being obsessive-compulsive, I would say."

Simon had limited knowledge of 21st century psychiatric terms. "Obsessive? Compulsive? What does that entail exactly?" he asked.

"Kevin came to the field from the archives department in the basement, and he was very meticulous in his work, a good quality—you certainly don't want someone there who might miss important data. But after working with him I could see that he had set impossibly high standards for himself, and he expected everyone else to adhere to those same standards as well, many of which were unnecessary or simply unachievable."

Simon was still confused about Kevin's motives. "What does that have to do with what's happening now?" he asked.

"Kevin is gay," Metzger said. Simon had since learned that "gay" was the modern expression for someone who, in his day, was homosexual but he didn't see how his sexual orientation would have any bearing on his current actions.

Metzger continued. "And he was working in, shall we say, an environment that wasn't what you might call 'inclusive'. On top of that he once confided to me that he had a very strict, evangelical anti-gay upbringing and evidently, ran away from home when he was a teenager," he said. "I think Kevin is bitter and very, very angry at the world."

While Simon pondered this bit of information, Dr. Hostin appeared in the doorway. "Simon! Here you are. I've been looking all over for you. Come with me."

Simon scooped up the photocopied book and he and Metzger followed Hostin, who brought them up to speed as they walked to his office down the corridor. Apparently, he explained, half a dozen of his colleagues, scientists who had been traveling had gotten caught up in Kevin's shutdown and were now trapped in time too. One of them, he said, Dr. Hugo Zambon, the Society's resident expert on disease had been focusing his studies on the effects of time travel on the body, specifically, why some travelers experience only minor illness, while others, like Kevin, become violently ill. But when the Coronavirus hit, he had switched gears directing his research toward ensuring that travelers who might be sick with COVID would not be able introduce the virus into the past and create a similar pandemic situation.

When they reached the door to his office, Hostin opened it and ushered Simon and Metzger in.

"Have a seat, gentlemen," he said.

Simon seized the opportunity to show him Eastman's book. "Dr. Hostin, I have something that might solve the problem, perhaps a way to turn time back on ..." but Hostin cut him off.

"Not now, Simon," he replied sharply, leaving both Simon and Metzger confounded.

" ... but, sir, it's George Eastman's book, *the* book, *The Photographic Guide to Time Travel*, that he wrote."

Hostin again waved him off as if the news was irrelevant. "Yes, yes, I've heard all about that, but we don't have time to decipher it right now. Time is of the essence! People are trapped, *my* people are trapped."

Simon glanced over at Metzger who shrugged, reflecting his own bewildered gaze.

"Now," Hostin continued, "as I understand it, Simon, you are the only person in the world currently who is still able to travel through time. Is that correct?"

Simon nodded. "Um, yes sir, I believe that is correct."

"Then you must go immediately and retrieve Dr. Zambon!"

⁓⁓⁓⁓⁓

Choppy seas ahead ... Simon knew something was wrong the moment he entered the photograph. Always there was pitch dark combined with a bit of swirling light seeping through that typically only lasted for a few seconds. This was something completely different, however. The caliginous abyss seemed to fully encase him; deeply, uncomfortably, like a nightmare. Blind, with the exception of the bright flashes, he could feel his body trembling, rocking, slowly at first and then tumbling and jerking back and forth wildly, a sensation he could only equate to being tossed about on a boat navigating choppy seas during a violent storm.

Just moments before, he had been gazing into a photograph of a building in Zurick, Switzerland, the location of a symposium where Dr. Zambon and several other scientists from the Society were attending. Simon began to feel something akin to sea sickness as the endless churning never let up. Cutting through the darkness, a crackling bolt of light pierced it and for a moment Simon could make out a series of running lights along a long tunnel or what sort of looked like a telephoto lens. As he drifted past the lights, he could make out places and people, he assumed from different times because of the settings and period clothes they wore. Like the strange specters he had encountered at the dead zone, he was now the one zipping in and outside of time.

At times, instead of passing on by he seemed to be pulled into a time for a few seconds like a voyeur—to places he realized he had been to before—1913, the Benson Hotel with Imogen, dancing and swaying together in the ballroom, laughing, kissing her neck, feeding her a strawberry in bed, then skipping to a frozen alleyway, a woman, Georgia Bitgood throwing her boot and hitting Teddy in the head, knocking him to the ground; vomiting violently on the floor of Imogen's office downtown after his first experience traveling; the scenes came faster and faster now—the Nuremberg trials, an antiwar protest, a diner in Kansas; then like watching a series of short movie clips, flickers of memories: Simon as a child, seated beside his mother laughing, twisting her curls around her finger; which faded and folded into someplace else he'd never been, a sign on a stone wall that read Crestview Sanitarium; a drab room and a woman strapped to a table, clenching a rubber heel in her mouth, her body convulsing as a bolt of electricity coursed through her; from there leaping to yet another time, he didn't know when or where, a balcony, two women, one older, one younger, talking, drinking tea.

As if sensing his presence, the younger woman, with incredible green eyes, turned and looked straight at him or through him, he wasn't sure. She was speaking to the other woman, but he could catch snippets of the conversation: "... a patient uprising at Crestview ... spirit you away to the safe house in 1930 ... even though it's 1937 now I've always meant to return .. to Montparnasse ... "

No sooner was he there, but he was whisked elsewhere, to a sunny day, seagulls soaring, the ruins of some structure by the ocean, the backside of someone with blond curls who slightly resembled Imogen. He was so close that he reached out to touch her but was immediately swept away again, and then abruptly the turbulence ceased. The wild ride was over, and he was standing now in a great hall. A person at a podium was speaking about the laws of thermodynamics. He had arrived at his destination, but for how long? He needed to find Dr. Zambon and the others quickly. The only thing he could think of to do was shout his name.

"Dr. Zambon, Hugo Zambon! Is there a Dr. Zambon here!" Everyone in the audience turned around to look at the person yelling at the back of the room.

"Excuse me, young man," the person at the podium said through the microphone. "What do you want here? You are disrupting our session!"

Simon didn't care. There was no time. "I'm looking for Dr. Hugo Zambon and two of his colleagues!" he shouted. "It's urgent." A slight man near the front sheepishly turned around raising his hand as he slowly arose from his seat. "I am Dr. Zambon," he said. The other scientists seated next to him followed suit.

"Dr. Zambon!" Simon called out, rushing toward him. "Come with me, please, sir. Dr. Hostin sent me to find you. Something terrible has happened. We need you back at headquarters." Without hesitation, Simon quickly gathered all three men into a body-hugging huddle next to him and instructed them to hold on tight to him and to each other, warning it might be a rough ride. "Ready?" he asked. The men indicated agreement and much to the surprised dismay of the attendees, Simon and the three scientists vanished from the room.

Closely observing the spot from which Simon had departed mere seconds before, Metzger and Hostin witnessed the turbulent return of Simon, Dr. Zambon, and his colleagues, Doctors Gerome Ludlow and William Perkins.

Although they were still tightly gripping Simon, their landing was anything but smooth. As though dropped from the sky, the three were tangled together, legs akimbo, expressions of anxiety, panic, and shock lining their faces.

"Thank god!" Hostin cried as he and Metzger rushed forward to help the men up off the tiled floor.

"Are you all right?" he asked.

"Okay ... I think," Ludlow said, looking around the room before grasping hold of Metzger's arm for help up.

Hoskin extended his hands to Dr. Ludlow and Dr. Zambon and helped them up. "I've been better," Dr. Zambon said, smiling weakly.

"How about you, Simon?" Metzger asked. "What happened out there?"

"I cannot lie," he said. "It was a bit rough."

The three scientists eyed each other, scoffing nervously. Rough was putting it mildly. The return trip was as chaotic and discombobulating as Simon's trip to retrieve them had been. Each experienced the nearly impenetrable darkness and choppy seas, the sensation of being tossed around like rag dolls. Simon couldn't be sure if the others were seeing the same people or reliving memories that he was but from the looks on their faces, whatever they saw had been harrowing.

Hostin wasted no time coddling them, however, and began to brief them, mobilizing the team, and issuing orders.

"So, here's what's happening," he began. "An employee of the Society, Kevin McCord, has found a way to shut down time travel, trapping hundreds of thousands of travelers.

It may be a power grab on his part, but putting innocent lives at risk is very, very serious and must be addressed. He has indicated that he will turn it back on if a cure can be found for the sickness that prevents some people from time traveling. Evidently, McCord suffers from this." Hostin turned to Dr. Zambon. "Hugo, you are studying the side effects of time travel, in particular, the illness issue, are you not?"

Dr. Zambon nodded. "Yes, that is correct."

"I need you to get on that; see if you can expedite it," Hostin instructed.

Turning to Dr. Perkins, a mathematician and cryptographist, he said, "Will, we have a copy of George Eastman's book. McCord purchased it from the people who had stolen it. We'd like you to take a look, see if you can make heads or tails of his calculations, and let us know asap if there is a formula there that might have clued McCord into how to turn time travel off."

"Simon and Frank, I'd like for you to accompany Dr. Ludlow, our forensic scientist to his office to review camera surveillance footage that was retrieved from the lab Kevin was using for his experiments. If there is something on there, we may be able to pinpoint what he was doing prior to the incident."

With their marching orders in place, the group dispersed. Metzger and Simon chatted as they followed Dr. Ludlow to his office. "Do you know where Kevin is now?" Simon asked as they walked.

"I'm not sure," Metzger said. "Some of the other agents were speculating that he might be holed up in the top floor suite where the shareholders meet. I mean, it's an entire floor. He has everything he needs, and security is tight up there."

After riding the elevator up to the fourth floor, Ludlow led them into his office/lab and offered them seats at a table in front of several large monitors. Metzger and Simon flanked him on either side as he turned on his computer, retrieved the footage that had been sent over from Kevin's lab, and clicked to open up the file.

An image of an empty lab popped up on the screen. "Wow," Ludlow said aloud as he was viewing the monitor.

"What is it?" Simon asked.

"This is a very large file. Looks like there is probably a good eight hours of surveillance footage here, at least. This might take a while."

Metzger and Simon looked at each other. "We're here for it," Metzger said, "Let's see what Kevin was up to."

19

Seated across from her at the small, wrought iron bistro table on the apartment's third-story balcony, Tiffany poured Dominique Flynn a second cup of tea. "I am so happy to finally meet you," she gushed. Nikki had snatched her from the sanitarium mere moments before she was to be lobotomized. She owed this woman her life. Not only was Tiffany in awe of the woman, but she was perhaps the most stunning creature she'd ever seen, particularly because of her unusual eye color—a shade of green the color of the Green Star Gladiolus, a perennial flower she remembered her mother growing in their suburban backyard garden— and a striking contrast to her darkish shoulder-length hair. Most intriguing though, was the calm she exuded, a certainty of purpose that was difficult to describe.

"So, tell me about yourself, Dominique," Tiffany said nervously, the words tumbling out willy-nilly. "I want to know all about you, and how you came to be at Crestview."

Nikki smiled and crossed her legs. "Please, call me Nikki," she said. She leisurely took a sip of her tea and when she spoke, her words were relaxed and measured. "I'm a traveler," she began. From there she told Tiffany her story. It started with her mother, also a traveler, who was married to an abusive man, she explained. Fearing for the life of her unborn child, she escaped to 1958 to live with her aunt in Florida.

"I wanted to be a nurse, to help people, but I found another way to help. Because I was a child of two timelines, I discovered I could travel freely, forward and backward without a photograph as an anchor, which meant that I could help people escape from bad situations," Nikki explained.

"When I read that there would be a patient uprising at Crestview in 1940, I traveled there, posed as a nurse, and was able to spirit you away to the safe house in 1930." She took another sip from her cup. "And even though it's 1937 now I've always meant to return …" Nikki's voice trailed as she turned her head to look at something. " … to Montparnasse…"

Tiffany looked at Nikki with alarm. "What is it?" she asked. "Do you see something?"

Nikki nodded her head. She seemed to be taken off guard. "Oh, it … it's nothing. I just thought for a moment that I saw someone … looking at us."

"Looking at us? Who?" Tiffany asked. Nikki tried to shrug it off, but Tiffany persisted. "Travelers can sense other travelers when they are nearby," she said. "But normally, you don't *see* them … like this."

"You saw someone?" Tiffany asked excited. "What did he look like?"

"Average height, straight and confident, dark hair," she described. It was a small detail, but one she had observed before. "It sounds odd," she said out loud, "but he was twisting a strand of hair with his finger."

Tiffany gasped and whispered, "A child of two timelines …"

"What do you mean?" Nikki asked. "Do you know who that was?"

"Yes," Tiffany said, "I believe that was my son."

〰〰〰

For days, they had been attempting to return home without success. The dismal reality was beginning to set in—they might actually be stuck here in 1973, indefinitely.

Imogen expended a deep, frustrated breath after yet another futile try. "No good," she said to Fletcher and Loretta. "I don't understand," she said. "How could this have happened? I mean, is it just us or is it happening to everyone?"

"My guess is everyone," Loretta said. "I can't go anywhere either."

Fletcher loosened his grip on Imogen's arm, walked over and plopped onto the worn couch. "As frustrating as it is for us, can you imagine what other travelers might be going through?" he said. "People stuck, people unable to go; maybe even sick or in danger and can't leave, or can't get medicine they need because it isn't available yet in that time?"

Imogen frowned at that bleak thought and she and Loretta nodded agreement. "At least we're in a good place,"

Imogen said, smiling at Loretta. "I can't help wondering if Simon is involved." During their stay at Loretta's house Imogen had time to fill her in on the details of their complicated relationship, his remarkable time-traveling abilities, and explanation of the Daguerreian Society's mission, which Loretta had never even heard of.

"You'd think that those Society people would be able to fix it," she said.

"Maybe they are," Imogen said, "But it's sure hard not knowing whether we should start making some contingency plans." She walked over and sat down on the couch next to Fletcher. "We feel bad about overstaying our welcome here, Loretta. Should we start looking for jobs?"

"Don't worry about that just yet," Loretta answered. "Honestly, I do love the company, so let's just keep trying; give it a little more time before you guys start making any plans to stay here permanently."

Because the delayed departure and the possibility that they might need to think about making this time and place their permanent home had consumed their thoughts and conversations, Imogen and Fletcher hadn't talked much about Imogen's mother or how either of them was feeling.

"I'm really scared," Imogen admitted after Loretta had left to go run errands, leaving them alone together in the bungalow.

"I know," Fletcher said, putting his arm around her and pulling her closer on the couch. "I am too, to be honest. I mean, seriously, what kind of lives can we even make for ourselves in 1973? Will we have to start all over? Do college over again?" he said. He searched her face for answers he knew she didn't have either. "It's just ... mind-boggling, really."

"The worst part, for me, is losing my dad all over again," Imogen said. "I just got him back and now I may never see him again. I'll never get to tell him what happened to mom ... It's like I'm nine years old again." She started to cry.

She looked up at him, tears rolling down her cheeks, so vulnerable, so fragile. He couldn't stop himself if he wanted to, he leaned in and softly kissed her lips, and Imogen kissed him back—like that first kiss in his apartment so long ago—a kiss bursting with so much raw, pent-up emotion and passion and need they were both surprised by the intensity of it. Fletcher pulled her up from the couch and led her to the spare bedroom. She lay back on the bed and he hovered close above her as she looked into his face. "This is wrong," she whispered.

"I know and I don't care," Fletcher said, kissing her all over.

∿∿∿∿∿

Neither spoke as they laid together on the bed afterward, staring up at the ceiling, spent, ragged breathing, and devoid of energy or thoughts or surroundings or reality, basking in the confusing aftermath of dozens of emotions and the physicality of sex, of what had just transpired between them.

Imogen spoke first. "That first day we tried to go home I went to Sutro Baths to tell my mom goodbye."

"I figured," Fletcher said.

"While I was out there, I started thinking a lot about time travel, you know, about whether it's worth it. All the ways Teddy hurt my family, whether I was really helping anyone, or just satisfying my own wandering soul." She paused. "I thought about Simon, too."

"I knew it would get around to Simon," Fletcher said sourly.

Imogen pulled herself up on one elbow. "Well how could it not?" she asked.

"I've been so selfish," she confessed, "always putting my wants, my needs first, never really listening to his. In the back of my mind, I knew he was suffering but not once did I offer to go look for his mother."

Fletcher felt a twinge of guilt. Simon was his friend, too, and he was the one who had planted that seed with him, asking him why Imogen had never offered to look for his mother when she easily could have.

Imogen got up and pulled her shirt on over her head. "This was wrong. It can't happen again."

Fletcher angrily got up from the bed and put his pants on. "That's just fine," he erupted, "because I can't do this anymore with you Imogen. I'm like some love-sick puppy, always following you around, wagging my tail and licking your face while you can't make up your goddamn mind about who you love!"

Imogen was conflicted and stunned by Fletcher's outburst. It was so unlike him. She had expected him to understand, to agree with her, like he always did ... *like a puppy dog*, she suddenly realized.

"I'm sorry Fletcher," she said, and meant it. "You're right. I haven't treated either one of you fairly. I promise, if we ever get back, to make this right. I'll tell Simon what happened between us and then I'm going to go look for Tiffany. I have to at least try. I owe him that much."

"What are you saying, Imogen? Are you're choosing me or him?"

Tears threatened to spill from the corner of her eyes. "I think I … I'm so confused."

Fletcher sighed, exasperated and tramped out of the room leaving her alone in an eddy of swirling, confusing thoughts.

20

For the last hour and a half, Agent Metzger, Simon, and Dr. Ludlow scanned the surveillance footage taken at the lab where Kevin had conducted his experiments. So far, they had observed a series of young people coming and going in what appeared to be scheduled appointments throughout the day. Kevin McCord sat down and interviewed each person first before having the individual focus on a photograph, ostensibly to attempt time travel. Although they were only able to zoom in so far, it was clear that the images, though similar, were blurry and mostly indistinguishable.

The first individual went into the photo, returned and appeared to be sick. A second, however, was unable to enter the photograph at all and was dismissed. The third subject came back sicker than the first and the fourth volunteer also was unable to travel. Kevin broke for lunch and returned an hour later. The pattern continued after lunch with the next two subjects. When the fifth volunteer returned, he was violently ill. Kevin was seen offering him a wastebasket to vomit into. The sixth volunteer was unable to enter the photo but curiously appeared to become quite ill anyway. The trio watched as the next subject, number seven, arrived at the lab. Because there was no audio they fast-forwarded past the interviews to the photo tests. But this one was not the same. McCord seemed to have extended the interview and foregone the test.

"I recognize that young man," Metzger said. "His name is Connor. He's an intern in my department." They observed Kevin and the young man Connor embrace, both smiling as he exited the lab.

"Strange that he wasn't a participant," Ludlow acknowledged.

"Maybe he was a friend," Simon posited.

"I don't think so," Metzger said. "I think Kevin may have changed his mind."

"What do you mean, changed his mind?" Simon asked.

"I mean, I think he was attracted to him and perhaps didn't want to put him in harm's way."

"Why would you think that?" Ludlow asked.

Metzger cleared his throat before speaking. He knew Kevin, but as a field agent, he was also a keen expert in observing and interpreting body language and behavior. "Just a guess, but it looked like Kevin was flirting with him." Ludlow ran the footage back. "See there, his entire demeanor changes when he enters the room." Metzger explained that Kevin's partner had recently broke up with him.

"Interesting," Ludlow said. "That information might be helpful when it comes time to negotiate with McCord."

They pushed ahead, fast-forwarding through the Connor segment and picking up at the point where the next subject entered the lab.

"Oh!" Simon chimed up, pointing at the screen. "I know that woman. That's Kevin's assistant, Brittany. I remember seeing her with him in the hallway."

Metzger nodded. "Yep, that's Brittany Kane, although she looks ... I hate to say it, but a lot better than I remember, dressed up more than usual."

It was obvious that the two knew each other. They chatted briefly and he pulled the photograph from a folder. She pointed at it and said something before sitting down at the table as the others had done. She looked at the photo and, in an instant, she was gone. But she didn't come back quickly like the others. The time ticked by. On the tape, Kevin paced around the room, and then they watched as the horror of what transpired next unfolded. What returned from the photograph was no longer Brittany; it was a monster, a mangled, ripped apart, husk of what once resembled a person.

All three men recoiled in disbelief as the grotesque remains splattered all over the floor.

"My god," Ludlow murmured, covering his mouth. Simon recoiled and looked away.

Metzger closed his eyes and shook his head from side to side. "Holy hell," was all he managed to say. Ludlow paused the recording, and they sat in stunned silence, unable to speak.

"I ... I never would have imagined he would take it this far," Metzger stammered.

"It looks like whatever he was sending them into went terribly wrong," Simon offered. "The others came back in one piece. What do you suppose was different about that photograph?"

"That's the question, isn't it?" Ludlow said. None of them was in a hurry to resume the tape, but Ludlow broke the silence. "Well, as difficult as it will be gentlemen, I think we must watch the rest of this, see what he does next."

He started it again and each of them cringed watching Kevin mop up the floor of what was once Brittany Kane and deposit her remains in another room. Shortly after, another young man showed up at the lab.

They skimmed through the interview to the part where he entered the photograph, and all three men held their breaths as they watched. Shortly after entering, where minutes before pieces of Brittany had been, the body of this subject landed violently on the floor. "Oh Christ," Metzger gasped. "Not again."

Curious, he was obviously dead, but his body was intact. Not even a trace of blood.

"At least he didn't die horribly," Simon said. "Yes, but why didn't he suffer the same fate?" Ludlow wondered out loud. They continued rolling the footage. To his credit, Kevin did seem despondent, at one point sitting with his head in his hands, crying, it looked like, but then he got up and methodically moved the body to the adjacent room where he had previously stowed Brittany, closed the door, and prepared to greet another subject, another girl, presumably an intern.

"Unbelievable!" Ludlow said, shaking his head. "Do you believe this guy? He sends two people to their deaths and he's going to keep right on going with the experiment?"

"I don't get it," Simon added. "He used to be a good guy. What happened to him?"

In this final segment, the volunteer disappeared into the picture but did not return. Kevin wrote something down in a notebook, called someone, and the footage later showed he and two other men moving the two bodies out of the lab in some sort of crate.

Dr. Ludlow stopped the tape and he, Simon, and Metzger leaned back in their chairs, each trying to process what they had just seen. Finally, Metzger spoke. "Can we run it back to around the 4:00 mark when Brittany arrived for her appointment?" he asked. "Yes, of course," Ludlow said. "Did you notice something, Frank?"

"Maybe," Metzger said.

Ludlow clicked the back arrow button and rewound it to that particular segment of the tape. They watched again as Kevin and Brittany chatted briefly. He took the photo from a folder, she pointed at it, and said something.

"Right there, stop it!" Metzger said. "Can you zoom in and slow it down?" Ludlow did as he was asked, and Metzger leaned in close attempting to read her lips. "Can you run it back one more time for me?" Ludlow did so and Metzger rewatched it. "I think she's saying, 'the two minute one,'" he said.

"The two minute one?" Simon asked. "Does that mean anything to you, Dr. Ludlow?

Ludlow pondered this information for a few minutes before speaking. He looked down at his tablet at the notes he'd been taking of times and observations from the footage.

"Possibly. I have a theory about what he may have been looking for and that number is a clue, but let's take what we know back to Hostin and compare notes," he said.

Tuesday morning, Simon, Frank Metzger and Doctors Zambon, Ludlow, and Perkins gathered for an emergency meeting with Dr. Hostin to report on their findings.

"Alright gentlemen," Hostin began, "What do you have to share?" He nodded first at Hugo Zambon to report first.

"I'm afraid there are no new breakthroughs in my side effects study. I've spent the last few days with my team poring over every detail and we're still at ground zero in terms of understanding why some folks become ill and others don't when they travel." Metzger meekly raised his hand in an effort at drawing Hostin's attention. "Sir, we might have some inform..." Hostin cut him off. "Yes, yes Frank, we'll get to you in a moment."

Hostin directed his focus next to Will Perkins, who had been tasked with deciphering the George Eastman book. "How about you, Will? Any luck with the Eastman book?"

Perkins cleared his throat. "Well, it appears that the calculations written on the scroll seem to suggest something analogous to frequencies of some sort, and there are several passages in the book where Eastman talks about briefly experimenting with double exposures. Otherwise, nothing conclusive."

Again, Metzger attempted to capture Hostin's attention. "Sir, I'm sorry to interrupt, but ..."

Hostin was irritated now. "Frank!" he said sternly, "You'll get your turn in a moment, after the experts have spoken."

Deflated over being brushed aside by Hostin, Metzger glanced over at Dr. Ludlow for affirmation, who gave him a reassuring smile as a sign to be patient; their turn would come.

"Thank you gentlemen." Hostin finally turned to address Metzger. "Okay Frank. I know that you and Simon accompanied Gerome to McCord's lab to view the surveillance tapes. Considering your enthusiasm to speak I take it you found something."

Embarrassed, Metzger was now hesitant to speak, but couldn't contain himself. "Kevin McCord murdered two volunteers!" he blurted. Audible gasps, dropped jaws, and stunned silence followed as the others struggled to digest this bit of shocking news. Visibly shaken, Hostin drew his hand up to his chin and searched for a response.

"You saw this? On the footage?" he asked.

"Yes," Metzger said, "and we uncovered information too that seems to correlate with the time sickness and the calculations found in Eastman's book, but for that I'll defer to your colleague, Dr. Ludlow."

"Tell us what you found, Gerome," Hostin prompted.

Dr. Ludlow opened his notebook and began his report. "As Frank mentioned, we witnessed the deaths of two young people and the disappearance of another. Evidently,

Kevin McCord had arranged some sort of study in the lab with some of whom may have been Society interns. We observed a total of nine individuals arrive at the laboratory. Assuming they were all capable of time travel, they were each given a photograph to view. I noted the schedule and results of the tests, for which I've made copies." Ludlow distributed copies to everyone at the table:

> Subject #1: Mildly sick – 30 sec
> Subject #2: Unable to travel
> Subject #3: Sicker – 1 min
> Subject #4: Unable to travel
> Subject #5: Violently ill – 1½ min
> Subject #6: Unable to travel but becomes ill trying
> Subject #7: Not tested
> Subject #8: Mangled/dead – 2 min
> Subject #9: Dead
> Subject #10: Does not return/time travel ceases – 2½ min

"At first glance, it would appear that McCord was trying to find a solution to the travel illness side effect that you have been studying, Hugo," Ludlow said.

"However, after looking at this schedule, to your point Dr. Perkins regarding Eastman's findings on frequency, it appears that it wasn't a cure for the sickness he was after."

"What exactly was he looking for then," Hostin asked.

Ludlow explained. "We know that the process of time travel involves the traveler concentrating on a picture to which their brain sends out a frequency that takes them to that time."

The others nodded understanding as he continued. "I believe that McCord was sending people into photographs that had been double exposed at different time intervals in an attempt to narrow down the discordant frequency that would turn time travel off."

"How did you come to this conclusion?" Hostin asked.

Ludlow gestured to Metzger. "Thanks to Frank here, who was able to read the lips of one of the subjects who died, we have part of the equation."

He explained how before she entered the photograph, his assistant Brittany had asked McCord if this was "the one at two minutes."

"You'll notice the times on the chart," he said. "Assuming that Kevin was using the scientific method to narrow it down between a range of numbers, if Brittany was at a lower number of two minutes, the subject before her entered a photograph with an arbitrary higher number, and we can assign likely corresponding numbers to each subject before and after her."

Perkins was incredulous. "So what you're saying is that the last subject in this list, the one who disappeared, entered a photograph exposed at a 2½ minute interval, the precise frequency that halted time travel?"

"That appears to be correct," Ludlow answered.

"What do you make of this Perkins? You've been studying Eastman's book. Does this have any connection?

Perkins leaned back in his seat and scratched his chin. "Hmmm, well it's possible," he said. "I mean, given the time it was written, Eastman's book offers a good bit of speculation on the origins of time travel. Still, there appears to be missing information. Some of the calculations appear to align with the notion of frequencies and it contains a vague hypothesis concerning double-exposed images."

Everyone at the table sat in silence, pondering whether any of this information might hold the key to unlocking the puzzle.

"Well gentlemen," Hostin said, "This has been illuminating. Thank you for all your diligent reporting; however, we'll have to assess and then reconvene for now."

The group started to get up, when Simon, silent throughout the meeting, inserted his voice into the conversation.

"Sir," he said, "Pardon me if I'm holding you up, but as you know, I was recently sent to the dead zones."

The mention of the dead zones seemed to pique everyone's interest, and they all sat back down in their seats.

"Yes, that's right, Simon, with all of this going on, we neglected to get your report," Hostin apologized.

Simon told the group about witnessing the people rapidly moving in and out of the zones, about how the ground vibrated, and large cracks were forming in the area.

"That's all quite interesting," Hostin acknowledged, "but I don't see how that ties in with our current situation."

"There was something else," Simon said, "… a high-pitched humming sound. I was there, in the dead zone, when time travel stopped," he said. "The people froze in place, the ground stopped vibrating, but the humming did not stop, although it slowed way down, and the pitch changed … almost like … a frequency? Could that have something to do with McCord's experiments?"

Excited now, Perkins was first to speak. "Yes! Of course, that must be it. Eastman's theory could not be proven at the time because there were no dead zones, but when they opened up, the actual frequency was exposed."

Everyone began talking at once until Hostin interjected. "Thank you all for your contributions," he said, addressing the group before singling out Simon.

"Time is ticking. How soon can you leave for the zones, Simon?"

21

As Dr. Hostin hustled Simon away, purportedly to prep him for a second trip to the dead time zones, Doctors Ludlow, Zambon, and Perkins headed off together down the hallway, shoulder to shoulder, deep in conversation about what they had learned, leaving Metzger awkwardly standing idle with his hands in his pockets wondering what his role, if any, might be in all this. It had been satisfying to be acknowledged for his contribution by Dr. Ludlow, but it was a small part, he knew.

Although Society employees were still in the dark about the McCord situation, things had calmed down somewhat over the last few days, and they had returned to their jobs. As Metzger headed back to his office, he noticed that the café had reopened. Why not stop in and grab a latte and muffin? he thought. The meeting had been long and trying, to say the least. But even more than that, he would never, ever be able to unsee what he'd seen on that surveillance tape. It replayed over and over in his head. The brutal state of that woman, Brittany, was stomach churning, like something out of a horror movie.

After ordering, he sat down at a table in the corner. Sipping his coffee, his thoughts turned to Kevin McCord. Despite the ghastliness, it had also been painful to watch him. Clearly, he was despondent, but the fact that he chose to continue with the experiment even after what had happened to his assistant nagged at Metzger. This wasn't the person he'd taken under his wing, the kid he had laughed and joked with and shared meals with on the road. He knew that no one was purely evil, but what he had done made it hard to see any good in him and he felt disappointed by him and for himself. Had he failed him in some way? Or worse, failed to see it? Could he have listened more, done something different that might have prevented this tragedy?

While these and other thoughts swirled around in his head, Metzger felt useless. The scientists seemed to have it all under control. Perhaps Simon would find the answers they were seeking in the dead zones. But what could he do to help? And then it occurred to him, nobody had discussed negotiating with Kevin yet. Maybe as someone who knew him better than anyone, he could get through to him. Get him to surrender without anyone else getting hurt. That's it. That's what I'll do! After taking a bite out of the uneaten muffin and washing it down with the rest of his coffee, he threw a $5 tip on the table and walked brusquely out of the café.

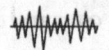

Metzger entered the dimly lit basement and flipped on the bright overhead fluorescent lights, flooding the room with glowing light. Dozens of computers and monitoring equipment, usually actively tracking data on the movement of time travelers around the world, sat eerily silent. Of course, they had sent the employees of the Department of Temporal Anomalies home, there was nothing for them to do, nothing to monitor or record. Metzger wasn't sure why he even came down here or what he was looking for, but it seemed like a good place to start, to poke around and maybe figure out where Kevin's head was at.

Kevin McCord had started his career at the Daguerreian Society as a data monitoring technician right here in this basement, spending many years collecting data, cataloguing it, tending to the Society's vast archives. He was the one who had first noticed that Simon was doing the impossible—making multiple jumps through time without the need of an anchor photo, the event that had catapulted his career as a field agent.

He next went into the large archives room and turned on the lights. A lot of the files had been digitized, but still there were row upon rows of cabinets, lined up like the stacks at the library still waiting to be scanned. He opened up a drawer and pulled out a folder labeled Odette Lumiere – 1858, an early narrative of the young woman's encounter with a time traveler. "Fascinating," he said aloud after reading the account. He was just placing it back in its place in the cabinet when he heard a voice yell out, "Who's in here?"

Metzger closed the drawer and followed the sound of the voice. Just outside the door stood a group of several young men.

"What are you doing here?" one of them demanded.

"I would ask you the same," Metzger responded.

"No one is supposed to be down here," another said.

"On who's authority?" Metzger asked.

A third stepped forward. Shorter than the others, his face red and pinched in an angry scowl. "Kevin McCord, that's who!" he said. "Who are you?"

"Ah, I see … well, where is mister McCord," Metzger inquired. "My name is Frank Metzger and I'd like a word with him."

They looked at each other confused. One whispered into the ear of the other and he pulled his phone from his pocket and walked away from everyone. When he returned, he said, "Mr. McCord will be here shortly."

About ten minutes later, Kevin himself strolled in through the doors. He smiled when he saw his old friend and mentor.

"Great to see you, Frank," he said cheerfully.

Metzger nodded. "Kevin."

"So … what can I do for you?"

"They sent me to talk to you, Kevin," Metzger lied.

Kevin snorted. "You? Why would they send you? A lowly field agent. I doubt you have any authority. Why haven't they sent in the higher ups to talk? What are they up to, those sneaky bastards? I know they're up to something. That's the reason for the delay. You better tell me, or I'll …"

"Or you'll do what, Kevin, throw a tantrum?" Metzger stated calmly.

For a moment, Kevin was speechless. For the past few days he'd gotten a small taste of power, of what it felt like to bully other people, and he was temporarily taken aback by Metzger's bravado.

"I know what you did, Kevin," Metzger said "… to Brittany and the others; I saw it on the surveillance tapes." All eyes turned to Kevin. It seemed clear that these minions evidently didn't know about what happened in the lab.

Kevin stiffened. Cleared his throat, and modulated his speech so the others would see that he was calm, reasonable, not rattled at all. "What are you talking about, Metzger? That's ridiculous. I didn't do anything to anybody. They are just upset that I figured out how to turn time travel off, that I'm smarter than they are, and they can't stand it."

Metzger continued the confrontation hoping to cast doubt in the minds of the loyalists Kevin had chosen to surround himself with—some likely paid, others disgruntled employees, Metzger surmised.

"You're not some evil mastermind in one of your comic books. And these are real people's lives that are at stake. Do you have any inkling of the misery people are suffering— travelers who are already in risky situations will die, people without their medications will die. There are a million potential scenarios, and you … you Kevin, are responsible for it. You've been there. You know what it's like. After all the years you spent here in the archives, I know how you took great care to make sure their memory was restored.

You cared about them. And as a field agent, you took a vow to protect travelers. What about that?"

Growing increasingly uncomfortable with the truth Metzger was speaking, Kevin tossed his hands in the air. "Stop! That's enough." He narrowed his eyes angrily at Metzger and shouted, "Tie him up ... now!

Before Metzger could react, the group pounced on him, knocking him down on the floor, and twisting his arms roughly behind his back. Someone grabbed computer cables and used them to secure him to one of the posts in the basement. More cable was wrapped around his chest rendering him completely immobile.

22

For the second time this week, Simon found himself in the town of Braunau am Inn, Austria, the birthplace of Adolf Hitler, facing the Pommer Inn on Salzburger Vorstadt 15, October 1889.

But this time it was not the same. The local townsfolk went about their business as before unaware of anything happening out of the ordinary, but the unseen forces of fellow travelers did not draw him toward the site this time. The ground beneath him was still and intact, and the hundreds of blurry phantom travelers that glitched in and out had disappeared. As before, he could make out the humming sound, last time a steady unbroken stream of sound—which he could now identify as a frequency—before Kevin McCord had managed to shut it down.

And yet, merely naming it wasn't enough to understand it. The mission was clear enough—find the frequency that will turn time travel back on, but how? He was a school principal for god's sake. Why had he been given this impossible task? He asked Hostin and the other scientists for advice, but their responses were vague at best. What was he supposed to do here? Think Simon. Okay, so he wasn't a scientist, sure, but perhaps he could *think* like one. He had taught science to schoolchildren. It was rudimentary science, but he understood the basics of the scientific method, of posing a question, developing a hypothesis, and then using available data to attempt to answer the question at hand.

Simon stood very still, emptied his mind of thought, closed his eyes, and focused in entirely on the sound of the barely audible hum. He immediately noticed that it sounded low-pitched and choppy, uneven as though two discordant notes were banging violently up against the other. When he had visited this site before the hum had been loud, sharp, high-pitched and steady, perhaps an indication that time travel was in the ON position?

He knew that McCord had discovered the discordant frequency by sending travelers into double-exposed photographs, but he had no photographs here, no lab. What might serve as a substitute of a double-exposed photograph for detecting the correct frequency that would turn time travel back on?

"Der Herr, Der Herr!" a child's voice rang out. Interrupted from his thoughts, Simon's eyes snapped open at once and he looked down to see a small boy tugging at his pant leg. A second boy of about the same age and stature stood a few feet away. He was holding what looked like the metal hoops from a barrel. In his other hand, a metal key-shaped stick. "der Herr, können Sie unseren Reifen reparieren?" the boy cried, pointing at the other boy.

Unable to understand German, Simon raised his hands in the air and shook his head. "I don't understand," he said. The boy began gesturing and pointing at the hoops, which Simon could see had become entangled. "Können Sie uns helfen, der Herr?"

"Ah, I see the problem," Simon said, smiling down at the boy. He walked over and stood facing the other youth. "May I?" he asked, as he reached for the hoops, which the boy handed over to him.

Simon remembered this game very well, having played hoop and stick often as a youngster. Manufactured toys were a luxury, so children of long ago invented simple games to entertain themselves. The goal was to keep the large hoop rolling upright by hitting it forward with a stick. Children could be seen rolling hoops down the streets, enroute to school, or during hoop races with other children.

Made of metal or wood, free hoops could be acquired from barrels as these two appeared to be. Barrel hoops, however, were difficult to roll because one edge of the hoop had a greater circumference than the other and it appeared that somehow during their game, one iron hoop, which was slightly smaller than the other had become entangled and became stuck. Using all his strength, Simon was able to disengage them and return each smiling boy his hoop.

"Danke!" they said in unison and darted away down the road, happily rolling their hoops with their sticks. Watching them go, Simon's thoughts began to drift. Two hoops merged together. Time as a circle. Two hoops, two boys, the motion of the hoop rolling a few seconds ahead of you. He pictured himself as a youngster playing the game in the late eighteenth, early nineteenth century—but not a regular boy—a boy conceived in 1997, but born in 1885, two times, two places, his origin.

Slowly, it began to click. If time travel truly was baked into his DNA and he didn't require an anchor photo, he also wouldn't need a double-exposed photo to be in two places at the same time.

He knew what to do.

Allowing his mind to wander he imagined himself floating between two times. "I am in 2020. I am also in the era that I grew up," he whispered. Back and forth, back and forth, and back and back and forth, concentrating on both places at once. Random images flashed before his eyes— of two places, two times—running down a dusty street with a hoop and a stick; his mother photographing him, telling him stories, twisting her curls between her finger; room 213 at the Benson Hotel with Imogen—flying in an airplane and listening to Pink Floyd through earphones for the first time, holding Imogen as she wept over her dead cat; the smell of her hair as he whispered goodbye to her at the airport …

The deeper he concentrated, the faster he began to move—like a human tuning fork—between two planes of time. As the imagery rose to a crescendo—a duration of precisely 2½ minutes—it gradually began to slow down, until finally dissipating altogether, replaced by a clear and high-pitched hum, the ON switch for time travel. At the same time, the ground again began to shift and rattle and crack beneath his feet. The incoming specters of travelers returned, rushing in and out of the dead zone again. Dizzy and drained, Simon's knees buckled beneath him. He collapsed to the ground and passed out.

〰〰〰

Despite being tied up, Metzger wasn't finished talking. "You don't want to do this," he implored him. "This isn't who you are. I know you. This will ruin your life, Kevin."

The more Frank talked, the more Kevin's rage began to build, until finally he blew up. "Fuck you, Frank, you don't know anything! My life is already ruined."

Kevin was clearly rattled, but that was what Metzger was hoping for, to get him to let down his guard, to feel *something, anything*, and hopefully realize the folly of continuing down this losing path. Kevin turned his back on Metzger, seemingly to regain his composure, before turning back around to face him.

Metzger wasn't sure but it appeared that something had struck a chord with him because he seemed to soften. Motioning the others to vacate the room, he pulled a desk chair up and rolled it across the floor positioning it in front of where Metzger was tied to the pole.

"Ever heard of 'pray away' the gay?" Kevin asked.

Metzger vaguely remembered watching an episode of *South Park* once about gay conversion therapy and he knew enough to know that people who were exposed to it were prone to increased mental-health issues like depression, low self-esteem, and suicidal behavior.

"Well, I'll tell you," Kevin said, "there wasn't much praying, but there was an awful lot of beating." He rolled his chair closer to Metzger. "When I was fourteen, my parents sent me away to a 'boys camp'—the Blessed Grace youth academy down in Georgia."

For the next twenty minutes, Kevin described the "camp," which was located in a remote part of the state, isolated, far away from prying eyes.

Drilled into his head that he was an abomination, that being gay was a sin, he was beaten with a belt and a bible with full written permission from his parents.

"The 'counselor' Mitch, had leather straps with names he'd given each of them, names like Mean Gladys and Twisty Spike and Elvis and Killboy," Kevin said. Each was different in thickness and weight and the level of pain it could efficiently administer. "They worked us hard all day, put us in isolation at night, and then made us sleep on the floor in our own piss."

At night, he said he spoke of hearing train whistles in the distance and dreaming of another life, somewhere safe, where he could just live, be who he was. A far cry from therapy, they eventually successfully broke him. He confessed his sins, admitted he was in fact not gay, never was, liked girls, loved Jesus, and so they let him go home.

"You joked about those silly Marvel comics," Kevin said, "but those characters saved my life." At home, damaged, defeated, he slipped into a world that he had control of; where he could pretend to be the hero, invincible. But when he got caught with a boy, his parents took his comics and games away. Threatening to send him back to the camp, he ran away for good. With help from friends, he was able to graduate from high school and college where he discovered he could time travel—another escape. He met Jackson and was hired by the Society.

Up until now Frank had sat silent and still, listening to Kevin's story, nodding when appropriate, hoping that by telling his story, being vulnerable, maybe he could reason with him.

"So your life was good then," Metzger suggested.

"It was," Kevin said spinning around a turn in his chair, "until it wasn't, until I got sick, and I couldn't go anywhere anymore, and nobody in this place gave a damn about that." His voice became louder, shrill, angry, bitter, someone who didn't know what to do with his anger.

"And not only that," he said, leaping to his feet and ranting at Metzger, "they were ruining it for everybody. I tried to tell them, to warn them, but would they listen? No, nobody cares what a lowly data technician down in the basement thinks!" Kevin was pacing back and forth now, agitated, on a tear. "I saw the anomalies—what are they calling them now? Dead zones—way, way before they ever did. And if they had just paid one iota of attention to me, found a cure for the sickness so I could travel again, none of this would have happened. I wouldn't have had to …"

"Murder two people?" Metzger finished his sentence.

Kevin stood still for a moment, saying nothing, staring at Metzger. His lips began to quiver, and Frank could see tears welling in his eyes.

In the shattered, childlike voice of someone who has been told his whole life that he did not deserve to exist, Kevin broke down and replied, "No! … Frank … YOU ARE THE BAD ONES, NOT ME. I thought this place was safe, but you fuck with people's lives." Kevin turned away and wiped his eyes with his sleeve, but Metzger could see the anger building again in Kevin's face. He opened his mouth to say something more when suddenly, a loud WHOOSH, and the computers in the basement began rebooting, whirring, starting up, every single one of the large monitors that lined the walls lit up at once like a meteor shower.

"What the hell?" Kevin cried as the computers began registering a series of loud bells and alarms and blips indicating that someone was traveling again.

"Nooo, no, this can't be happening," Kevin whined, the panic steadily rising. He turned to Frank and shouted, "I stopped time travel!"

"It's all over Kevin," Metzger said evenly. "Simon must have figured out how to turn it back on,"

"No one knows the frequency but me!" Kevin shouted like a toddler that isn't getting his way. "I'm the only one who knows the frequency!"

Moments later there was a loud bang and shouting outside the doors, and in a rush, Daguerreian Society security along with the police pushed into the room at once and grabbed Kevin. Handcuffing his hands behind his back, the arresting officer said, "You are under arrest for the murder of Brittany Kane and Joel Young, and the disappearance of Megan Parker."

Security untied Metzger, and he watched a subdued Kevin being escorted from the basement. "You have the right to remain silent," the officer recited the Miranda Rights. "Anything you say can and will be used against you in a court of law. You have a right to an attorney. If you cannot afford an attorney, one will be appointed for you."

23

Megan, the last volunteer intern Kevin sent into the double-exposed void was dead. Within the first hour she had lost her mind completely, and shortly after that she'd succumbed to fear-induced stress cardiomyopathy, literally dying from fright.

Florida man, Angus Hunter, who waded into the swamp to evade the police, became stuck in the murky waters and was later eaten by a hungry crocodile.

Thanks to quick-acting lifeguards, Emiliano Romero was scooped up just in time from the swirling eddy left behind by the monster wave. Miraculously, he suffered only a slight concussion from his surfboard hitting him in the head. He returned to his own time and vowed to take fewer risks.

Hours after many failed attempts to get back to his beautiful Emily, a distraught Thomas Mayfield, convinced that life was not worth living without his beloved, was found swinging from a rope tied to a wooden beam in his living room.

Although Maeve Stewart felt that London was a quite pleasant place to reside, she'd forgotten that her heart medication was not available to her in 1878. She later collapsed from a heart attack in a local store and died.

Evie Aaronson was arrested for being a subversive and sent to a labor camp. No documented record was ever found for her in Germany, and although relatives reported her missing, she never returned home to her Brooklyn, New York apartment. The kaffeehaus, later destroyed in WWII air raids, was never rebuilt.

After spending several days at Loretta's house in 1973, Imogen and Fletcher were finally able to come home.

⁕⁕⁕

Upon arrival in Imogen's kitchen Fletcher immediately went limp, slipping to the tiled floor as though his body was absent of any bones to hold him up. Imogen wasn't feeling well either, weird and dizzy and sort of confused, but she had enough foresight to grab the garbage can just in time to prevent Fletcher from throwing up all over the floor. She crumpled to the floor too and sat cradling his head as they both tried to adjust to their bumpy reentry.

Niles and Jade, watching TV in the living room, heard a commotion in the kitchen, jumped up and dashed toward the noise. Peering cautiously around the doorway, Jade behind him, they both screamed with surprise and joy. They were back! Simon had said he wasn't sure if they would ever return, but here they were.

"What is it, Niles?" Jade asked twisting around him to have a look. "Oh!" she gasped. Imogen and Fletcher lifted their heads to look up and Fletcher threw up again.

"Imogen!" Jade cried as she rushed over and put her arm around her shoulder. "Are you okay?" Niles placed his arm around Fletcher's waist and helped him to his feet.

"Bring the trash can," Fletcher managed to say as Niles guided him to the couch in the living room. Jade helped Imogen up and got her situated on the loveseat.

Jade rushed into the kitchen and returned with two tall glasses of cold water, handing them to Imogen and Fletcher who were both still struggling to catch their breath. Fletcher took a sip and hung his head over the trash can positioned between his legs. Still feeling light-headed and out of sorts, Imogen took a drink and dropped her head backward against the couch as Niles and Jade hovered over them concerned and wondering what more they could do to help.

After a few minutes, Imogen raised her head and took a second sip of water. She had been sick before when returning but never so discombobulated as she felt this time.

"Dad," she suddenly asked, "Have you seen Simon?"

Niles sat down beside her and took her hand. "He was here looking for you last week."

"You saw him?" Imogen asked, turning to face him.

"Uh, no," Niles faltered. "I wasn't here. I mean, he called me. I was in Detroit."

"Michigan?" Imogen was confused. "What were you doing in Detroit?" And then she realized that her friend Jade was there. "What are you doing here, Jade?"

Niles avoided her question and instead answered, "None of that is important right now. Simon wanted to know if you were traveling because he said the universe had collapsed or something and time travel had stopped, trapping people …"

"Yes, yes, that's right," Imogen interrupted excitedly. "We couldn't get back for days and days. We tried … but what did Simon say after that? Did you tell him we were stuck in San Francisco?"

"I told him, but I didn't know *when* you were there or anything and then he said he had to go and that was it."

⎍⎍⎍⎍⎍⎍

Exhausted, Imogen and Fletcher opted for naps. A few hours later, Imogen got up to go to the bathroom and noticed her dad sitting alone in the living room. "Dad?" she asked as she peeked into the room.

Niles set the book he was reading down. "Hey sweetie, you're awake. How are you feeling? Better?"

"A little," Imogen said. "Where's Jade?"

"She said she had some errands to run, she'd be back later."

"Oh, okay," Imogen said. "I'll join you in a sec."

A few minutes later, Imogen came back into the living room and sat down in a chair facing Niles.

"Would you like me to get you anything?" he asked. "Iced tea? I could make you some coffee."

"No, no thanks, Dad," she said. It would not be easy, but she knew that the conversation she had been dreading needed to happen, sooner rather than later.

"Dad, I have some news," she began, "about Mom." Judging by his daughter's serious tone Niles braced himself for the worst.

"Well, I'll just say it," Imogen said. "It turns out Loretta's book was based on Mom. She used to frequently travel to San Francisco to visit Loretta and another woman, around '64, '65, I think it was."

Imogen explained how Francis had initially gone back in the hopes of meeting photographer Imogen Cunningham. She did and they became friends and it was through her that she met Sylvie, who became her lover. Niles listened without changing expression or commenting, nodding every so often.

Imogen purposely skipped the parts she'd written about in her journal but did mention that Teddy had developed a crush on her. "Teddy," Niles muttered under his breath. It was the first time he had spoken.

"Yeah," Imogen continued, "Teddy." She paused a moment before beginning the next part. "He followed her back there and when he found out she was having an affair with a woman, he freaked out, I guess." The story tumbled out so fast now, Imogen barely took a breath between words. "She tried to get away from him. She got on her bike, and he chased her to Sutro Baths."

Imogen paused again before continuing. "It was the day Sutro Baths burned down. Teddy may have set the fire to cover it up." Niles drew in a heavy breath, trying not to let his mind conjure up images of what Teddy might have done to his wife.

"Loretta and Sylvie knew they couldn't report a man or a murdered woman from another time," Imogen said. She paused before delivering the last blow. "Sylvie reported Francis missing though. Loretta said they later found charred remains at the site, but they couldn't identify them."

Tears streamed down Imogen's cheeks as she finished the story. "I'm so sorry, Daddy," she cried, first reaching out for his hand but then rushing over to embrace him. They sat like that, the two of them together for a time, locked in their shared sorrow, wounded yet again by the same hateful person that had caused so much pain and grief to their family.

When Niles finally broke away, he said, "So that's why he destroyed both of our photos, he wanted to cover up what he'd done to her."

Imogen nodded. "Yes, I think so."

Imogen and Niles decided to get out of the house, take a walk, get some fresh air, talk things out, remember Francis. As they walked, Niles admitted that although he was surprised that it turned out to be a woman she was having an affair with, they had been experiencing a lot of problems. "Your mother was complicated. She hid her feelings, and I think she wanted more than I could offer her," he said sadly. "She loved books and music. She was a great photographer, and sometimes she could be really funny."

"Oh yeah?" Imogen said.

"I remember this one time telling her I wanted to catch a re-airing of *The Sound of Music* on cable TV and you know what her response was?"

"No, what?" Imogen asked.

Niles chuckled. "She said, 'Why don't you just turn on the stereo if you want to hear what music sounds like?'"

Imogen snorted. "Wow, corny, but actual proof there that she had a sense of humor!" Imogen stopped walking then, cocking her head to one side as though deep in thought. "A really random memory of Mom popped into my head just now," she said.

"What? What is it?" Niles asked.

"It's so weird," she said. "I think it might have been the very first time that I ever time traveled. "It's fuzzy because it was so long ago, but knowing now what happened to her, it makes more sense. I think I was about four and I was looking through Grammy's photo album. Remember that old one she had?"

Niles nodded. "Yes, of course I do."

"Well, I recall finding a picture of Mom standing on a beach, and the next thing I knew I was there ... in the picture. There was sand and I remember it smelled fishy like San Francisco. She looked down at me and the tips of our fingers touched. She seemed surprised to see me, but happy too, and she asked me what I was doing there and then it all faded away and I was back in Grammy's chair looking at the photo album again. I always thought it was just a dream I'd had, but now I think, it must have been real."

"And she was happy, you think?" Niles asked.

"Yeah," Imogen said. "I think she really was."

After dinner Niles and Fletcher retreated to the living room to watch TV as Jade finished loading the dirty dishes in the dishwasher.

Imogen sipped a cup of tea at the table. "You didn't have to do that, you know," she said.

"I know, but you cooked dinner," Jade said, and besides, I'm worried about you. You look a little pale."

Imogen patted her cheeks. "Not surprised. That return trip was a lot," she admitted. "I don't know if it was because of what happened with the whole time shutting down and then coming back on, but I could barely keep hold of Fletcher. It felt like we were being tossed around like a couple of socks in the spin cycle."

Jade was concerned about her friend. Not only pale, she looked tired, but she didn't want to pry. "Well, I'm glad you made it back safely," she said. "We were so worried about you."

The two sat in silence until it became uncomfortable, and they both started to speak at once. "You first," Jade prompted, amused. "Tell me how you're doing. Your dad told me a few things, but I'd like to hear it from you."

Imogen was still exhausted from the emotional conversation she'd had earlier with her dad. Having to deliver the news about what happened to his wife, her mother, was probably one of the hardest things she'd ever had to do. Yet, it had also been cathartic in a way. It would take a while for them both, but it was true what people said about closure. She was certain that it was what they both needed to move ahead in their lives, and yet, there were many lingering emotions.

"Is it horrible that I don't feel as sad about her as I should?" Imogen asked.

"Gen, you were nine when she disappeared," Jade said. "She's been gone a long time."

"I know, but most of my memories of her are not happy ones."

"What do you mean?" Jade asked. "I thought your parents were really happy together."

"They weren't, as it turns out, but ... it was me also," Imogen clarified.

"I remember her pushing me away, off her lap. 'You're a big girl now,' she said, 'too big for mommy's lap.' I guess I made creases in her skirt," Imogen said, sadness and longing creeping into her voice.

"I remember wrapping my arms around her waist, her peeling them off of me and walking away ... leaving me there wondering what I did wrong that my mother didn't like me enough to want to hug me." Jade frowned. "I wanted to love her," Imogen continued, "but she wouldn't let me in."

"Don't beat yourself up over it too much, Gen," Jade said. "Just because she was like that when you were nine, doesn't mean that she might have changed at some point in the future. You said yourself, you didn't know what was going on with her, and besides you barely had enough time together to build a relationship."

"Thank you," Imogen said. Having her dad and Jade back in her life was something she would never take for granted. Feeling emotional all of a sudden, she reached out and wrapped her arms around Jade. Jade leaned into her and squeezed back, hoping to give her friend just a little bit of what her mother could not. "You always know the right things to say to make me feel better," Imogen said.

Jade smiled at her friend. "That's what friends are for, right?"

Imogen took another sip of her tea and sighed. There was more to talk about. "What?" Jade asked.

"I suppose dad told you about Simon."

"That he's been gone for a while, yes," Jade said.

"Not just that, Jade, did he tell you about the baby?"

Jade nodded. "He said you miscarried."

Imogen tried to hold back tears, but her voice began to crack. "He didn't even know I was pregnant," she blurted.

"Oh Gen, I'm so sorry." Jade reached out again and took Imogen's hands in hers. The floodgates open, Imogen poured the story out to her friend.

"He never called," Imogen blubbered as wet, soppy tears dripped from her eyes. "Why didn't he call me Jade?"

Jade wasn't sure how to comfort her. She had only limited knowledge too about what Simon was doing in Chicago. The only thing she could think to say was, "Maybe they wouldn't let him. It's a 'secret' government society, right? I mean, who knows what crazy, stupid rules they had going on there."

Imogen wasn't really buying that explanation—he had his cell phone; he could have called—but Jade's theory seemed sort of probable. "You think so?" she asked.

Jade squeezed Imogen's shoulder. "Sure, honey," she reassured her. Jade listened mostly silently except to nod or offer a word of encouragement here and there as Imogen poured out her grief over the loss of her mother and the baby, how unexpectedly hard losing a baby would really be, how she grieved alone, without Simon, for a child they would never know.

"I can't put into words what it feels like," she confided, trying to hold back another round of tears. "Until it happens you don't understand how much love you have for this little person growing inside of you."

She told Jade about going to the community pool, how it had saved her, calmed her, but even though she'd managed to cope alone, she had concerns about her and Simon's future together. "I'm afraid it's my fault that he doesn't want to come home," Imogen said.

"What do you mean?" Jade asked.

"Ever since he came back with me from 1913, he talked about wanting to find his mother," Imogen said.

"And?"

"And basically, I blew him off. I was always caught up in things I was doing—sometimes what we were doing together. Mostly, I heard him saying it over and over, but I wasn't listening.

"I was crazy about him, sure, but at the same time, I was impatient with him. I wasn't prepared to stay in 1913 with him, yet when he came to my time, I expected him to just … I don't know … adjust… I guess. Even though I knew it had to be so overwhelming for him—cars, television, airplanes—all these things that I took for granted were completely new to him and I left him floundering, Jade. I expected my life to continue on as if nothing had changed, when the life of the person I claimed to love had been completely turned upside down."

"But he did adjust, didn't he?" Jade asked. "It seemed like when I visited that time he was doing okay."

"He was good at keeping it bottled up inside," Imogen said. "The truth is besides all that, we never got a chance to have a normal life together because every second it seemed like there was some kind of drama or distraction—Teddy, Mimi Pinky and Carl, and the court hearing, Dad coming back, and then the break-in at the pawn shop. And then he was just gone … whisked away to Chicago. Part of it was me, too, just being distracted by Kansas and all the different cases I took. I let him down, Jade."

"You were both going through a lot, Imogen," Jade said attempting to reassure her that she wasn't to blame for everything.

Imogen shook her head. "There's more," she said. "Fletcher and I slept together."

"You what?" Jade was surprised by this. "I always thought that the two of you were just good friends."

Imogen looked away, hung her head, feeling ashamed and guilty. "I'm not proud of it," she confessed, "but Fletcher, he's always been there for me, Jade, always. He has stuck by me through thick and thin," she said. "Honestly, with COVID and being pregnant and then the miscarriage, I don't know what I would have done without his patience and support."

Imogen continued. "We've always been friends, but we had a thing in college, and later on, he asked me to marry him."

"Wow. I didn't know that," Jade said, "but I'm glad he was there for you."

"He was," Imogen said. She began tracing the sentimental journey of memories they shared from their first meeting in college to how he'd been there for her when Grammy died, and they'd stayed up all night talking about science and history and literature and philosophy and their dreams for the future.

It started with a kiss, and then making love—how she adored him, but she was young and dumb and immature and foolish and unsure and unready, yet Fletcher hung in there, even after she had met Simon. He checked up on her.

"One night, he picked me up at the bar and took me home when I was roaring drunk and ranting about how much I missed Simon!" she said, chuckling at the memory.

He kept her secret about time travel. Brought her a white kitten named Luxe. She knew Fletcher wanted to hate Simon but was surprised how much he liked him and how they became friends. It had taken the pressure off her for him to have another friend besides her. And Fletcher was a very good friend to Simon. He risked his life to save theirs when the thieves broke into the pawn shop.

"During the COVID lockdown he entertained us. He was funny and sweet, and when I lost the baby, he took care of me, forced me to get up out of bed and eat and to go to the pool. He helped me through it without expecting a thing in return," she said.

Jade didn't mince her words. "You love him, don't you."

Imogen stared blankly, processing the truth of what Jade had said out loud. It dawned on her that, like Simon, she had brushed Fletcher's feelings aside in the very same way. Too busy chasing after the other shiny thing to notice the precious gem hiding in plain sight.

"Don't you see, Imogen. He was right there in front of you the whole time."

She did see and it worried her. "I think maybe I do … love him," she said. Maybe not in the whole fireworks, bombs bursting in the air way that it was with Simon, but in a different way, more like a slow burn kind of love, like a plot in one of Loretta's romance novels.

Imogen clutched Jade's hand. "How did you get so smart anyway?"

"Gosh, I don't know," Jade said.

"Okay, your turn now," Imogen changed the subject. "Why was Dad in Detroit and why are you here now?"

Jade looked away anxiously, taking a deep breath before responding. "So … well, Niles, your dad, and I were friends online," she began.

"Uh huh," Imogen said trying not to smile.

"And … well … " Deciding to just dive right into it Jade clapped both hands together and flatly stated, "Okay, we started chatting. Initially, I was curious about the time he spent with my mother and sister and me. I wanted to know more about my father and what happened, from Niles' … your dad's perspective.

"And then COVID hit," she said. "I was working from home, had a lot more time on my hands, and we started regularly emailing and chatting. And well, there was just so much going on, the masks, Black Lives Matter, protests, you know, it was such a crazy summer, and the more I got to know Niles … the more I liked him."

"He's old enough to be your father," Imogen responded. "You know that, right?"

Jade rolled her eyes. "eeee yeah, technically, yes, he is, but … but, chronologically, because of getting stuck in the loop, he's the same age as we are now. I caught up with him."

"True," Imogen conceded, "but …"

"But … he lost a lot of time, Imogen," Jade added. "He may be older, but I'm telling you, his mind is as sharp and curious as any thirty-two-year-old."

Imogen could see in Jade's eyes that she so wanted Imogen to understand and to accept their odd relationship. Yeah it was weird, but love is love even when it seems wrong or impossible and, what the heck, stranger things had happened in her own life.

"So …" Imogen said. "I'm just thinking, you know, that if you two get married that will make you my stepmother, right?"

"Oh my god!" Jade exclaimed, breaking into uncontrollable laughter, "you're right! How stupid weird is that?"

Imogen started to laugh too. "Pretty stupid weird!" she agreed.

24

Only vaguely aware of being awake before he opened his eyes, the first thing he felt was the cool sensation of a wet cloth pressed against his brow. Simon pulled himself up and stared into the face of a woman he did not know on a lumpy couch in an unfamiliar place. Startled, he instinctively grabbed her wrist. "Where am I? Who are you?" he demanded.

The woman didn't seem to be bothered or frightened. "I'm Dominique Flynn," she calmly replied. "You may call me Nikki."

Simon let go of her wrist, embarrassed he'd overreacted, and leaned back against one of the soft cushions. "Why am I here?" he asked.

"You ask a lot of questions, Mister Simon Le Bon Elliot," Nikki said.

"How do you know my name?"

Nikki set the cloth aside on the end table beside the sofa and said, "I've known about you a while."

Simon glanced around the high-ceilinged room he appeared to be in. The décor was ... interesting, he thought. Parisian-style, an odd assortment of rugs, plants, cushions, curtains, apparently of an earlier era.

"Alright," he said addressing this mystery person who had somehow plucked him from the dead zones and dropped him presumably in Paris, date unknown and knew all about him. "Perhaps we can start at the beginning. Last thing I remember I was in Austria. Now I am here. How ...?"

"You collapsed, passed out, and I brought you here, Simon," she said.

"Where is here?" he asked.

Nikki stood up and strode smoothly across the room to stand beside a large wooden cabinet along the wall. The black slacks and knit shirt she wore seemed to reflect a thirties or forties style, by Simon's estimation. What he hadn't noticed before was how incredibly stunning she was. It seemed clichéd—she was tall with impeccably quaffed shoulder-length hair, striking facial features—red lips, dark eyebrows, and the most unusual green eyes. A fleeting memory of a girl in a bookshop with eyes that color raced through Simon's mind. Now he was staring, but Nikki didn't seem to care. She stared right back at him as though accustomed to men gawking at her. From a silver case that was lying atop the bureau, she pulled out a cigarette and lit it, drawing the smoke in. She exhaled and as the puff of smoke escaped her lips, she replied, "Here is Paris."

"And the year ...?" Simon prompted.

"1937," she replied.

A recent but rather hazy memory triggered in his mind, of traveling, choppy seas, the green eyes, which sort of made sense now, and a message whispered. "Montparnasse, 1937?" he asked.

"Yes, that's right," she said.

"I saw you!" Simon said as the memory crystallized fully in his mind. He reflected back on the crazy trip to find the scientists, how he'd seen fleeting glimpses of people and places that he'd been to. Simon was confused though. He had never been to Paris before.

Nikki offered an answer. "Travelers sense other travelers that are nearby," she said. "I happened to be nearby."

"So you are a traveler then. Like me?" he asked.

"Yes," she replied, "very much like you."

"By that do you mean you can travel freely without a photo …"

"Yes, Simon. Like you, I was conceived in one time, born in another."

Simon took a minute to ponder this bit of information before speaking. "As I recall, you were with another woman," he said. She was older, wearing a shawl. Is she a traveler as well?"

Nikki blew out a puff of smoke and extinguished her cigarette in the ashtray. "No, but I know that she would very much like to meet you."

⁓⁓⁓

Simon followed Nikki down a narrow hallway where she pointed to a door on the left. Simon hesitated before lightly rapping on the closed door. A small voice from inside said, "Entrez vous."

Inside, a demure woman wrapped in a colorful silk dressing robe sat facing an elegantly carved mirror attached to a waterfall vanity. Her hair, a few silver strands poking out, was pulled up into a small bun and held in place by a jewel-encrusted butterfly shaped comb.

"Hello?" he inquired.

At the sound of his voice, the woman turned slowly around in her seat to face him. "Simon!" she cried. "It's you, my son, my baby." It took a moment to recognize this older version of the woman who had held him as a child, wiped his tears, made up stories to tell him, and protected him the best way she knew how. Overcome with sudden emotion, Simon rushed forward to her.

Kneeling in front of her, he wrapped his arms around her resting his head in her lap. "Mama," he cried.

"My darling sweet boy," she said.

〰〰〰

After their emotional reunion, Tiffany guided Simon back to the living area. They had much catching up to do. It was a long story, but for Simon, it all began with Imogen.

"I met a woman," he began. "She was from the future too, like you, and we fell in love. Her name was Imogen Oliver," he said.

"Imogen, an unusual name," Tiffany said. "It is vaguely familiar to me. I remember hearing of someone by that name many, many years ago."

"It should. She is Niles Oliver's daughter," Simon said.

"The photographer?"

"Yes."

"He took my senior portraits. She was just a little girl then, as I recall." Tiffany was curious. "And what does Imogen look like now?"

"She has curls like you mother, blue-gray eyes, a small gap between her teeth, and a smile that lights up the room."

Tiffany smiled at his description, but then seemed to remember something. "It's funny, I seem to recall an odd encounter once with a woman that fits that description, at the mercantile, when you were just a baby Simon. I was pushing you in an old straw-woven stroller. Without a husband, I was a bit of a pariah in that town."

Tiffany chuckled even though Simon was certain it was likely a painful memory for his mother. "Anyway, this girl, she noticed you and complimented me, said that you were prettier than the 'Gerber' baby, which I thought was an odd thing to say at the time, but then this rather large woman with a huge hat approached me in the store, pointed at you, and asked me if this was my 'bastard child.'"

Simon cringed hearing that word. "Oh, my," he said, thinking, so that's where it had started; later on, the children at school had mercilessly taunted him with the slur.

"At any rate, I'd never seen her before or ever again after that, strange because it was quite a small town in those days, and well, the Gerber baby didn't exist in advertising until much later."

"I can't tell you if it was Imogen," Simon replied. "It could have been. She traveled a lot, as did both of her parents."

"Shortly after I met Imogen ... " Simon hesitated. "I met my father."

"Your father?"

"Yes, Teddy Diamond."

"Oh." Tiffany's face paled at the mention of his name. "I have not thought of Te ... *him*, in years, she said. "That makes sense that he knew your Imogen. Teddy worked for Mr. Oliver. That's where I met him. He must have learned how to travel from him."

"Niles did not teach him," Simon said. "He was spying on the Olivers."

Tiffany sighed. "Of course he was, the toad," she hissed with disgust. "I never told you the truth about what happened, Simon, and when I'm through I will never speak of it, nor say his name again," she said.

"He raped me," she blurted, "and when I told him I was pregnant, he blamed me for it. Besides Herbert, I've never told anyone that." She pulled a handkerchief from her pocket and dabbed at the corners of her eyes.

Simon was sure that Teddy could not be any viler, but it distressed him to know that his cruelty went even beyond what he knew. He took his mother's hand in his and gently squeezed it. "He'll never hurt you again, mother, I promise."

"How do you know," she asked.

Simon told her the parts of the story that she didn't know, how Niles had found some of the photos she had left for someone to find and confronted Teddy and that in a panic that he could be caught, he destroyed Niles and Imogen's mother's anchor photographs, trapping them in the past as she was.

Tiffany was distraught. "Oh mercy, I knew he was dangerous, but I had no idea he would hurt anyone else."

He explained how when Teddy discovered that Imogen could time travel, he was afraid that she might figure out what he had done to her parents and started tracking her through time. "He followed her back to 1913, where I was," Simon explained. "That's when we met and fell in love. We also met Herbert and learned your story."

He told her how they stopped Teddy from killing Imogen but when he traveled back home, she followed him and that's when Simon tagged along.

"We cornered him at his mother's house, and he escaped through another photograph," Simon said. "But we believe he is dead."

"How can you be sure?" Tiffany asked.

"The photograph was of a beach in Bikini Atoll, where in 1954 they were testing the atom bomb. It's not likely that he survived the blast," Simon said. "Nothing there did."

They sat in pained silence for a minute or so as Tiffany processed it. "Good," she said finally. "I'm glad he's dead. And we shall never speak of him again." Simon smiled and patted her hand. "And you, going to live in the future," she added. "It's redemption in a way—you getting to live the life that Teddy stole from me."

Hoping to lighten the mood after talking about Teddy, Simon asked, "So you knew back then about television and airplanes and history, all the things and you never once told me?"

"How could I explain something like that to you Simon? You were a child. I was desperate to get home, that's all I could think about. I wasn't even sure that if someone from the future actually did come and rescue me that they could bring me back or that I could take you with me, but hope was the only thing I had to cling to, and I paid dearly for speaking about it, that's why Herbert had me committed. I nearly died for speaking my truth."

"He deeply regretted his actions, mother. We spoke of it. You were his friend, and he felt that he betrayed you."

"He did betray me."

"He didn't want to."

"It doesn't matter now."

He was hesitant to ask her, but he had to know. "What happened to you? At Crestview?"

"It was hell," Tiffany said without hesitating. "There were shock treatments, straightjackets, solitary confinement, rotten food, bad smells ... so many bad smells, but as bad as it was," she continued, "I made friendships. And they had books, a library. I found escape in books. For a few years I retreated into the stories. I no longer spoke of the future. It helped me cope with confinement, but then I met some, what you might call, militant patients. They spoke of the unhealthy conditions and the unfair treatment. I became anxious and more vocal again and it got me into trouble. Dominique rescued me before I was to be lobotomized. That is how I ended up here, safe."

The graphic images of the atrocities his mother endured in the sanitarium made Simon feel nearly physically ill. He turned to her and said, "I'm here now and all that pain is behind you. I'll take you back to your time, or any time you want. I can rescue you finally," he said, his voice starting to crack.

"Simon," Tiffany said, turning and looking into his pleading eyes. "Son, you don't understand. For years, decades, I longed for this day, for someone from the future to show up and take me home, but the truth is, I no longer want to be rescued. That place, in the future, is nothing but an old memory. It's not home anymore. This is my home now. I like it here. In this time. I have friends. I've made my peace with the past, I forgive Herbert. I may even eventually find mercy for Teddy, I think. Because if things had been different, I wouldn't have you and I might not have ended up here where I'm supposed to be."

"But this isn't where you're supposed to be, Mother," Simon asserted. "It's not safe here. You must know that you cannot stay beyond 1940. Paris will fall to the Nazi occupation!" He paused before saying, "You're supposed to be with me, your son." He was weeping now. Years of longing for his mother's touch, dozens of pent-up emotions spilling like a waterfall over a steep cliff. Tiffany tenderly comforted her son again, letting him cry it out.

〰〰〰

The three of them—Tiffany, Simon, and Nikki sat at the bistro-size table on the balcony enjoying morning tea and a freshly baked batch of croissants Lili had whipped up for them in the kitchen. Nikki had been retelling the story of how she was able to extract Tiffany from the sanitarium in the nick of time.

"And you say you read about the patient uprising at Crestview?" Simon asked Nikki.

"Yes, that is correct," she answered.

Simon was interested in how she was able to travel freely without being detected. When he had done multiple jumps, apparently it had set off all kinds of alarms at the Society.

"Have you heard of the Daguerreian Society?" he asked.

Nikki, who Simon noticed was dressed informally today in a pair of trousers and a loosely fitting cardigan sweater, casually recrossed her legs.

She reached over and picked up the silver case, removed a cigarette from it and lit it before responding.

"Yes, Simon, I am aware of the Society people."

Simon was surprised. "You are?"

"Yes," she said, leaning back coolly.

"And are they aware of you?" he queried.

Nikki set her cigarette down in the ashtray and said, "They've never contacted me, no."

"And how can that be?" Simon inquired.

"I suppose I fly under their radar," she said coyly.

Simon was both intrigued and conflicted and he felt incredibly attracted to her. "Tell me more," he said, leaning in and turning on a bit of the old Simon Le Bon charm.

Tiffany patted Simon's hand as she rose from the table.

"Mother, where are you going?"

"I'll leave you two to chat," she said as she got up and retreated inside.

When she was gone, Simon looked over at Nikki and asked, "Do you think you can convince her to come back with me?"

"No, I'm afraid not. Your mother has a bit of a stubborn streak."

"I know," Simon agreed, raising his eyebrows.

"Don't worry though," she said. "You can visit her whenever you like and keep an eye on things from afar."

"But you'll be here with her, right?" Simon asked.

Nikki shook her head. "No, I can't stay ... I ...?

For the first time in a long while, Simon felt a flutter of something like anticipation stirring inside him. Not only that, but months and months of trying to get Imogen to at least make an effort to find his mother, it occurred to him that this woman had risked everything to save her.

"Come back with me then," he suggested on impulse, "to the Daguerreian Society."

"No ... oh, no." Nikki insistently shook her head. "Why would I do that?"

"Because you're like me," Simon said. We may be the only two people on the planet that can travel without having to be tethered to an anchor, even when time is shut down. Someone just tried to end time travel. He nearly succeeded. If I hadn't been able to do what I do, millions of people would still be trapped. The two of us ... together ... we ... "

"So, what are you saying?" Nikki asked.

"I don't know," he said, retreating, shaking his head, frustrated by an unexpected inability to express himself. He didn't know why he was asking a complete stranger; someone he'd only just met to go with him. He didn't know her, didn't know anything about her ... and yet, he wanted to. It was like the universe was urging him to do so. No, he argued with himself. It was crazy. Dumb. He loved Imogen and she loved him ... she did, didn't she?

"Look," he said, "I know this whole thing is weird for you and we just met, but ... well, you see, I have a life with someone in Oregon," he confessed.

"I expected that you probably did, Simon," she said, "but so do I, except my life is in New York."

Simon grimaced, embarrassed. What a fool he was for assuming that she wouldn't also have a life of her own. Of course, she would.

Nikki placed her hand on Simon's. "Listen, how about this? I'll go with you." She nodded her head back and forth as if she herself couldn't believe what she was agreeing to and lowered her eyes. " ... if you'll first go someplace with me. Will you come with me?"

Simon stood up, paced, put his hands in his pockets. "um ... okay, sure, of course."

"Let's go."

"Right now?"

"Sure," she said. "You know how time works, Simon. We can stay as long as we want, get to know each other better. When we return, it will be as though no time has passed at all. Your mother won't even notice that we were gone."

25

They arrived outside a Brooklyn walk-up in present-day New York. Nikki led Simon up the stairs, inside the building, and down a hall to apartment 107.

"This is where I live, well some of the time. I'm a bit of a nomad," she explained as he peeked into the kitchen, and poked his head into the other rooms. The apartment was small, sparsely decorated, clearly functional but with only the bare necessities, like a hotel room designed for people who came and went often. A second room served as her office complete with a desk, computer, two large monitors. "This is where I work," she said, adding, "I have apartments that I keep elsewhere too, in other times, places that I can go to when I need time to slow down. I'd like to take you to one of those places."

It shouldn't be this easy for a strange woman to just lead him around to parts and places and times unknown Simon thought, but for some reason, he didn't mind. It felt right and he truly wanted to know more about her.

"So, where to next?" Simon asked.

Nikki smiled. "You'll see."

The warmth of the sun and a slight breeze welcomed Simon and Nikki to Neptune Beach, Florida, a small, quiet coastal community nestled on the northeast coast of Florida between Atlantic Beach and Jacksonville Beach.

Nikki let go of Simon's hand and took a moment to take in and admire his outfit. "You look great," she said approvingly. Simon's attire had transitioned to a cool bark cloth Hawaiian shirt, white trousers, and a pair of brown leather Huaraches.

"So do you," Simon said, smiling at Nikki in her breezy sleeveless sun dress, sunglasses, and wide-brimmed straw hat with a yellow ribbon.

"So, where are we?" Simon asked.

Nikki pointed to the yellow beach cottage where they stood. "This is my house." The cottage, complete with shutters, a window box filled with flowers, and a picket fence, could not be any less charming. Simon figured they must be close to a beach. He could smell the salty air. Simon would soon learn that it was 1950 and this house in was just a few blocks from the Atlantic Ocean.

"Come," she said, taking Simon's hand and leading him up the wooden stairs to a small porch.

Inside, exposed beams, vaulted ceilings, and hardwood floors, a braided rug made the cottage feel warm and beachy and cozy. As far as furniture and décor, it had a minimalist quality, Simon noticed, that is, unless you overlooked the built-in shelves filled with hundreds of books. There were a few well-placed art pieces on the wall, a typewriter on a desk, and over in one corner of the room, a record player with a pile of albums stacked next to it.

When she saw him looking at the records, she walked over to it. "What music do you like to listen to, Simon? jazz, blues, pop?" Before he could answer, she had already selected a record from the pile, put it on the turntable, aligned the tonearm, and placed the needle down on it. The cool jazz groove of Charlie Parker's "Summertime" filled the small living room.

She turned and as she walked away, said, "I don't have anything here in the house for us to eat. We'll have to go to the market, but I'd like to change into something a bit more comfortable first."

While she was gone, Simon got up and browsed her book collection. At a glance, he could see that her tastes ran the gamut from fiction to nonfiction, literary to contemporary. Faulkner and Hemingway, Wellek's *Theory of Literature*, Henry Miller's *Death of a Salesman*, *Being and Nothingness* and *Existentialism*, by Jean-Paul Sartre, Kerouac's *The Town and the City*; and *The Natural Superiority of Women* by Ashley Montague. In addition, there were dozens of poetry books written by Robert Frost, Ezra Pound, William Carlos Williams, e.e. cummings, T.S. Eliot, Wallace Stevens, and others.

Nikki returned a few minutes later wearing a pair of lime-green pedal pushers and a striped top. At the market, they picked up provisions for dinner and on the walk back Nikki took Simon for a stroll along the exquisite white sand beach. Simon removed his huaraches and let the soft sand squish between his toes. As they walked, in the distance, Simon noticed bright lights emanating from the area.

"What is that light in the distance?" he asked.

"Oh, that's the boardwalk at Jacksonville Beach. There's a Ferris wheel and a Merry-Go-Round, a promenade with games and hot dogs and cotton candy. All that," she said. "We can go if you'd like."

Simon shook his head. "No, not tonight. I think I'd rather go back to your place and eat and maybe pop open that bottle of wine you bought."

⎍⎍⎍⎍⎍⎍

After dinner, Simon and Nikki went out on the porch and sat down together in the swing to drink their wine and stargaze.

Simon took a sip from his glass as they gently rocked back and forth in tandem. "This is nice," Simon said. "Do you spend a lot of time here?"

"hmmm, when I can," Nikki said. "I come here when I need to recharge."

"Why here?"

"I grew up here."

"Here, in Neptune Beach?"

"No, in Miami," she said. It was getting dark and cooling off, and Nikki shivered.

"Are you cold?" Simon asked.

"A little, would you mind grabbing my sweater from inside, on the chair?" Simon went inside and returned with the sweater and draped it around her shoulders.

Nikki settled back against the swing. "My mother is a traveler," she began. Simon listened as she told him when her mother, Emily was in her twenties she had been married to a violent man. Pregnant and fearing for herself and the life of her unborn child, she escaped to another time in the past.

"She went to 1958 to live with my Aunt Olivia, mother's sister, in Miami," Nikki explained. Olivia, who could also travel, apparently met her Cuban husband Camilo there and had decided to stay. "It was safe for mother there and that is where I was born."

"What year did your mother depart from, if I might ask?" Simon said.

"Twenty thirteen," Nikki answered.

"Ah," Simon responded. "I was conceived in 1997 but was born in 1885, which makes you a bit of an old soul too then? Like me."

Nikki acknowledged their shared experience. "Yes, I suppose I am," she said, pausing a moment to smile at him before resuming her story.

"I grew up in Miami but when I was eighteen, mother and I decided to return to 2013 for me to attend nursing school. I wanted to heal people, but I found another way to help," she said. "As you know, as a child of two timelines, I discovered I could travel freely, forward and backward without a photograph as an anchor. I decided to try to help people escape from bad situations."

"I'm a bit confused though," Simon said. "If you could help people this way, why did you not help my mother when she was abandoned in 1885? I'm sure they must have posted publicly, a missing person report."

"I'm sure they did," Nikki said, "but even if there had been something in the paper about her being missing, I still would have had no way of knowing where to look for her."

Simon nodded, understanding. "Oh yes, that's true."

"But ... when I read that there would be a patient uprising at Crestview in 1940, I knew that I could travel there, pose as a nurse, save her and others, and take her back to the safe house in 1930."

"And I am so grateful that you did," Simon said, followed by a puzzled look. "Why didn't I know that I could do this?"

"I don't have an answer," Nikki said, "other than that perhaps it's because you were not raised around other travelers as I was growing up."

"I want to show you something." She removed a pair of pair of tortoise shell eyeglasses from her pocket and unfolded a piece of paper—a newspaper story chronicling the abuses at Crestview.

Simon lurched forward suddenly, startling her. "Oh my god, it's you!" he said. "You're Abby with the green eyes ... from the bookshop back home in Portland. You helped me find a book of poems!"

Nikki sighed. "I am," she confessed. She had not intended to go into this part of her story yet. The last thing she wanted to do was scare him away thinking she had been stalking him, but the cat was out of the bag. "That time in the bookstore was not the only time we met. I had a feeling. There was something about you, that you were, as you say, another old soul, like me."

"Not the first time? What do you mean? We've met other times, too?" Simon asked.

"Travelers are drawn to one another, Simon. I was drawn to you and I ... " She looked away, embarrassed. "I watched you from afar. I suspected you might be a traveler, but I wasn't sure and, of course, I had no idea that we shared the common element of being conceived in one time, born in another." She looked down at her hands in her lap. "I'm sorry."

Simon lifted her chin, forcing her to look up and make eye contact with him. "Don't ever be sorry, Nikki. I'll never regret meeting you. How could I? You saved my mother's life. You saved my life, for gods sake! I shudder to think what might have happened to me if you hadn't followed me to the dead zone." As he looked into her eyes and she looked back at him, in that moment, something potent passed between them. Simon felt something shift inside him. It troubled him and he pulled back, stumbling over his words. "Uh, I'll go get some more wine," he said as he got up from the porch swing and disappeared inside the house.

Over the next few days, they spent hours talking about books, art, music, travel, history, listening to records, drinking more wine, and getting to know one another.

One night as they sat together on a blanket laid out on the sand gazing at the horizon, the light from the moon reflecting off the crashing waves of the Atlantic, creating a magical, surreal sort of moment, Nikki leaned her head against Simon's shoulder and sighed. "I could stay like this forever."

Simon felt the same. The last few days with Nikki had been superb, it was a rush to finally find someone who understood him, someone with whom he felt so comfortable. He tried to avoid making comparisons between Nikki and Imogen, but it was becoming abundantly clear that his life with Imogen stood in stark contrast with what he imagined life with Nikki could be. With Imogen, life was a constantly changing landscape. Sure, it had been fun and exciting at times, but also extremely frustrating. From what he could tell so far, Nikki was the embodiment of calm. He felt completely relaxed in her company. He didn't feel like he was on pins and needles all the time, always afraid of saying something that could be misunderstood. But even more than that, there was an instant connection. They clicked. The things he wanted, the dreams he had, seemed to gel with hers.

He burrowed his feet into the soft sand and looked up into the starry skies. "We have to go back soon," Simon said.

"I know," Nikki answered in a voice filled with sad.

"Tomorrow."

"Okay."

26

After several protracted rounds of tearful goodbyes and promises to come back and visit soon, Simon and Nikki left Tiffany behind in Paris 1937 to return to present day Daguerreian headquarters in Chicago. First stop: Hostin's office to meet with Metzger and the doctor to be briefed on what had transpired during Simon's time in the dead zones.

"Great work," Hostin and Metzger said at the same time, congratulating Simon when he came in.

Simon savored the respect and kudos coming from his colleagues. "I'd like you to meet Dominique Flynn," he said as Nikki followed him into the office. Nikki shook hands with both men, and they sat down. "Nikki is a traveler," he said, "like me."

Hostin's eyebrows shot up. "Like you? ..." he asked. "In what way?"

"As in, the *same* as me," Simon clarified. "She can travel to multiple places without restrictions, without an anchor photograph."

"Really?" Hostin said, pursing his lips and cocking his head sideways. "Interesting. "May I ask how you two happened to meet?"

"Ms. Flynn saved my life," Simon explained. He briefed them on his journey to the dead zones to find the right frequency to reopen the door to time travel that Kevin had managed to close. He described the barely audible low humming that he detected even though everything else had shut down, but it wasn't until he helped a couple of boys disentangle their barrel hoops that he was able to make the connection of time being a circle which got him thinking about pairs and double-exposed photos and his origin—as a child of two alternate times. As he concentrated, his body physically began to work as a sort of tuning fork until it landed on the correct frequency that turned time travel back on.

"When it came back on, the high-pitched sound from before came back, as did all the incoming and outgoing travelers," he said. "Unfortunately, it took a toll on me physically. I must have passed out and the next thing I knew I woke up on a couch in 1937 Paris to this woman, who also reunited me with my mother." He gestured to Nikki and smiled warmly at her. After Simon had finished his report, it was Nikki's turn to speak. She filled them in briefly on her backstory, how she had also straddled two different times and had been using her unique ability to rescue people in dire, life or death situations.

"If you'll excuse me for interrupting," Metzger said, "but when we first discovered Simon, all kinds of bells and whistles and alarms went off here at the Society. If what you're saying is true, how did you manage to fly under our radar all this time?"

Nikki shrugged her shoulders. "I'm sorry, but I really don't have an answer, I can't say why I was never detected."

"A regular power couple, you two make," Hostin said, grinning.

Clearly uncomfortable by Hostin's wildly inappropriate observation, Simon quickly switched topics. "So, what happened to Kevin?" he asked, looking over at Metzger.

"Kevin was arrested," Metzger said.

"How did you get to him?" Simon asked.

"Well, I had this idea that I'd go down to the basement, you know where he used to work and just poke around a bit, see if I could figure out a way to negotiate with him if I could get near him and some of his lackeys caught me and tied me up. They called Kevin and he came down from the upstairs suite where he was holed up and …"

Hostin wasted no time chiming in, "And Metzger's butt-dial saved the day!"

"Huh?" Simon asked.

Metzger explained that while he was negotiating with Kevin, he was sitting on his phone which was in his back pants pocket and he inadvertently butt-dialed another agent, who was able to track his phone and notify the police.

Simon laughed along with them, but then became serious again. "I'd like to talk to him, to Kevin, if I could?" he said.

"You can later," Hostin said, "but first you need to come with me."

Simon, Nikki, and Metzger dutifully followed him as he led them upstairs to the suite located on the top floor. Hostin pushed open the large conference room door and ushered Simon into a room full of all the Society's board members, standing and applauding him.

Simon was not expecting this at all. "What's all this?" he said, confused and unsure why he was the recipient of such overwhelming adoration. After the clapping subsided, a smiling Josie Mendoza, Daguerreian Society president approached Simon and reached out to shake his hand.

"On behalf of the Society, we'd like to sincerely thank you for your contributions, Simon," she said, which brought about another rousing round of applause. She gestured to Simon and the others to join them at the long conference table.

"Going into the dead zone alone, putting your life at risk for members of the Society as well as for the benefit of tens of thousands of travelers who were stranded out there, was a completely selfless act of bravery," Mendoza gushed. "We can't thank you enough, Simon."

Unaccustomed to this level of praise, Simon simply nodded and tried to hide his discomfort as everyone clapped some more. Thankfully, she directed her focus away from Simon to address the group.

"In response to the recent security breach and the senseless murders of three innocent people, the Daguerreian Society is proposing plans to implement a completely new and more secure structure of operation that will ensure that people like Kevin McCord will never be able to tamper with time frequency again.

Rather than simply monitoring travelers, the Society will no longer be in the shadows as we plan to not only oversee time travel but to regulate it as we would "normal" travel via the issuance of passports. Our newly obtained information on time, frequency, and dead zones will provide our researchers with the tools to effectively activate time travel capabilities in everyone as well as greatly minimize associated side effects such as time sickness.

Finally, in an effort to reverse the damage in the dead zones, we plan to close off those areas to tourists indefinitely."

When she had finished speaking and the clapping died down, Mendoza turned once again to address Simon.

"Simon, as we move forward with these big changes, we'd like you to be part of the planning and implementation. As such, we are pleased to offer you a permanent position here at the Society."

Again, Simon was flattered by all the attention he was receiving. From lowly school principal to power position in the Daguerreian Society, wow, who would have thought such a thing could ever happen to the likes of him? Humbled and unprepared for it, his immediate instinct was to give others the credit.

Simon arose from his seat and said, "Thank you, Ms. Mendoza."

"Josie. Please call me Josie," she interposed.

"Uh ... Josie," he continued. "Again, thank you for ... all this. I appreciate your offer but I'm afraid I cannot accept ... " A collective gasp erupted in the room. " ... your offer," he continued, " ... unless it includes my colleague." Simon turned to Nikki urging her to stand up.

Shocked by Simon's public acknowledgment Nikki hesitantly rose from her seat and nodded meekly at the assemblage. "Um ... hello," she said.

"Like me, Dominique Flynn is also a multiple jump traveler," Simon said, "and where I go, I would like for her to go, too."

⎯⎯⎯〰️⎯⎯⎯

They both were feeling slightly giddy when they exited the meeting room together. "Oh my goodness," Nikki gushed. "What have you done?" she asked as she playfully poked Simon's side.

Metzger and Hostin were jubilant and pleased as well. "What do you say we all go grab a cocktail!" Hostin suggested.

Nikki looked at Simon. "Sure," he said, "that sounds great, but just give me a second, okay. I need to make a call."

Simon pulled out his phone and broke away from the group. Nikki pretended not to watch him as he nodded his head up and down in response to the person on the other end that she knew was Simon's partner Imogen.

"I'm coming home," Simon said into the phone, "but I have one last thing I need to take care of."

Over drinks, it was decided that Nikki would temporarily stay in Simon's suite at headquarters.

"Are you sure it will be all right?" she asked, concerned that he was making arrangements without the necessary permission.

"It will be fine," Simon assured her. "I promise I'll be back soon." He felt awful making any promises without knowing first how things would go with Imogen, but he had to say something.

They had discussed this. Nikki knew that Simon had unfinished business with Imogen, and there was always the chance that he would decide to return to his life. She wasn't altogether prepared for that scenario, but she hoped for the best even though he was the one after all who had gotten her swept up into this whole "she's with me" job thing at the Society.

Metzger had offered to take Nikki to the suite and Hostin was planning to drive Simon over to the jailhouse to meet with Kevin, but Simon pulled her aside.

"I'm truly sorry for dragging you into all this, Nikki," he said, apologizing again and touching her shoulder.

"Simon," Hostin called out, "c'mon if you want a ride to the jailhouse!"

Nikki leaned forward and gave Simon a gentle peck on the cheek. "We'll figure it all out," she said.

〰〰〰

Hostin and Simon chatted casually as they headed downtown to the Chicago PD. "How do you reckon they're going to regulate time travel?" Simon asked.

"I don't know, honestly," Hostin answered. "It's going to require a lot of work; I know that much."

"It seems like a huge undertaking." Simon thought about his mother and others who had decided to remain in the past. Would they be able to return if they wanted to? There were so many unanswered questions. He sighed and replied, "Well, I hope it will all work out."

Hostin turned into the parking garage. "We shall see," he said, "we shall see."

Inside the jail, Simon was led to a small room with two chairs separated by a table. A few minutes later, Kevin, wearing a neon orange jumpsuit, was led into the room by a guard who uncuffed him, instructed him to sit down in the chair opposite Simon, then walked over and stood next to the door.

Simon didn't waste any time asking him, "Why did you do it, Kevin?"

"Why would I tell you?" Kevin mumbled without emotion.

"Was it worth it?" Simon demanded.

Kevin looked bored. "It was science," Kevin answered, "and that's all."

Simon leaned back in his seat, placed his hands on the table, and spilled it. "You're a bad man, Kevin."

His face remained unchanged. "But I'm really not," Kevin said calmly, although Simon noticed his eye twitching a bit.

"You murdered people," Simon countered.

"Not intentionally."

"But you did kill them, Kevin." A violent image of Brittany's mangled body sprawled across the bloody laboratory floor flashed through Simon's mind, and he struggled to temper the anger he felt. "Don't you feel any remorse at all, for their families, not to mention the countless others who perished because of your actions?"

"Oh, don't be so dramatic, Simon," Kevin answered nonchalantly. "I do care. Contrary to popular belief, I'm not a monster."

With that, Simon was done. He shook his head in disgust, got up, and headed toward the door to be let out.

"I should be Captain America," Kevin said, " ... not you."

Confused, Simon turned back and looked at Kevin. "Captain? ... Who?" he asked.

Staring straight ahead, Kevin answered, "Why, Captain America, of course, only the best and most noble hero in the entire Marvel universe." And then, as if he was lost in a daze, he slowly turned his head, looked directly at Simon, and speaking in a dull, emotionless, eerie voice, said, "It should have been *me*, Simon ... *me*. I was trying to make it right again."

Simon gestured to the guard to let him out immediately and left without looking back.

27

Simon lingered for a moment at the curb before heading across the lawn to the porch, gazing at this house that he had called home, a place that always felt comfortable and warm and welcoming the way a home should. He knew Imogen would be inside waiting. Her car was parked in the driveway.

He sighed and pushed the door open, entering the foyer to Imogen waiting for him under the archway, arms crossed.

"Hi," he said, awkwardly handing her a bouquet of flowers he'd hastily picked up at the supermarket before coming over. "I'm sorry I missed your birthday."

"It's not all you missed," Imogen said, getting right to it. "Why didn't you call?"

He had hoped she wasn't upset, but the fact that she wasn't welcoming him home with open arms wasn't entirely unexpected. "They wouldn't let me," he said in his defense. "They took my phone; said they didn't want me to be distracted. Turns out they were more security conscious than they let on." Imogen rolled her eyes. He hated it when she did that.

"Distracted, huh?" Imogen replied sardonically as she turned around and stomped into the kitchen to find a vase for the flowers. Simon watched her rummage through a cupboard looking for one suitable for the bouquet. Becoming agitated when she couldn't find one, tossed the bundle of flowers into the sink and covered her face with her hands to obscure her tears and frustration.

"Oh Imogen," Simon said, rushing over and pulling her into her arms. He hated to see her unhappy. It was the last thing he wanted to do, but the more he tried to console her, the more she cried.

Still, she stood stiffly, her arms at her side, hesitant to reciprocate Simon's embrace. Simon loosened his arms from around her, stepping back to look at her.

"What's wrong, Imogen? I know it's been a long time. What can I do to make things right?" he pleaded.

She pursed her lips, measuring her words carefully before speaking. "It's just …"

"It's just what?" Simon asked.

"It's just that you come back here after being gone for months and you act as if nothing has happened, that nothing has changed."

"Much indeed has happened," Simon admitted, "but tell me, what has changed between you and me?"

She could feel her emotions overriding any rational thought and the words came tumbling out before she could stop them. "I needed you and you weren't there for me!"

Under attack, Simon lashed back at her. "Well, I could say the same. You've never been there for me, Imogen ... ever!"

"What the hell are you talking about Simon?" Imogen was mad, really mad now. "I've done nothing but coddle you. Ever since you came back here with me, I've been there for you, helping you adjust, being patient with you during your depression, and through all the times you were sad and frustrated. I always tried to be there, always, Simon!"

Simon appreciated all that Imogen had done for him, but he didn't realize until now how much she resented it and likewise, in the heat of the moment, his feelings bubbled to the surface and spilled over.

"Well, if you were so patient and understanding, like you say, then why didn't you *ever* offer to help me find my mother?"

Imogen let out a gasp. "Your mother?"

"Yes, my mother! I asked you, begged you repeatedly to help me find her and you always had other things to do, some excuse for not being able to do it. I have a case, I have to deal with *my* feelings, me, always me," he mimicked her words. "Fletcher even asked me why you didn't offer to help ..."

"Fletcher!" Imogen roared. "What business of it was his?" She was so angry right now she could strangle both of them. And then, she leveled the bombshell. "I had a miscarriage, Simon."

This news he was *not* expecting. It felt like she had sucker-punched him, and his face revealed every bit of the shock and anguish that suddenly exploded inside him. "I

... I don't know what to say," he stumbled. "Oh my god, Imogen, I didn't know you were pregnant ... I would not have gone had I known."

She immediately regretted her words; wished she could take them back. This was not how she had wanted to tell him, but in her stupid, stupid rage she knew this news would wound him in the worst way possible. His reaction said it all. Tears began to stream down Simon's cheeks.

He bent over, gutted, his hands over his face, weeping, grieving the loss of their child for the first time. She had time to come to terms with it, of course, but this was a shock for him. She instinctively reached out to comfort him, wrapping her arms around him and holding him, full of remorse for losing control.

"I didn't know, Imogen," he sobbed. "I would have come home; you know I would have."

"I know you would have," she consoled him, gently caressing his head with her hands. "I'm so, so sorry, Simon." They stood together like that in the kitchen for a while, tears streaming and mingling together, clinging to the other as they grieved as one.

Hours passed. They cried. They listened as each talked. Imogen told him about finding out she was pregnant shortly after he had left and that she was excited to tell him, but the weeks went by with no word from him and then COVID hit, and they were quarantined, but that it had also provided her much-needed time to reconnect with her dad.

Simon described arriving at headquarters, how they had set him up in a fancy suite and he began a battery of tests. "The suite was nice. I had a fantastic view of Lake Michigan. The tests were arduous. I had to wear a silly helmet all the time to monitor my brain activity."

Imogen talked about the miscarriage. "Thank goodness I was not alone when I miscarried," Imogen said sadly. "But having Niles there, and Fletcher ... Fletcher forced me to get up out of bed and go swimming at the pool. I don't know what I would have done without them."

"I wanted to call you. I missed you," Simon confessed, miserable again for having not been there when she needed him most. "I tried repeatedly to talk to the people in charge, but no one would give me any answers. Then, when the pandemic hit, they put the Society on lockdown as well, which meant none of its agents or employees could travel anywhere. They were concerned, rightly so, about travelers who were sick with COVID spreading it to populations in the past."

Imogen told him that the three of them had visited Bakunawa during the quarantine. "We thought about that too before we went," Imogen said. "I remembered you telling me something about it once, but none of us were sick, so we figured it would be okay."

"That's right, the scientists knew that disease works the same way that taking something back in time does; it becomes the period equivalent, but COVID wasn't like a normal flu epidemic, so they were cautious about avoiding introducing the disease via a sick traveler into the general population of a time in the past."

"I guess you learned a lot about time travel while you were there though," Imogen said.

"More than I wanted to," he chuckled. "I was glad when they finally gave me something to do, though. They sent me to a place called the dead zone." He described the problem with people traveling to certain regions to try to alter history.

Imogen regrettably understood. "I know about that," she said. "I tried to change history in Kansas with those girls and you know how that turned out."

Simon explained how travelers had, for example, attempted to go back in time to kill Adolf Hitler as an infant in Austria, and with so many people visiting the same location over and over, the universe eventually pushed back.

"... and when I was there Kevin shut down time travel," he said.

"Kevin?" Imogen reacted, surprised. "The agent from the Society that came here to talk to us? The funny one that explained everything to us in Marvel Universe terms? That Kevin?"

"He's not so nice," Simon answered dismally. "He murdered people."

"No shit?!" she gasped. "So, that was why we couldn't come home from Loretta's in 1973."

"Loretta?" Simon asked, "Who? ..."

"You remember that author I told you about, Loretta Ross, the one I met in Kansas?"

Simon wasn't sure. "I think so ... maybe ... I don't know."

"Well, it doesn't matter. She was a traveler like me," Imogen said. "And I found a book that she wrote with a plot that seemed oddly familiar, like I already knew part of the story."

"Familiar how?" Simon asked.

Imogen presented him with a quick synopsis of the book *She Left Her Heart in San Francisco*—a woman in the late sixties having an affair is confronted by a jealous boyfriend who shows up and tries to kill her.

"Fletcher and I went back to find out if the book had been written about my mother."

Simon sat silently and listened to Imogen's story of discovering that her mother had been traveling to San Francisco to see Loretta's roommate, that sixteen-year-old Teddy, who had a crush on Francis, followed her to San Francisco and killed her when he found out about her affair with her lesbian lover, set fire to Sutro Baths, and when he returned, destroyed both Niles and Francis' anchor photographs to cover up what he had done.

Simon was stunned and distressed. What a devastating end to a decade's long mystery. He sighed and placed Imogen's hand in his. "I'm so very sorry, Imogen," he said. He was surprised by how composed she was. She squeezed his hand. "I've come to terms with it," she said. "She has been gone from my life for a long time."

"I'm glad, but I am sorry that Teddy—someone who I'm unfortunately related to—managed to ruin so many lives. Even after he was dead and gone, he has still managed from the grave to be the villain in both of our family's story."

"Yeah," Imogen agreed.

They sat quietly for a moment, thinking about all they had been through, each caught up in their own thoughts until Simon finally spoke again.

"When I was in the dead zone, somebody saved me," he began. "Her name is Dominique Flynn. She has special abilities, like me ... and she helped me find my mother."

Shocked by this unexpected news, Imogen gasped. "You found your mother?" she asked.

"Yes," Simon answered.

Imogen's excitement quickly turned to sorrow. "I failed you where she didn't," she said, glumly.

"Not intentionally," Simon said. "Nikki didn't know that it was my mother, but she led me to her."

"Is she okay?" Imogen asked. "Your mother?"

"She's good, really good," he said. He explained how Nikki had managed to rescue her from Crestview Sanitarium and that she was living in Paris in 1937.

Imogen felt a mixture of emotions—thrilled that Simon had finally reunited with his mother, sorry that someone else named Dominique, who Simon obviously knew well enough to call by her nickname "Nikki," had been the one to help him find her. "I'm so happy for you Simon," she managed to say. "I'm glad Nikki was there for you."

Sensing a bit of irony, Simon called her out. "I don't know if you noticed, Imogen, but while you were telling me your story, you kept talking about how Fletcher was there for you. He was the *one* that was there for you, wasn't he?"

Imogen looked away, struggling with how best to respond.

"Fletcher and I are close, it's true" she confessed. "We always have been, you know that, but …" she paused … when we thought we were going to be stuck in 1973 for good … well, things happened … between us."

She turned back, searching Simon's face for a reaction, but he seemed to be taking it better than she expected. He pursed his lips, nodded, paused before saying, "Things have changed, haven't they, for both of us. Not just the loss of the baby."

Imogen wasn't sure what to say. "A lot has happened. Yes, we've changed, grown apart, I think."

"But I don't think that's all of it," Simon said. "I think maybe the time apart caused us to question what we both really wanted and needed."

Simon let go of Imogen's hand. "They offered me a job at the Daguerreian Society," he said. "In Chicago."

Imogen knew without asking that Simon had already accepted the job, but letting him go didn't feel quite as difficult now that each had given the other unspoken permission to live their own lives.

Imogen searched for something to say. "Well, probably, the strangest and maybe the best thing to come out of all this was Dad and Jade getting together!" she said.

It was Simon's turn to be surprised. "Isn't he old enough to be her father?"

That made Imogen chuckle. "That's everyone's first reaction," she said. "When he was stuck in the time loop, he didn't age, and Jade grew up, and somehow, now they've managed to meet in the middle. And it works for them, I guess."

It was getting late, shadows were beginning to creep along the walls, and they were running out of conversation, but Simon had something else to say before he had to go. "Despite everything we've been through, I want you to know that I'll never regret loving you, Imogen," he said. "One might say our timing wasn't right."

"Hmmm, one might," she agreed.

"If I hadn't brought you here, you could have lived your life the way it was supposed to be though," she said.

"If you hadn't, I would have never experienced the wonders of time travel, never found out what happened to my mother. I might have stayed a school principal, married Georgia Bitgood, and spent a lifetime of us making each other entirely miserable."

The memory made them both laugh. "Or avoiding shoes lobbed in your direction."

"Yes, avoiding all the potential shoes," he said, grinning. "Listen," he said. "I was standing at the precipice in 1913. Had I stayed, I may have been called off to war or died of the Spanish flu. And besides, I grabbed hold of you, remember? It was my choice, Imogen. Mine. And now I have a purpose in my life; a mission, something I could never have imagined in my wildest dreams."

"Are they planning to crown you Time Lord, Master of the Universe?" she joked.

"Nah," he said chuckling. "I don't think so, but time travel as we knew it will change, for sure. No more running off for photo shoots with Andre in Paris, or to ride the

Ferris Wheel at the World's Fair in Chicago in 1893; no more escaping to remote islands, or visiting the Benson Hotel in 1913 on a whim. The wild, wild west of time travel is over, I'm afraid."

"In that case, I'll probably hang up my PI hat," Imogen acknowledged. "I've been thinking about becoming a professional photographer for a while. Instead of finding missing people and lost things I think I might just stick to creating memories for them."

"Would you tell Fletcher goodbye for me, too," Simon asked. "I always knew he loved you and had I not been here to disrupt the natural order, the two of you may have found each other sooner."

Imogen sighed, unsure how to respond. She hoped they could change the subject, but apparently Simon wasn't done with this one just yet. "Hey, do you remember that film we watched together, *Excalibur*?"

Imogen nodded. "Oh yeah. I loved that movie." Whenever the 1981 film on the legend of King Arthur turned up on one of the streaming services, she made a point to rewatch it.

"Do you remember that part where Lancelot and Guinevere are riding horses down a path through the forest?" Simon asked.

"I sort of remember that scene," she said, "but I'm not sure."

"Well, Lancelot says something to Guinevere like he will love her as his queen, but also as his best friend's wife, but then he says 'while you're alive, I will love no other.'" Simon paused before adding, " … and I feel the same, Imogen. I know Fletcher will take good care of you. But you'll always be my girl."

"Wow," was all Imogen could manage to say. "Way to melt a girl's heart."

Just then Simon's phone began to vibrate. He removed it from his pocket, read the incoming text, and said, "I have to go."

"Off to save the world?" she asked.

Simon flashed one of those alarmingly charming smiles of his, like the one that had melted Imogen's heart the first time they met on the street so long ago.

"Something like that."

Instinctively, she reached out to him, like she had so many times before, wrapping her arms tightly around his neck. They held each other for a time in a lingering embrace, until they both reluctantly let go and walked out to the front porch together.

"Will I ever see you again, Simon Le Bon Elliot?" she teased through tears.

"Yes, Imogen Oliver, of course you will," he said "... but remember, in the future you'll need a passport if you want to be a time tourist."

THE END

EPILOGUE

- The Daguerreian Society merged with Amazon to form Time Tourists, Inc., a highly regulated, commercialized, and absurdly lucrative enterprise.

- Like normal overseas travel, all time tourists must apply for a passport as well as submit a travel itinerary stating where they are going and for what purpose (e.g., Going back in time to kill baby Hitler: DENIED. Traveling back to research your graduate theses on the dustbowl: APPROVED). No exceptions allowed.

- Some places in the dead time zones, like Braunau am Inn, Austria, were closed off to tourist travel while the universe healed itself.

- A booming lockbox industry sprang up to accommodate the expanding need for time tourists to secure their [approved] souvenirs and treasures gathered while visiting the past for later retrieval in the future.

- Sales of metal detectors skyrocketed as treasure hunters searched for potential hidden artifacts that other time tourists might have stashed/buried in random places.

- Daniel (D.B.) Cooper cashed out before the 1929 Wall Street crash and disappeared to a time unknown. Imogen donated the money he stole to several charities promoting education, helping children, and studying climate change.

- Niles and Jade welcomed a baby boy, making big sister Imogen no longer an only child.

- Imogen and Fletcher bought a house in the suburbs. She photographs babies and families and flowers and he builds tiny houses.

- Nikki and Simon frequently visit Tiffany in Paris, despite the "no exceptions" rule, because, well, they were exceptional.

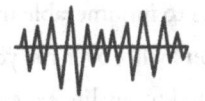

ACKNOWLEDGMENTS

Sixteen years ago, it started with a fuzzy idea—what if a person could walk into a still photograph and go back in time? I would like to thank the readers who decided to come along with me on Imogen Oliver's intrepid journey—from the first book, *The Time Tourists* through her continuing misadventures in *The Yesterday Girl*, and now *The End of Time*, which completes the trilogy.

All the love to my person and partner in crime, Jeff Bolkan for supporting and encouraging me, and keeping me on track.

Much love to my special friend and muse, Gail Curtis, who was there from the start, reading and critiquing all three books, catching typos, asking good plot questions, serving as a human thesaurus, and forever cheering me on.

Lots of gratitude for my family: To my sister Carol Niblett for making me the coolest ever time-travel themed quilt and for the ongoing love and support of my three grown children, Cory Huffman, Kaylee Crum, and Daniel Stoltey. Thank you to my mom, Marian Nelson, for saying 'I love you' to me every week over the phone, and for reading my books even though they have some bad words in them. To Dad, Russ Nelson—for all the good memories.

Finally, many thanks to innumerable friends, family, professors, and coworkers who, over the years, have shaped, influenced, or contributed to my life experiences in good and bad and big and small ways.

ABOUT THE AUTHOR

Sharleen Nelson, a magna cum laude graduate of the University of Oregon's School of Journalism and Communication, recently retired from her position as University Communications Editor & Writer at the UO.

During her 30+ year career as a journalist she has interviewed numerous individuals from a wide range of backgrounds including academia, science, politics, and the arts, among others. She has edited more than 100 books and written hundreds of magazine and newspaper articles on a diverse range of topics in the fields of travel, entertainment, arts, education, science, and technology.

She served as an editor and writer on a variety of magazine staffs, including *Spectroscopy*, *Video Store Magazine*, *The Maratime*, and *Oregon Quarterly*, and is an award-winning photographer and accomplished graphic designer.

She is the author of *The Time Tourists*, *The Yesterday Girl*, *The End of Time*, and co-author of *Dye. Run. Don't Die.*

More Books from GladEye Press

*The Time Tourists
The Yesterday Girl
Sharleen Nelson
Follow the adventures and missteps of time-traveling PI Imogen Oliver as she recovers lost items and unearths long-buried stories and secrets from the past in this exciting trilogy!

*The Fragile Blue Dot
Ross West
"Perceptive tales that boast memorable characters and a potent, sweeping, message." ~Kirkus Review

Veteran science-writer and journalist Ross West's collection of award-winning short fiction touches on the human aspect of living in a world on the brink of ecological disaster.

*Dye. Run. Don't Die: A Love Story
K.G. Kolsen
Chased by shadowy figures, Winnie and Jimmy re-unite somewhere between Oklahoma and Colorado and embark on a wild ride filled with disguises, stolen vehicles, murders, truck-stop perverts, a sex-cult, deadly shootouts, and rediscovered love.

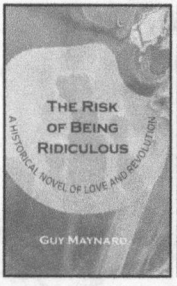

The Risk of Being Ridiculous
Trial
Guy Maynard
Join 19-year-old Ben Tucker through confrontation and confusion, courts and cops, parties and politics, acid and activism, revolution and reaction. *Ash Valley*, book three in the trilogy coming soon!

*Available as an ebook on Kindle Unlimited.

All GladEye titles are available for purchase at www.gladeyepress.com and from your local bookstore.

*Federation of the Dragon
*Footman of the Ether
Jason A. Kilgore
Dragons, mages, elves, humans, and other creatures populate the magical lands of Irikara in books one and two in the epic Heartstone Series. Available in both trade and deluxe hardback!

The Midnight Show: bohemians, byways, and bonfires
Camille Cole
During the early days of Oregon's famous Country Fair, the Midnight Show was a stage shared by icons of the counterculture, lovers, children and families, and those of us finding our way through.

Tripping the Field
Ian Jaydid
Empiricist scientist, Prof. Michael Huxley tumbles, stumbles, strides, and crawls through the jungles of South America, the mountains of Tibet, and the backwoods of Colorado in search of enlightenment and hope of saving the world from a religious cult that has discovered a dark shorcut to the power of quantum realities.

A Recipe for Dying
Patricia Brown
The old people are dying in the small coastal town of Waterton, but no one seems to notice—after all, that's what old folk do, isn't it? Eleanor and her delightful assortment of friends, most of whom are getting up in age, set out to discover what is going on in this first book in the Coastal Coffee Club Mysteries series.

COMING SOON *from*
GladEye Press

Ash Valley
Guy Maynard
In this final installment in the Risk of Ridiculous Trilogy, Ben Tucker, his soulmate Sarah, and a community of like-minded friends forge new bonds while seeking tranquility far away from Boston at a commune in the rugged Pacific Northwest.

Quilts of a Feather
Arlene Sachitano
The Harriet Truman/Loose Threads Mysteries are back! The fourteenth book in the series is the best ever! Your favorite characters, new riddles, and a new publisher!

Dying for Recipes
Patricia Brown
Who has stolen Eleanor's recipes? Whip up all the delicious dishes as you follow the clues in this special Coastal Coffee Club Mysteries cookbook!

Black and Tan Fantasy
Randall Luce
In the turbulent and often violent nascent civil rights movement of the Mississippi delta, racial identities, culture, and attitudes collide and shift in this taut drama.

Far Side of Revenge
Anne Dean
A fictionalized account of the life and rise of Brian Boroimhe, King of Ireland.

RERELEASES FROM JASON A. KILGORE
The First Nova I See Tonight
Star pirates, alien lovers, tentacled mafiosos, this space opera offers a return to the beloved "zap gun" stories of the past!

Around the Corner from Sanity: Tales of the Paranormal
Fourteen short stories of spine-tingling horror will scare you AND tickle your funny bone!

Guide Me, O River and other poems